Delphine stood just inside the room. She could hear a man's heavy breathing, but apart from that it was quiet, the light dim. It was a small room, but well furnished, and on a bed a man lay asleep. His arm was raised to cover his eyes, a bandage wrapped round his wrist. Assuming the wound it covered was the reason Mr Oakley had brought her to the tavern, she moved towards the still figure.

She opened her mouth to speak, but at that moment she was unable to utter a word. This was a man the like of which she had never seen before. A sheet covered him up to the waist, beneath which he was naked. His body was perfect. He was lean, his muscles hard, his dark chest broad, his shoulders strong.

Sensing her presence, he slowly lowered his arm and opened his eyes—an extraordinary midnight-blue. Delphine's heart turned over. They remained fixed on her face, and she could feel her cheeks burning, but she could not look away…

AUTHOR NOTE

MISS CAMERON'S FALL FROM GRACE was an exciting book to write—what I like to think of as romantic suspense. All my novels are historical romances set in varied backgrounds, and I'm equally comfortable writing stories in the seventeenth, eighteenth and nineteenth centuries. I love inventing characters whose stories are worth telling, and I like my heroines to be strong-willed, with a spark of life and determination.

As in my other books, my heroine has hopes and ambitions—until she meets Lord Stephen Fitzwaring, and then she has hopes and dreams of a different kind.

I wanted to write an intensely romantic story. I hope I have achieved this in my latest novel, and have managed to create an enjoyable escape for you, the reader.

MISS CAMERON'S FALL FROM GRACE

Helen Dickson

First published in Great Britain 2012
by Mills & Boon, an imprint of Harlequin (UK) Limited.
Large Print edition 2012
Harlequin (UK) Limited, Eton House, 18-24 Paradise Road,
Richmond, Surrey TW9 1SR

© Helen Dickson 2012

ISBN: 978 0 263 22528 0

Harlequin (UK) policy is to use papers that are natural,
renewable and recyclable products and made from wood grown in
sustainable forests. The logging and manufacturing process conform
to the legal environmental regulations of the country of origin.

Printed and bound in Great Britain
by CPI Antony Rowe, Chippenham, Wiltshire

Helen Dickson was born and lives in South Yorkshire, with her retired farm manager husband. Having moved out of the busy farmhouse where she raised their two sons, she has more time to indulge in her favourite pastimes. She enjoys being outdoors, travelling, reading and music. An incurable romantic, she writes for pleasure. It was a love of history that drove her to writing historical fiction.

Previous novels by Helen Dickson:

THE DEFIANT DEBUTANTE
ROGUE'S WIDOW, GENTLEMAN'S WIFE
TRAITOR OR TEMPTRESS
WICKED PLEASURES
  (part of *Christmas By Candlelight*)
A SCOUNDREL OF CONSEQUENCE
FORBIDDEN LORD
SCANDALOUS SECRET, DEFIANT BRIDE
FROM GOVERNESS TO SOCIETY BRIDE
MISTRESS BELOW DECK
THE BRIDE WORE SCANDAL
DESTITUTE ON HIS DOORSTEP
SEDUCING MISS LOCKWOOD

Chapter One

Summer—1810

It was not Delphine's habit to visit bordellos, but she had a duty to ensure that Maisie, who had disappeared from the orphanage, was safely with her mother. Granted, this particular bordello was of a most prestigious kind, but although the location was not beyond criticism, it was certainly no place for a lady. The genteel world of Delphine's mother and sisters, however, had begun to matter less and less of late.

Delphine was usually accompanied by one of her mother's footmen who drove her in the carriage, but today he had duties at the house so she'd gone to the orphanage alone. Two of the children had gone down with temperatures and a rash. After isolating them and on the point of leaving, one of the warders had informed her that Maisie was missing. Delphine had a good idea where she could be found—there was nothing for it but to go after her.

The evening was warm and sultry and oppressive, the kind of oppression that comes before a storm. Mrs Cox's was an imposing three-storey building, and torchlights burned on each side of the red-painted door. Delphine was admitted to this house of assignation by Fergus Daley, the man Mrs Cox employed to keep order within the house and the rougher elements of the district out. The purple livery he wore looked out of place on his huge frame. The bones of his face were pronounced, with a lantern jaw sharp enough to cut paper. His crooked nose, which had been broken several times during his years as a pugilist, and his eye sockets set deep beneath his heavy brow gave his face a sinister look. But now he smiled, for Miss Cameron was a regular visitor to the house when she was looking for young Maisie.

'Welcome to our house of pleasure, Miss Cameron,' he greeted jovially in a deep, baritone voice, his expression warm and welcoming.

'House of depravity, more like, Fergus,'

she replied in hushed tones as she placed her brown-leather bag containing medicaments and dressings on the hall table, 'but don't tell Mrs Cox I said so.'

'Wouldn't dream of it, miss,' he replied, giving her a conspiratorial wink. 'I think I know why you're here—and I don't think it's to sell your body for what pitiful rewards a common man could offer you.'

'How right you are, Fergus—not even for the king himself. I can only hope my parents never learn I come here.'

'Not from me, Miss Cameron, and while you are here, you are solely under my protection.'

'That's a comfort to me, Fergus,' she said, standing back to allow an inebriated gentleman to sway past and disappear into the salon, his clothes in some disarray. During business hours there were always gentlemen present.

'If it's young Maisie you're looking for, she arrived an hour since.'

Delphine uttered a sigh of relief. 'Thank goodness. I do wish she wouldn't run away like that. If only she knew how much trouble she causes. She's just a child. She shouldn't be here.' What Delphine said was true. She'd been doing her charity work in and around the area of Covent Garden and St Giles long enough to know that wealthy and depraved gentlemen of the city would pay a fine price for girls as young as Maisie.

Fergus nodded towards the curved staircase. 'She's with Meg—or the Luscious Delphine as she's calling herself these days.'

'She does seem to have taken a fancy to my name,' Delphine remarked, laughing lightly, 'although last month it was Gorgeous Louella and the month before that Sweet Angel. I find her peculiar taste in names rather odd. She seems to change it whenever another takes her fancy. It must be very confusing for her clients—but I suppose it adds to her mystique. Can I go up?'

He nodded. 'She's no clients tonight—which you can put down to Will Kelly. He was here earlier.'

Delphine glanced at him in alarm. It was no secret that Fergus had no liking for Will Kelly, nor the devious and often brutal way he went about procuring girls for Mrs Cox's brothel. 'Has he hurt her?'

'You'll see for yourself—but I swear I'll swing for the bastard if he lays a finger on young Maisie and he knows it, if you'll forgive me for saying so, Miss Cameron. Go on up. I'll have to tell Mrs Cox you're here.'

'Then I'll disappear before she sees me.' Delphine was hoping to avoid seeing the strict madam of this establishment.

With such an impressive array of whores available, Mrs Cox's business profited from well-heeled and aristocratic customers. Mrs Cox—if that was indeed her name—always dressed plainly in a black gown, her greying hair pulled severely back into a knot at the back of her head: the very picture of respectability. She might have been someone's grandmother, but Delphine knew she was not. Mrs Cox had lived a life and knew how to make it pay.

She was very proud of her establishment. Some of the girls were brought to her from the provinces by the ruthless procurer Will Kelly, who took a fair cut of the profits from the brothel's immoral earnings. Mrs Cox chose the other girls from poverty-stricken backgrounds and girls whose indiscretions had made them outcasts from their own kind. She taught them how to give pleasure by offering clients temptations to which they could yield. Love didn't come into it—what went on in Mrs Cox's establishment made a mockery of love.

From the spacious hall—which was hardly what one would expect of a bordello, with its light oak-panelled walls and black-and-white-tiled floor—Delphine, hearing excited ribald laughter and raised voices, glanced into the main salon where young women in various stages of undress were lolling about on sofas. She had been to the house several times during the day and thought nothing of it.

Tonight, the sight of scantily clad female bodies both shocked and excited her. The flimsy garments clung to their figures, showing off curves of pearly flesh gleaming in the soft light. The tantalising half-sight of their bodies weaving into the heady scents of perfume was more arousing to the gentlemen pawing them than nakedness would have been. The girls were taking refreshment with clients before going upstairs. Sometimes the gentlemen preferred girls to come to their places of residence, a service they were charged extra for—and as for what happened after that, well, it was no business of hers.

The salon was elegant with its dark-blue carpet and crystal chandeliers. Occasional tables and padded chairs were scattered about and scarlet-velvet curtains, deeply fringed with gold, hung at the windows. Venetian mirrors adorned the walls, along with gilded lewd pictures of nudes in elegant poses. There were ferns in jardinières so tall they almost reached the high ceiling; plinths on either side of the room held beautiful, life-sized Italian marble statues of male nudes of such quality one would expect to see them in the house of a nobleman, not in a bordello.

Lifting her skirts slightly Delphine began to climb the stairs. The air was sweetened by perfumed candles. Reaching the top, she went down one of the two landings, halting at the door at the end. Knocking gently and hearing a voice telling her to come in, she opened the door and entered a rose-pink boudoir. Its furnishings were surprisingly cosy; facing Delphine was a dressing table littered with cosmetic pots, perfumes and a silver-backed hairbrush, the border of the gilt mirror carved with cherubs.

Meg was reclining on a low couch, toying with her dyed red hair. With her big blue eyes, full soft lips and luscious form, there was little wonder men couldn't resist her. Expecting her visitor, for she knew Delphine would come after the child, she gave her husky laugh and stretched luxuriously like a cat, raising a shimmering leg and admiring its shapeliness whilst watching Delphine out of the corner of her eye, trying to gauge the effect of the voluptuousness barely contained within her violet-silk robe. When she registered neither shock nor horror in Delphine's countenance, she rose, drawing the robe tight about her body.

'I suppose you're looking for Maisie.' She nodded towards the ten-year-old child asleep on the bed. 'She went to sleep straight away. I didn't want to wake her.'

'No—of course not. I had to come, Meg, to make sure she was safe. I know Mrs Cox thinks I ought to mind my own business, but anything could have happened to her.'

A wry smile twisted Meg's lips. 'Mrs Cox? Don't be fooled by her.'

'I'm not.'

'She's a trollop as old as sin, but she's right. You should mind your own business,' Meg remarked, sitting back on the couch.

'I come here because I care.'

'Why should you?' Meg said, with a haughty toss of her head. 'You with your fancy name and fancy clothes and all your airs and graces. Why would someone like you care about people like me and my Maisie?'

'Because I do. I do care about you and Maisie, otherwise I wouldn't be here—and as for my name, you appear to be making good use of it.'

'Aye—maybe. I like it, that's why, but I don't own it and there's the difference. You don't belong here.'

'Neither do you, Meg. None of the girls do—and Maisie certainly doesn't.' Delphine glanced across at the sleeping child curled up against the pillows. She was an extremely pretty child, with large green eyes and an abundance of light blonde hair, and she remained devoted to her mother, despite her neglect.

Meg shrugged. 'I can't help it if she keeps on coming. And as for the others, it's become a way of life for them—most of them driven to it by one hardship or another.'

'Don't make it a way of life for Maisie. She deserves better.'

'I have to make a living,' Meg replied, her voice hard and flat.

Delphine crossed the room and crouched on the floor beside her. 'You don't have to stay here.

Take her away, Meg. Somewhere decent. I'll help you all I can.'

'I don't want charity; besides, I can't leave. You see, this is where I want to be—where I *choose* to be.'

'Why? Because it excites you? Because you can't leave Will Kelly? For heaven's sake, Meg, look at you,' Delphine hissed, taking one of Meg's arms and shoving up the sleeve to reveal a host of bruises, some purple and some yellowing with age. 'He's a cruel, overbearing bully. I simply cannot for the life of me understand why you tolerate his ill treatment.'

Meg shrugged, jerking her arm out of Delphine's grasp and pulling down her sleeve. 'I've had worse. He does care for me.'

'Nonsense. He merely seeks to use you. If he cared for you, he would not have brought you here. You know full well, Meg, he may be all flattery and honey when he's sober, but once he starts drinking—well—I'm the one who patches you up. I've seen the results of his behaviour once too often. Oh, Meg, please think about it.'

'I try not to think. I accept what there is.'

'Don't give him the chance to hurt you again. I implore you.'

Meg's face clenched up like a fist as she fought to keep her voice under control. 'I need no instructions from you on how to conduct myself.'

'Of course not—but really I am most concerned about you.'

'Save your concern for someone else,' she grumbled ungraciously. 'I'm quite capable of taking care of myself.'

'Are you?' Delphine pressed. 'I beg you to go away somewhere—for Maisie's sake as well as your own. She is but a child and deserves better than this. You once worked in the theatre as an actress, touring the provinces. Could you not go back? It has to be better than this.'

Meg's lovely face became almost ugly as she looked down at Delphine. 'I don't know what you're trying to gain by this,' she said nastily, 'but I'm not going anywhere. I can look after myself—as I've always done. I won't leave Will. I can't.' She looked away. 'That's the way it is.'

Unable to understand Meg's loyalty and devotion to Will Kelly, Delphine's heart sank with defeat. Meg had grown partial to Will's silken tongue and good looks whilst on tour with an acting troupe; when he'd offered to take both her and Maisie to London and a better life, she'd packed her bags and gone with him—to Mrs Cox's place, to become one of her whores. Now she was at the service of any lecherous rogue with gold in his pockets and Maisie stayed in the nearby orphanage. Will was the first man Meg had loved. She would do anything to keep him. He had been the first male to reject her, scorn her, beat her, awake in her all the fury of which only hell has the like, yet she would not leave him.

'And Maisie? Can you look after her?'

Meg's eyes narrowed and anger sparked in their depths. 'I know what you're thinking, but don't,' she said fiercely. 'I'm her mother—not a good mother, I admit, but I am still her mother. Do you think I'd let any one of the dirty brutes who come here touch her? I'd kill her and myself before I let that happen—after killing the man who tried.'

Delphine nodded. 'I know you would. But there are men who come here who would take a young girl—whether she was willing or not.'

'They won't. You don't understand one thing about me. Do you think I don't worry about Maisie? That's why I put her in the orphanage. If anything should happen to me…' She swallowed audibly, weakening and allowing her emotions to show. 'I worry about what would happen to her.'

'Nothing is going to happen to you, Meg, but if it did, then I would do my utmost to take care of her.'

Hope welled in Meg's eyes as she gripped Delphine's hand. 'Would you?' she whispered. 'Would you do that for me?'

'Of course I would.'

'You promise?' Meg urged, her eyes dark with anguish.

For the first time Delphine heard a tremor in her voice. She was conscious of strong conflicting urges—though she ached to vent her impatience, she was tempted, too, to put a sympathetic hand over Meg's. She resisted both compulsions and forced herself to think calmly for a moment about the promise she was about to make should anything happen to Meg. Her heart sank precipitously at the thought.

'Yes, Meg. I promise. I would see that she came to no harm.'

'Thank you.' Her voice trembled on the words, and she looked away, jaw clamped tight. Then she looked back at Delphine, eyes bright and tearless. 'You should go. I'll see Maisie gets back to the orphanage. I've no customers so she can stay with me tonight. I'll take her back in the morning.'

Delphine rose, standing for a moment in grave silence. 'Very well,' she said eventually, gazing at the sleeping child. 'But think about what I've said, Meg. Take Maisie away and put this place behind you.'

Without another word she left, exceedingly vexed by the interview. She was anxious of the influence this place would end up having on Maisie, for deep in her heart she knew Meg would not leave while Will Kelly continued to have a hold over her.

She paused, hearing a moan, and lingered at the top of the stairs, transfixed. Someone had left a bedroom door ajar in his haste to bed his companion. Overcome by a strange sense of curiosity, she moved hesitantly towards it and peered through the crack.

One of the girls was doing what she was paid to do. Delphine flinched, about to draw back—but she could not.

At first she felt shock, then she felt her body growing warm. Her spirit seemed suddenly quite apart from her body. Like a rabbit before a stoat, she was mesmerised. Two naked bodies, arms and legs entwined as they writhed and sprawled on the bed, moved in a voluptuous rhythm. Against her will, Delphine felt her body respond to what she was seeing. Her pulse was beating faster; every nerve seemed to tingle.

She drew a long, shuddering breath. What was happening to her? The two people she was observing were strangers to her. How could their impassioned movements awaken these dark longings in her blood? Loose women, she knew from her mother's lectures, were the only women who took pleasure in such things. Attempting to calm her mind as well as her body, she shrank away, her body trembling. She felt like a little girl at a keyhole.

Suddenly she was snatched from her preoccupation by the sound of a voice close at hand. It was a loud, brutish voice, belonging to a heavily built man with thick fair hair and a coarseness that dominated his heavy features. As he ascended the staircase, his dark gaze assessed her with a scathing vulgarity. He wore a coarse linen shirt stained with food and ale, and dark-velvet trousers fastened with a wide belt.

This was Will Kelly, a swaggering, ill-

mannered brute who drank, gambled and se-
duced his way through life. He had close-set,
foxy, clever eyes that missed nothing and a way
of looking at Delphine that made her flesh crawl.
He carried with him a smell of the poverty-rid-
den streets that turned her stomach. When she
had first laid eyes on him, his manner had con-
veyed to her that this was a man of intense cun-
ning, utter ruthlessness and terrible danger.

He watched as she approached him, standing
with his feet wide apart and his huge fists resting on his wide hips, his grey eyes cold and unfriendly.

'So! What have you been up to, Miss Cameron?
Interfering again?'

'Not at all,' Delphine replied haughtily, determined to remain unruffled, even though beneath
her skirts her legs were trembling at his nearness. 'I've been to see Meg—and there's no need
for you to shout; my hearing is perfectly sound.'

'Not thinking of entering the profession, are
you?' Moving closer, he reached out his gnarled,
dirty fingers and gripped her chin roughly, turning her face from side to side, showering her with
spittle as he spoke. 'You're comely enough, I'll
give you that—a tempting wench.' He grinned

lewdly. 'I'm a reasonable man. We could come to an understanding.'

Delphine glowered at him, pushing his hand away. 'Do not touch me. Do you honestly think that I would consider giving myself to the likes of you and the men who frequent this place? Never.'

He laughed sneeringly. 'I've met many haughty women like you, Miss oh-so-high-and-mighty Cameron. There was a French bitch who considered herself a prize for the most handsome rogue in Paris once. In a matter of days she came crawling, begging me to take her to bed. Then there was a beauty from Kent. Oh, yes, she was an arrogant bitch. But little more than a week of my hospitality brought her to see the light and she came to me willingly,' he boasted with a triumphant laugh.

'Do you mean to frighten me with that repugnant account of your conquests?'

His eyes raked her boldly and a repulsive smile twisted his lips. 'If I wished to frighten you, I would drag you into an empty room and listen to you scream. I'm a strong man and I can't say I don't enjoy a fight, but I do not wish to frighten you, only to point out the advantages of my protection should you decide to join the ladies in Mrs Cox's fine establishment. You'll not find boredom here.'

'That will never happen. I came here to find Maisie and for no other reason.'

'Ah—young Maisie,' he drawled, an interested, dangerous gleam entering his narrowed eyes. 'Now, there's a pretty little thing. She'll be a beauty one day—' his gaze narrowed '—just like her mother. Imagine how popular they would be, working together—mother and daughter.'

Delphine went cold, suddenly fearful for Maisie. Was this to be her lot, her destiny? No, not if she could help it. Will Kelly's eyes were watching her sharply. Deliberately she considered his gaze, but she knew that he none the less sensed her deep, desperate need to protect Maisie. She had given him a weapon.

'You leave Maisie alone, Will Kelly. She is nothing but a child. Meg would kill you before allowing you to get your filthy hands on her daughter.'

'Meg would have no say in it. If she opposes me, she'll rue the day. Don't fool yourself. Maisie is in my hands. She'll make a fine whore—just like her mother.'

'Never. At least, not while I have breath in my body.'

Without another word Delphine swept past him. As she made her way down the stairs she felt both angered and unsettled by her encounter with Will Kelly, but nevertheless she considered Maisie safe for the time being.

She was also affected by what she had witnessed prior to Will's arrival. The air around her still shimmered with the heat of what she had seen. Her whole body had ignited and she was still afire. It was a wonder she didn't burst into flames.

There was no sign of Fergus in the hall, so she picked up her bag and opened the door herself. A man stood on the doorstep, about to raise the heavy brass knocker.

'Excuse me. My name is Nicholas Oakley. I'm looking for a lady by the name of Delphine,' he said in a pleasant voice.

Delphine looked at the stocky, broad-shouldered, neatly dressed man. 'I'm Delphine Cameron. May I help you?'

He didn't look like a man who would visit a bordello, nor did he look ill. In fact, he appeared healthier than most, his face weathered by wind and sun, but hale and full-fleshed.

Mr Oakley was thinking along similarly approving lines as he considered her. She was wearing an open jacket of brown velvet with brown ribbon around the edges and a coffee-coloured dress and brown poke bonnet with tendrils of deep-red hair escaping its confines. Most prim, he thought—in fact, she didn't look at all like the red-haired siren the landlord of the Blue Boar had described to him when he'd enquired about a clean and comely lady with whom his master might pass the night away while he was in London. But then, these ladies of the night were full of surprises.

The landlord had assured him that Mrs Cox's establishment operated affluently and was one step above the other brothels—and such was the excellence of Delphine's technique that she would make love an entire night without ceasing, at his master's pleasure.

He smiled, a sudden charming smile that quite transformed his big face. 'I believe you can— or perhaps I should say you can help my master. Yes, indeed! I am sure you can be of great help.'

'Would that not depend on what is wrong with him?'

He raised one of his bushy eyebrows. 'In a manner of speaking. All I can say is that he's in great need.'

'Is he sick?'

'I suppose you could say that. My master—I am what is termed as his batman—the Colonel Lord Stephen Fitzwaring is home on leave from Spain, where he's been with Wellington fighting the French. Fighting has taken its toll on him, I'm afraid.'

'I see,' Delphine replied, thinking rapidly. She was sure that she didn't see the half of it—whatever *it* was—but on the face of things, if the man was wounded then, even though it was beyond her capabilities to cure him, she would make an assessment of his condition and ask Dr Grey, who often ministered to the children at the orphanage, to take a look at him.

'Mr Taylor, who keeps the Blue Boar at the end of the street, assured me there is no one better equipped to relieve my master's—er—' he coughed as he sought the appropriate word '—discomfort.'

In her complete naïvety and gullibility, Delphine

smiled broadly, finding it hard to believe her charitable deeds had attracted so much attention. She
was acquainted with the landlord of the Blue
Boar—a kindly man who donated regularly to
the orphanage—and if Mr Oakley's master was
suffering from some kind of discomfort, then it did
not strike her as odd that Mr Taylor would recom-
mend her. She had waved to him from across the
street earlier and, aware of Maisie's habit of visiting her mother, he would have known she would
be at Mrs Cox's establishment.

'If you will come with me, I will take you to
him.' Mr Oakley was watching her with interest. 'I am sure you can accommodate each other.
My master will be most generous.'

At the mention of money and considering how
it could benefit the orphanage, Delphine looked
at him levelly. 'Indeed I hope he is. I do not give
my services for nothing.'

His brows went up at that. 'My master would
not expect you to. Dear me, no! Though, I must
say, most persons of your profession seem to care
for everyone.'

'Not everyone, Mr Oakley. Only those I believe can be helped. Your master is an amenable
gentleman, I hope?'

'Most of the time. There are times when he looks far more fierce than he really is.' A smile touched the corners of his lips. 'Don't mention that to anyone else, or you'll ruin his reputation.'

'Reputation?' Delphine tipped her head to one side, casting him a sideways glance. She was becoming more intrigued by Mr Oakley's master by the second. 'Does he have one?'

'Of the worst sort,' he averred flatly, shooting her a teasing look.

'Then spare me the sordid details. I shall be seeing him for no other reason than to make him feel better. Is there no woman in his life to look after him?'

'Oh, yes,' Mr Oakley replied. 'In Spain, a beautiful, voluptuous *señorita* is most enamoured of him and often keeps him company, but Spain is a long way away. My master is one of the finest men I know. He has a most tremendous strength of mind and a will that has carried him through many a battle. Because he is so strong-willed, he seldom encounters opposition from anyone—unless it be from the enemy Bonaparte!—which is why you may occasionally find him somewhat... dictatorial.'

'I see,' Delphine said stiffly. 'Thank you for

that insight into your master's character, Mr Oakley. I shall remember it. Where is he?'

'I left him abed at the Blue Boar. Are you prepared to come with me now?'

Delphine held up her bag and smiled. 'I have everything I will need in my bag.'

Mr Oakley raised his brows in awe as his mind conjured up the delectable items that bag might contain; items she would no doubt use to titillate his master.

Delphine was not thinking logically. The mortal danger she might be incurring did not enter her mind. She had long ago acquired the habit of ignoring other people's advice and plunging into situations with no thought for the consequence.

'Lead on, Mr Oakley. Let us see if we can make your master feel better, shall we?'

But time was of the essence for Delphine. If she hurried, she would make it home in time for her mother's musical evening; woe betide her if she was late. Her charity work often provoked trouble with her mother. Privileged by birth, Delphine had been drawn into such pursuits by her Aunt Celia, who had instilled into her the duties of a gently born woman to the less fortunate. *The Devil finds work for idle hands*, she had said, then she had smiled, adding, *or I should say, there is always work for a spare pair of willing hands*. In an attempt to invest her empty life with meaning, Delphine had been more than willing. She was the youngest of five children— all girls—and, disappointed that the last of their last offspring had not been the much-wanted son, her parents had not even bothered to announce her birth.

Neglect bordering on rejection beat a bitter note in Delphine's heart. All her life, doubts had drummed heavy blows upon the crumbling walls of her confidence. In her parents' eyes she could never be the woman her sisters were: beautiful women who attracted men wherever they went.

She did not like to dwell on her inadequacies, but when she was in the presence of two exquisite creatures like her twin sisters, she was painfully aware of her unfashionable reddish hair, her too-large mouth and the light scattering of freckles across cheekbones that were much too high.

From childhood she had been trained to detachment, but she was none the less human and thought life in her parents' house very cruel and so very lonely that she had long ago made up her mind to be her own woman. She would defy convention and be true only to herself.

And so she had thrown herself into her charity work, becoming closely involved with the homeless and destitute children and venturing into dark places not one of her four pampered older sisters could have imagined.

Most of her work was carried out with other charity workers at the orphanage in Water Lane. Not all the children were orphaned; some, like Maisie, had been abandoned by their parents. When she wasn't at the orphanage, Delphine was forever organising fund-raising events and annoying her mother by lobbying her friends for donations. From the beginning, charity work had given a purpose to her life. She could breathe, could live, could give of herself at last.

On entering the orphanage for the first time, the things she had seen had upset her terribly. Her aunt, a spinster who had made charity her life's work, had a natural air of authority, which she shared with her brother, Delphine's father. She had told Delphine that to do this work well she must remain detached. She must not let emotion get the better of her. If she did this, she would control others—and herself.

Delphine had taken this advice and used it as best she could. Working among the poor, she was surprised at the intensity of her feeling and compassion, so long suppressed, and wondered whether her work was in fact altering her, turning her into a more passionate human being.

Her skin still burned from what she had seen at the bordello; her face felt as if it were glowing with fever as she followed the stranger. She hated the streets at night. There were ghosts in these streets that sometimes made her tremble with fear. It was all a million miles away from her mother's genteel world; violence was endemic in London. Muggers and cut-throats roamed the streets virtually unchecked; anyone who walked alone at night took a serious risk.

Delphine decided that, once she had seen the gentleman, she would ask Mr Oakley to order her a chair or a hackney to take her home. Her eyes were cast down to the ground, but the night above stretched black and clear and infinite, the stars burning with their own fire.

They reached the Blue Boar, entering by a back doorway. It was a busy night at the inn. She followed Mr Oakley up a narrow staircase.

He stopped at a door and opened it, standing back for her to pass through.

'I shall leave you to it.' Without another word he left her, closing the door as he went.

Delphine stood just inside the room. She could hear a man's heavy breathing, but apart from that it was quiet, the light dim. It was a small room, but well furnished, and on a bed a man lay asleep. His arm was raised to cover his eyes, a bandage wrapped round his wrist. Assuming the wound it covered was the reason Mr Oakley had brought her to the tavern, she moved towards the still figure.

She opened her mouth to speak, but at that moment she was unable to utter a word. This was a man the like of which she had never seen before. A sheet covered him to the waist, beneath which he was naked. His body was perfect. He was lean, his muscles hard, his dark, furred chest broad, his shoulders strong. Sensing her presence, he slowly lowered his arm and opened his eyes—an extraordinary midnight blue. Her heart turned over. They remained fixed on her face and she could feel her cheeks burning, but she could not look away from him.

This man was quite exquisite, perfect, and

Delphine, untouched by any kind of passionate emotion, felt her heart take flight. She was aghast at herself, staring like an ignorant girl. When he saw her a slow, appreciative smile curved his firm lips. It was such a wonderful smile and Delphine, poor naïve innocent, felt a thousand emotions explode inside her head all at once. She was lost. Bewilderingly, heart and soul, lost.

'Well, well,' he drawled groggily, 'what have we here? Such a prize I did not expect. Oakley has surpassed himself. What kept you?'

Delphine realised suddenly that she had been holding her breath from the moment she had entered the room. She had come with the sure knowledge that this man was ill. Now she lost some of her certainty. The gentleman was most handsome, about thirty-one, haughty looking, his body as lean and supple as a sword. His finely chiselled features were clean-shaven and golden skinned. His thick, curly gleaming black hair— slightly flecked with silver at the temples—was dishevelled and those midnight-blue eyes now gazed warmly into hers. His voice—slurred with sleep or alcohol, she could not decide which, but strongly suspected it was the latter—was deep and golden like his skin.

'I—I came as soon as Mr Oakley asked me to.'

'Good old Oakley. Always a man of his word, is Oakley—and I can see he's done a handsome night's work finding you.' Thrusting the sheet away and exposing his nakedness, in one swift movement he was off the bed and walking slowly, deliberately, around Delphine as she stood rooted to the floor, drowning in a well of embarrassment. He touched her with only those deep-blue eyes, yet they were enough, boldly, rudely evaluating every angle of her assets. He paused in front of her and smiled broadly, extremely pleased with what he saw.

A cold dread grew deep inside Delphine and she clutched her bag to her bosom, trying hard to focus her eyes on something other than his nakedness. She was beginning to wonder what she had let herself in for. Outwardly she appeared calm, but the emotional frenzy raging within her was beginning to sap her strength. She was both tired and confused; she was also angry that Mr Oakley had lured her into a trap.

'I was under the impression that you were sick or injured in some way,' she said crisply. 'Since that does not appear to be the case, I will bid you goodnight, sir.'

He laughed softly, barring her path of escape
with his naked body. 'Not yet, my sweet. What
is your name?'

She raised her head, jutting her chin. 'Delphine.
Delphine Cameron.'

'Delphine.' He sighed. 'A lovely name—a fitting name for a lady. I am Lord Fitzwaring. My
friends call me Stephen. Can I offer you some
wine?' He indicated a decanter on a small table.

'No. I would rather not.'

Stephen chuckled, taking her bag and carelessly tossing it into a chair by the bed. Before
she could protest he had whipped off her bonnet and removed the pins holding her hair up,
watching hungrily as it tumbled over her shoulders. The glow of the lamp brought out the fire
and vibrancy in the thick tresses. He marvelled
at her beauty. Long, wavy hair the colour of rich
mahogany framed a perfectly proportioned face,
her skin a creamy hue. Even through the fog of
alcohol he concluded the girl was beautiful. Her
cheekbones were high beneath large and slanting eyes, dark brown, mysterious and magnetic
and flecked with green. Her nose was small and
straight, her mouth soft and sensitive, luscious
and pink.

'Well,' he murmured, 'I am well satisfied with Oakley's choice.'

He moved closer, slipping his arm about her narrow waist and drawing her into his arms in one rapid movement. At his touch, a tingling, magnetic touch, she was drawn to him as the needle on a compass is drawn north. But Delphine had no compass to guide her through this strange, alien territory, a dark and seemingly dangerous place she had stumbled blindly into. It was her fault, she thought despairingly. If anything awful should happen to her, she would be to blame. Except that she did not know quite what she had done wrong, or what she might have done differently to prevent it.

Covering her mouth with his, Stephen engulfed a stunned Delphine in a heady scent, not unlike brandy. Too shocked and surprised to resist, she trembled, holding herself rigid in his arms. She felt as if she were detached, seeing herself from outside her own body; in this trance-like state, she was amused when she felt him deepen his kiss and from a low level of consciousness grew a vague feeling of pleasure as she became caught up in the moment. She had never been held so close by a man before. It was an extraordinary sensation to feel the heat of his body so close to hers, to feel the muscles in his chest and arms and legs, his slim hips pressed to her own. Had the circumstances been different, she might even have enjoyed the sensation.

When he raised his head there was fire in his eyes. With swift dexterity he removed her jacket and took her in his arms as she stood frozen in stunned silence. Once more he proceeded to kiss her lips, with a hunger that alarmed her. When he released her, she was astonished to feel her dress fall away, settling about her feet. As his arms once again enfolded her in a grip of iron, her body full against his, Delphine little realised the devastating effect her soft flesh was having on him as he crushed his mouth to hers, invading, demanding, taking everything with a sensual, leisurely thoroughness, aching to sample the woman more meticulously.

Delphine's mind reeled from the intoxicating passion of his kiss, from the smell of him—a combination of sandalwood, alcohol and bodily scents—and the touch of his skin. The trembling weakness in her limbs attested to its potency. It really was a very strange situation, she thought coolly, her mind numbed with shock, and he, a very strange man—and, following what she had paused to watch at the bordello, she was in a very strange mood. She was conscious of her increased pulse rate—due to nervousness and trepidation, no doubt—but what to make of the weakness in her legs and the warm, glowing feeling low in her belly she truly did not know.

Reason began to flood back to her as she felt his hands wander all over her body. She fought and twisted within his embrace, for with sudden clarity it dawned on her just what he had in mind. She quickly realised her disadvantage; his grip was no longer like iron, but like finely tempered steel, and her struggles were in vain, for it was impossible to free herself. Still holding her, with an easy pull on the fastenings of her chemise he separated it from her body, spilling the full glory of her breasts before him. The only garments that remained were her drawers and white silk stockings.

Smothering a shocked gasp, at last Delphine managed to extricate herself from the embrace, at the same time catching both his hands and pushing him back.

'Sir, your eagerness astounds me,' she gasped, clutching her precarious modesty close, pressing the fullness of her bosom upwards until it fair besotted her assailant's senses, 'but I am not who you think I am and I really must go.'

A half-frown, half-smile crossed his face. 'I know not where your duties call you, sweet Delphine, but they can wait. At this moment—' Delphine saw the hard, flint-like gleam in his eyes '—I must have you.'

His arms scooped her up and, in a single lunge, they were on the bed. The heady scent of her gentle perfume, mingled with the essence of pure woman, filled Stephen's head and warmed his blood. The heat of his hunger spread with eager bounds through his loins.

Delphine started violently as her bare thigh brushed his and she felt the scorching heat of his flesh. She rolled away from him and came to her feet on the far side of the bed, but was halted in her intended flight when he rolled after her, shot out his arm and with a deep and throaty laugh jerked her back on to the bed. Her naked breasts were crushed against his chest as he bore down on her, his lips upon her neck insistent, his breathing uneven. With definite panic rising, she pushed hard and for a moment was free of him.

'Sir, please,' she begged with quiet desperation,

managing to keep her voice from betraying her alarm. 'Let me go for just a moment. There will be plenty of time later,' she cajoled in the softest tones. 'I shall return as soon I am able.'

'Don't be a tease.' His eyes were dark and heavy-lidded with desire and he smiled with wicked enticement as he divested her of her drawers. 'If this is a game you play, Delphine, I ask you to stop it now. Your maidenly blushes are a conceit. I want you—why else would you be here?'

Smothering a shocked gasp, again she moved to the side of the bed, and again he caught her round the waist with a strength that did not surprise her. Though she shoved at his hands, she could not escape; purposefully he drew her toward him. Kneeling on the mattress, he lowered her to its softness and, before she could move, his arms came down like sinewy pillars on either side of her, trapping her between them. He lowered his weight until he lay upon her, pinning her beneath him; it seemed that every move she made only abetted his unswerving seduction. She could no longer escape that long blade of passion that seared her thighs and made her quake. Raising his head, he stared down into her eyes and smiled slowly.

'I will have you now, Delphine. I will pay you your dues when the sun comes up, so do not disappoint me and I shall make it worth your while.'

'Oh,' she gasped, feeling his hardness searching, probing; feeling the heat of his maleness. 'What am I doing?'

He chuckled against her throat. 'If you don't know, sweetheart, who am I to tell you? You are a whore, my pet, and tonight you are mine.'

Delphine heaved beneath him, straining against the broad expanse of his chest, but his strength overpowered her struggles. It was too late now, he couldn't draw back, not now, not with that urgent need, swollen and throbbing, demanding release.

A burning pain exploded in her loins and his face pressed harder against hers. Tears filled her eyes and she tasted blood as she bit her own cheek. Then his hungering mouth found her lips and he kissed her long and deep. The pain started to subside as he began to move within her, savouring each passing moment of pleasure.

With her eyes closed tight, Delphine lay unresponsive. She resolved that she would resist any intrusion of physical delight from anything his body would do to her. If she remained still, he could not reach her. His long-starved passion grew; he could no longer control himself. She was unaware how long it lasted, but when he pulled away from her she turned, pulling the covers over herself, covering her used body from his gaze.

Chapter Two

The second time he took her, a strange, new feeling began to bloom within her, a feeling she could neither quench nor deny. Delphine's world began to tear itself free of all restraint. By now she realised her mistake in coming to his room, realised that he took her for a whore, but feeling the entire force of his will-power surrounding her, tempting her to do what she should not, she could not leave him.

He kissed her throat and murmured soft words. He touched her breasts with his fingertips, exploring their shape. Lightly, gently, and with the greatest of care, he squeezed her nipples until they began to throb and swell, and tiny threads of warmth began to radiate from them, spreading, growing, melting through her. The touch of his hands on her flesh destroyed her self-control; the heat of his kiss seared her lips, devastating her senses, rousing sensations that flamed through her body. She clung to him as she fought to cling to her sanity, trying to fight emotion with reason, but common sense eluded her.

Fear was gone now, gone completely, and she moaned softly as his hands continued their sweet torture. When he entered her she felt something new, something incredible, and she began to move as he moved, wrapping her legs around his, lifting her thighs and catching his hair in her hands, pulling it, throwing her head from side to side as the fountain welled within and began to brim.

To feel this way, to want this stranger with a hunger she could not believe, sapped all sense of honour. The desire that flared between them was so unexpected that it was in itself a seduction. One minute she was a tiger, the next a kitten, clawing, purring as the beauty became unbearable and she was lost, soaring into an oblivion that loomed ahead, awaiting with shuddering intensity. It came closer; he filled her fully and she held him inside her and clasped him and caressed him. She was completely absorbed, and through the veil of that absorption, a speck of light appeared, sharp as a star in a midnight sky. As it grew, she knew it to be something within herself, something that distinguished these moments of intimacy from everything that had gone before; she knew that she was linked to this man by something magical they both possessed—he to express, she to receive.

She was stunned by these thoughts at first, then fearful of what they could mean to her future; at that instant, as if he sensed the change in her, he opened his eyes and the pinpoints of fire in their depths linked with the light shining from hers.

'What are you? Are you some kind of sorceress, or are you an angel, that you can make me feel this way?'

Again he claimed her lips and she could not have drawn away had her life depended on it. Then she felt a bliss so bright, so blazing, she knew she couldn't possibly endure it, not a moment more. He shuddered and she was torn into a thousand shimmering shreds and cast into the abyss of ecstasy.

Dear Lord, what was happening to her—the helper, the do-gooder? Like some dreadful, insidious disease, the low life of the brothel had begun to infect her with its dark promise. Gone was the shining simplicity of her father's house and the dignity and elegance of her mother's world. What she felt now was every rotting desire that drove those who had anything to do with Mrs Cox's bordello. Having been bedded by a complete stranger, having responded wantonly to his demands made her no better than they were.

He fell asleep with Delphine in his arms. Forgetful for the moment of how the situation had come about, the feel of him so firm and strong infused her with a sense of security. Its curious comfort made her spirit dissolve like ice in a noonday haze. It was the first time any person had ever held her and the unexpected need of a lonely girl to be held broke loose and mingled with untold fears about her empty future. They found their outlet in tears.

She wept with the stranger's arms fast around her, breathing in the essence of him, and in so doing—even though she did not know this man, her only knowledge of him carnal—she sensed part of his spirit was empty, lonely and bereft, because, like her, he, too, had no one.

Though there was no strength left in her limbs, she sought to hold fast to the moment lest she lose some portion of it to the oncoming demands of sleep. But her eyelids were heavy, and she felt herself drifting away.

Stephen opened his eyes and quietly studied the face on the pillow beside his own, taking pleasure and becoming lost in the exciting beauty of her. Long sooty lashes fanned flawless skin, her mouth softly pink and tempting. A wealth of hair the colour of ripe chestnuts, streaked with red and a deep burnished gold, spread over her shoulders and breasts, dewy white as though they were lit from within, glowing and gleaming in the soft morning light. She lay limp against him and he shifted slightly in bewilderment, staring at the flecks of blood that stained the sheet they lay beneath.

He was confused by the memory of her reaction to last night; even though his brain had been befogged by alcohol, he remembered her own confusion when she had entered the room—and her inexperience in bed. Why had she allowed Oakley to bring her if she was a virgin? Was she compelled by poverty to take up the occupation of prostitution? He sighed, resting his head back on the pillow and closing his eyes. A virgin was the last thing he'd been expecting last night. They often spelled trouble and he always made an effort to avoid them, taking his pleasure with experienced creatures.

On his first night in London after months of fighting in Spain, after a night in an overcrowded tavern, he had instructed Oakley to find him a lively wench with emphasis on comeliness and cleanliness. No, he thought, looking at the woman asleep in his arms, a virgin had been the last thing he'd expected—and, he observed, as his eyes coursed slowly over her figure, admiring the well-turned hips, sensuous thighs and gracefully curving back, she was a beauty at that. At that moment, more than anything he wanted to take her once more, but in the cold light of day, his senses returning, he could not. Had she then made the smallest gesture that she was willing, he might have taken her quickly, but she was no longer merely a body, a thing of the flesh.

Her expression was one of peace, of perfect tranquillity. He put a finger gently to her face and brushed a wisp of hair from the sweet curve of her cheek. She did not speak or move, only opened her eyes. They darkened almost to black as the pupils dilated.

Delphine stared up at him, her mind slowly coming together from the depths of sleep, and saw that she nestled against a warm, hard chest. Stephen Fitzwaring was looking down at her, his breath stirring the hair on her brow. There was no denying that he was handsome, physically magnificent. She might even have dreamed of such a man at one time, but never in those dreams did she imagine that she would be made to fulfil his basest desires.

That was the moment when she realised full well where she was and what she had done—what she had *allowed* to happen. She had been bedded by a complete stranger. The passion that had earlier heated her blood with lust now blazed into fury and shame. The infatuation that had betrayed her honour was decimated by her own disgust. A gasp of anguish tore itself from her lips before she could strangle it. Throwing off the protective arm, she sat up, clutching the sheet over her bosom, her body trembling, her hair falling in soft disarray over her shoulders.

'How do you feel this morning?' Stephen asked, as though she had been his willing partner in carousing the night away.

'How do you expect me to feel?' she whis-

pered hoarsely, wriggling to the edge of the bed
and lowering her legs over the side, amazed and
shocked to find she was still wearing her stockings. 'I want to get dressed.'

'If you must.' His eyes passed over her with a
leisurely ease and he reached out a hand to caress her thigh, laughing softly when she shrank
further away from him. 'Would you like me to
help?'

'Please don't touch me again,' she managed
to utter, horrified and shocked to the core of her
being by what she had done. 'You've done your
worst—you've defiled me, you—you *lecher*—
now leave me alone.'

He heaved himself out of bed and, to Delphine's
relief, pulled on his trousers. 'Such cruelty. And
if I don't?' he teased, walking round the bed to
stand in front of her, hands on hips, not touching,
but near enough that she was trapped and could
not move without coming into contact with him.

'I'll scream the place down.' Tall though she
was, he topped her by a full head.

'I doubt that would do any good.' He grinned
quite devilishly. 'Oakley knows better than to
interrupt me when I'm entertaining a lady.'

'A lady is exactly what I was—my life one

of chastity and restraint, before I encountered you,' Delphine cried wretchedly, pushing him away and beginning to pull on her underclothes, though she found it impossible to stop her violent shaking and her thin petticoat offered little protection. How she wished he would complete his dressing and put on a shirt. 'What you have done to me makes me feel like a…a scarlet woman.'

The silver, early-morning sunlight drifting through the window glowed on his bare chest, showing him lithe and dangerous like a panther. Her nerves stretched taut, she raked her trembling fingers through her hair, combing it as best she could before securing it in a knot in the nape of her neck. Leaning on the bedpost with his arms folded across his chest, Stephen continued to watch her. When her gaze fell on the blood that stained the rumpled sheets, her cheeks flushed scarlet: her shame was complete.

Stephen shifted his gaze from her angry face to the bed, then back to her, and their eyes met. She was a most desirable young woman, but with a subdued, ladylike composure. The bold ones always drew immediate attention, yet they could not always keep it. Delphine Cameron was of prime quality and, until her encounter with him, unsullied. His awakened passion had made him more forceful than he'd intended and he did not recall her saying no.

'I now understand the truth of your inexperience, Delphine. I do not know why you agreed to let Oakley bring you to me—that is your affair—and if you are now full of regret then that, too, is your affair, but I cannot regret trying you before other men. Nor do I feel any guilt over the pleasure you have given me—although if you choose to be a woman of pleasure, then you need to be taught the finer arts of the profession. You are very beautiful. Such spirit and passion—a woman worthy of being loved. It would be a task for any man not to want to make love to you.'

Delphine's face reddened at his words, at what he incorrectly imagined she aspired to be. But she could not escape the fact that the second time he had made love to her had held some surprises, for she had not found him quite so loathsome then. And now, at this very moment, she wanted more than anything to run her hands across his muscled shoulders and down his chest. Her gaze lingered about his narrow waist and hips and taut, flat stomach. She trembled, her eyes darkened and instantly slid away from him, as if the temptation was more than she could bear.

She reeled with self-disgust at what she threatened to become—that most despised of all women: a loose woman. She had sampled the pleasures of the flesh, craved it. She was dissolute, wanton—but it was this stranger who had made her so. He had unleashed that wantonness within her and now she was afraid of herself.

'You were like a breath of fresh air,' he went on softly, 'after an evening spent in an overcrowded tavern. You have the kind of beauty that would tempt a saint.'

'In matters of debauchery you don't need anyone to lure you.' She bestowed on him an accusatory glare before lowering her gaze, reluctant to meet his eyes as she hurriedly fumbled with her bodice. She turned aside to hide her nakedness from him, but his hands came to assist, fastening the catches of her gown. When his fingers lingered on her neck she gasped and moved away, casting a quick nervous glance at him, fearful of what might happen if he came at her again, for she was absolutely certain she could not withstand his persuasive, unrelenting assault.

'Please do not touch me again—I beg of you,'

she pleaded. 'You have done me a grave injustice. Have you no conscience? I am not a strumpet, nor do I wish to be.'

Stephen's eyes narrowed at her words, the seeds of doubt beginning to take root. 'But Oakley found you in a whorehouse, did he not? That was his intended destination last night.'

'Yes, that was where he found me,' she confirmed, her voice ragged with emotion, 'but I was there looking for a missing child. Working at the orphanage and treating young and old for minor ailments is my profession, Colonel Fitzwaring, not prostitution. Your Mr Oakley led me to believe you were sick and in need of attention. I now fully comprehend the misunderstanding— on both our parts. Mr Oakley was looking for a woman by the name of Delphine, a woman at the bordello who has assumed my name for no other reason than because she happens to like it. It is unfortunate for me that I did not comprehend this at the time.'

Stephen nodded his head slowly as he began to understand the mistake. 'Yes, it was—and very stupid.'

'How could I know that I was about to fall prey to a degenerate, unprincipled libertine?'

Stephen scowled. 'That bad?' he asked softly. 'No matter. It's too late for recriminations now. The deed is done and there is no going back.'

'And I am totally ruined,' she said, her voice thick with recrimination. 'You callous beast. I am flattered that you found a romp on the bed with me entertaining, Colonel, but I truly wish you had sought a woman who would appreciate your advances rather than one who loathes you. Does it not concern you that you raped me and that I do not wish to be here?'

Stephen studied her with a great deal of interest. 'It is beginning to and I cannot say that I blame you. Although, as I remember it, you had plenty of time to warn me of my error before we got to bed.'

He stared down at her. He was sorry for what he had done, for not bothering to find out more about her and for not taking the time to make love to her properly as she deserved. He longed to explain away the extraordinary circumstances and his own behaviour, to lay the blame elsewhere, but he could not. He shook his head and the shamefaced, penitent cast of his features softened. His eyes were steady and honest, and he did not avoid her gaze as he spoke.

'I will not lie to you, but last night I truly believed you were—'

'A whore,' she provided for him coldly.

'Yes—that. Men are weak creatures, Delphine, when their manhood is involved, and cannot resist a beautiful woman. But I swear I would not have touched you had I known you were chaste.' A small smile broke across his features and he moved to stand closer to her. Before she could protest, he took her hands and drew her to him. 'However,' he murmured, his eyes lingering on her lips, 'I did touch you—and more than that. And now I am reluctant to let you go. So a kiss before you leave me, Delphine—something I can remember you by. Let us see if I can thaw some of that ice from your lips.'

So saying, he lowered his head and placed his lips on hers, kissing her long, almost lovingly, arching her body against his. He ravished her mouth, savouring the honey sweetness of her lips and the intoxicating nearness of her body, and all logical thought flew from his mind. He held her to him, luxuriating in the feel of her, the warmth of her, her desirability. One of his hands rested in the small of her back, holding her to him, fusing their bodies together so that Delphine was aware of his arousal. It was becoming increasingly difficult to imagine her leaving him just yet. Damned if it wasn't. But Delphine had other ideas and took his bottom lip between her teeth to nip it fiercely. Cursing, he set her away from him, tasting blood in his mouth.

'And you call yourself a soldier—a commander of men?' Delphine exploded in disgust, choking on sobs and angered by the tears that blurred her eyes. 'Where have you learned your manners, Colonel? In the hovels of Spain?'

Ignoring the pain from his injured lip, with his hands on his hips he stared into her tear-bright eyes. 'So the kitten has found its claws. You have a sharp tongue, Delphine, and teeth to go with it. You cut me to the quick. I do not recall any such protestations when we were in bed.'

'You wouldn't,' she uttered derisively. 'You were disgustingly drunk.'

His gaze travelled the length of her slim, lissom body, her breasts rounded beneath the tight bodice of her gown. The tall, shapely figure could not be hidden even when she was fully clothed, nor could her natural grace be disguised.

'Not so drunk that I did not know what was happening,' he replied, softening his tone. 'The second time I made love to you, I would go so far as to say you found pleasure in the act.'

Infuriated, Delphine swung her bag at him, missing his face by a mere inch when he sprang back. He had not expected physical violence from her.

'Next time I shall not miss,' she promised heatedly.

He cocked a sleek black brow. 'Is there to be a next time?'

'Only if we should have the misfortune to meet,' she cried, angrily wiping away her tears with the back of her hand. 'Touch me again and you will be singing in soprano for the rest of your life. Now kindly call your Mr Oakley and have him order me a carriage. The sooner I am gone from this place—and from you—the better I shall feel.'

Deeply touched by her obvious distress and cursing himself for being the cause of it, in an attempt to ease her wretchedness he said, 'As a gentleman I can hardly send you on your way without escort. I do not wish to pry, but if you will name your destination, I will deliver you there without further ado. I assure you most humbly that you need have no fear of me.'

'Indeed? Forgive me, but I must disagree. I prefer to see myself home.'

'As you wish. You are not my prisoner. You may leave directly if you so wish.'

'I cannot do that. I entered your room unobserved; I would die of shame if anyone should see me leave.'

'Then I will get Oakley. I would go myself, but I fear these tight breeches leave nought to the imagination. The embarrassment would be all mine.'

Delphine's eyes travelled downward innocently and she was immediately sorry. Blood rushed to her face and she turned away. He was right; his physical state could not be concealed. She was thankful when a hesitant knocking came at the door.

Stephen smiled, amused by her discomfort, and went to open it. 'I must pay recompense to the time you have given me, Delphine. What is the going rate?' As soon as the words had left his mouth he regretted them. Hurt and humiliation filled her eyes.

'How would I know that? As I have told you, I am no whore. You owe me nothing. I have my pride, Colonel, and will take nothing from you.

However, a generous donation to the orphanage on Water Lane would not go amiss.'

'I will see to it.' His eyes darkened and he frowned slightly, his gaze holding hers. 'For what it's worth, I do not blame you for being angry. I feel wretched about the way I treated you. My conduct was inexcusable.'

His frankness startled Delphine and for a moment she was caught off guard. 'Yes, it was,' she said softly.

'Subtlety is not my strongest suit, I fear, but if you wish to slap my face, it is at your disposal.'

Delphine slowly shook her head, still startled. 'I would not blame you.'

As they stood silently looking at each other, Delphine felt a curious sensation for this man stir deep inside her—this man she had every reason to despise. He would escape retribution for what he had done to her, for she knew she could never speak of the shameful night past. Her body trembled so violently that she almost swayed off her feet. Last night she had suffered the depravity of a man. Last night had also provided a chilling insight into her own body and how wanton she could be.

When Stephen turned from her, Delphine saw

her reflection in a cracked mirror across the room. Rage and fury roiled within her and bitter tears stung her eyes. Traitor, she silently spat at her image. You let him bed you. Shameless hussy! Have you no honour?

No answer came.

Stephen opened the door to admit Mr Oakley, who smiled sheepishly at her, but she returned the smile with a glare, whereupon he turned to his master, quite confused. A penitent smile curved Stephen's lips. Perplexed, Mr Oakley glanced at the bed, his eyes widening when he saw the stains on the sheets. Stephen met his gaze and nodded the silent response to his unasked question.

'It would appear you were mistaken, Oakley. This Delphine is not the Delphine you sought. It is unfortunate, but there we are. Arrange some transport for her, will you, and I am sure she will appreciate it if you see that she leaves the inn without being observed.'

Putting on her bonnet and picking up her bag, Delphine couldn't exit the room quickly enough. She followed in Mr Oakley's wake, hoping never to have the misfortune to see Colonel Fitzwaring again. A fierce hatred for the man burned inside her with an all-consuming intensity. She would never forget what he had done—and certainly never, ever forgive him.

She was still in a state of considerable shock after what she had endured, but seated in the hackney on her way home to Mayfair, she had yet to comprehend the full magnitude of what had transpired. A conflict raged inside her between shock and anger. Shock that such a thing should have happened to her, and anger against Colonel Fitzwaring for having done it—the most dreadful thing that could happen to an unmarried girl of her class. She froze as the situation and the seriousness crystallised in her mind. It seemed, suddenly, as if all her innocence had vanished. Indeed, there was a fearsome new depth to life that she had never known before.

Delphine was the daughter of Lord John Cameron and his wife, Evangeline, and they lived in one of the elegant houses lining Berkeley Square. Delphine was on the point of letting herself in when, as if on cue, the door was opened by Digby, the butler Delphine had known all her life.

'Good morning, Digby,' she said, entering the

hall. She had no doubt that, like everyone else in the house, he would be curious to know her reason for remaining out all night—and with not a word to anyone. God help her if the truth came out. 'Is anyone risen, or are they still abed?'

'Lady Cameron is in the drawing room. She was most concerned when you failed to come home last night and rose early. She instructed me to tell you to go straight in the moment you arrived.'

Delphine's heart sank. She had wanted to bathe and change her clothes before she faced her mother's wrath, but it would seem there was nothing for it.

'I see. Then I shall go in. In the meantime, have one of the maids prepare me a bath, will you, Digby?'

Delphine's mother was seated in her favourite chair by the window. Although it was still early, the day promised to be as hot as the one before; the room was already sweltering and her mother was fanning herself. Of medium height and slender, her greying dark hair perfectly arranged, Lady Cameron's anger was palpable to Delphine the moment she entered the room. With compressed lips the older woman looked her over in a strained, suspicious manner and began wielding her feather fan more swiftly, a sure sign of exasperation. Its quiet swishing in the silence of the room jarred Delphine physically. She crossed the room and clung to the back of a chair to steady herself.

'Good morning, Mama. I apologise for giving you cause for concern.'

'Concern?' she snapped crossly. 'You knew perfectly well that I wanted you to attend my musical evening last night. Not only did you fail to attend, but you didn't even bother to send word that you would be out all night! This is most improper. Where have you been? I demand to know. And just look at you. Your clothes look as if they have been slept in.'

'I—I was at the orphanage until quite late. Two of the children have gone down with something. I stayed to help. By the time I'd finished it was too late for me to get home, so I decided to remain there the night.'

Her mother's eyes narrowed with angry suspicion. 'I do not believe a word of it, Delphine. You are lying; I know that for a fact. When you failed to come home I sent a footman to the orphanage to fetch you. He was told that you had already left. I shudder when I think of the type of people you consort with. Celia has a lot to answer for.'

'It wasn't Aunt Celia's fault.' Having been caught out in a lie, Delphine knew she would have to tell her mother some of the truth. 'I—I went in search of a child who'd gone missing.'

'And did you find her?'

Delphine nodded. 'Yes.'

'Where?'

'She—she had run away to be with her mother—at Mrs Cox's bordello, at the other end of Water Lane.'

'I see. So her mother is a fallen woman. And are you telling me that you actually entered that establishment?'

'Yes,' Delphine answered quietly. Her mother was a woman who had led a sheltered life in the exclusive part of Bath until her marriage. Her world consisted of daily promenades around Mayfair, shopping and sipping tea with her friends in the pleasure gardens, her evenings one long round of entertainment. She had never been to places like St Giles or Seven Dials, those stewpots of disease and depravity. She had never seen women like Meg or children like Maisie.

She would never understand as Delphine and Aunt Celia did that Meg and women like her were driven to sell themselves on the streets out of desperation. She would never know how those women suffered.

'The fist attribute of a lady is ladylike conduct, whether in public or in private, and conduct of all kinds must be governed by good manners. You, Delphine, have shown neither. *Why* do you have to be like this? *Why* can you not look to your sisters for example?'

'I am not like my sisters, Mama.'

'No, you are not. You are too outspoken, too disobedient—too much of everything, and you do things that no respectable young lady would contemplate doing. Courting danger, traipsing about the streets at night with cut-throats and ruffians on the loose and suffering all weathers.'

Delphine's eyes grew moist with unshed tears. 'Exposure to the elements is not suffering,' she replied. 'It is nothing compared to the pain of rejection. To be rejected by a father and mother for not being the son they had hoped for: that is true suffering.' The words slipped from her mouth before she could check herself and her mother looked surprised and more than a little discomfited by her perception. Delphine felt as if a part of her had died. Her need to be loved and adored burned as brightly as ever, but her innocence was gone.

Pulling herself together with an effort, she continued. 'I should not have spoken to you so, but your questioning has drawn from me that which we have never spoken of before. I have always been sensitive to the fact.'

Her mother got to her feet, her body ramrod straight, her head up. Her breathing was fast, her whole face alight with the force of her anger.

'Your father and I have tried and tried with you, Delphine,' she said. Her voice was tinged with sadness, but edged with self-righteous complaint. 'We have done our best for you—given you everything. All you seem to care for is your charity work—there scarcely seems room in your life for anything else. I don't know where it has come from, this fondness you have for simple folk. It may be counted a credit to your wisdom that you are fair and show consideration to them. Alas, this cannot hold true for those most near and dear to you.'

'I am sorry, Mama,' Delphine said awkwardly.

'I do love you and Papa and all my sisters, but I also enjoy what I do.'

'Sorry!' Her mother's voice was scornful. 'Perhaps if you had been a dutiful daughter you would not feel so rejected. I am still waiting for you to explain where you have been all night. Am I to suppose that you stayed at that—that bordello?'

Delphine blanched and looked away. Lady Cameron came to stand in front of her and, taking hold of her chin, forced her face back round. Her eyes probed, delved into those of her daughter, trying to read in them the truth. She wrinkled her nose as though she could smell the physical contact. She knew.

'You did, didn't you?' she asked in shocked disbelief. 'Were you with a man? Answer me!'

With a pain in her heart almost too heavy to bear and tears not far away, Delphine nodded, unable to stop herself from telling her mother every sordid detail of what had happened to her. In the telling, she remembered when Lord Fitzwaring had taken her a second time, how she had stilled, knowing the struggle was over. He was the victor—though against a smaller opponent. She had known the relief of it, and in doing so had become aware of the smooth firmness of his flesh, his perfect body above hers, the strange attraction she felt for him and her own insatiable desire.

The end of tension from the struggle had given her a strange physical thrill. She'd realised with horror that despite her rigid self-control during visits to the bordello, she could fall prey to sensual delight as easily as the woman she had observed making love to a stranger; she had understood in that instant that men and women were drawn to each other for the sensations they could enjoy. If a man or woman found delight in the sensations, this was part of the way they had been created, part of nature's law, and could not therefore be considered unnatural. But her mother would not see it that way.

Lady Cameron listened in horror to the words that tumbled from her daughter's mouth. For a moment, only utter shock and uncertainty registered on her face. Then her eyes began to gleam as they had done on the day her eldest daughter had married Lord Rundell and her whole expression changed, leaving her face blank, but decisive. Behind the mask of dignified respectability, the ambitious mother had taken over, greedy for her children and determined both to avoid a scandal and to make the best out of an intolerable situation.

'The man is a colonel, you say, in Wellington's army. What else? Is he rich? Titled? What?'

'He is Lord—Lord Stephen Fitzwaring. That is all I know about him.'

'Your behaviour was reckless and totally irresponsible. Now you must pay the price. He will have to marry you, of course—and he will, if he is a gentleman, which I am beginning to doubt.'

Delphine had never seen her mother's face as it was then. Her eyes were hard, looking through Delphine as if she were a whore rather than her own daughter. Her eyes dropped to Delphine's waist and then back to her face.

'What if there is a child? Have you considered that?'

A cold, dreadful shock seized Delphine's every nerve and the blood drained from her face. In her innocence she had not thought of this; lying beneath Colonel Fitzwaring, she had not considered the full consequences of his act.

When Delphine opened her mouth to speak, her mother held up her hand, quivering with fury and indignation. 'Be quiet. What you have done is nothing short of wicked. It pains me to say it, you—you Jezebel. I shudder to think how your father will react to this. You are a disgrace.'

John Cameron was a short, stocky man of Scottish descent, with whitening tawny hair and a temper that was easily roused. He was summoned right away and when he'd heard what his wife had to say, his anger was like an explosion.

'I always knew no good would come of your visiting that orphanage—however good your intentions. No,' he blustered, red to the ears and puffing out his barrel chest, 'you've made your bed. Lie on it. You are absolutely ruined unless the man marries you. You do realise that, don't you, Delphine?'

She straightened up and looked directly at her father. 'I have made a mistake, a grievous and awful mistake, and I will have to live with the consequences—but marriage?'

'Absolutely. Thank God the man's credentials are fitting.'

'He won't marry me.'

'We'll see about that. If Fitzwaring thinks he can ruin my good name by seducing one of my daughters and then go flitting off back to Spain, he is grievously mistaken. He'll pay for it; I'll make damned sure of that.'

Helplessness, bleak as the grave, descended on Delphine, but she was powerless to speak, powerless to stand against the combined forces of her parents when their minds were made up.

Two days later her father summoned her. Fully expecting another scolding, she proceeded to her father's study, patting her hair into place. He was standing with his back to the fireplace.

'Come in, Delphine.' He nodded towards the tall man looking out of the window with his back to her. With his feet planted firmly apart, his hands behind his back, attired in his military uniform of scarlet jacket and white trousers, he stood stiff and unyielding. 'You are already acquainted with Colonel Fitzwaring, of course.'

Delphine's heart gave a fearful leap. Her initial surprise at her father's summons was stirred into a sudden tumult of emotions by Colonel Fitzwaring's presence. He turned and looked at her with those incredible midnight-blue eyes of his. The glare of his red jacket hurt her eyes; for one wild, unreasoning moment her life flared into vivid, lively colour, her familiar surroundings fading away into the background. She was conscious of an unwilling excitement. In fact, much to her annoyance, she was very much aware of everything about him—the long, strong lines of his body, the skin above the jacket, tanned and healthy—and she was surprised to see faint lines of weariness on his face.

Conscious of those searing eyes on her, with trembling fingers she clutched the neck of her gown, remembering that dark gaze and its seeming power to strip the clothes from her, leaving her body bare. Yes, she remembered him. She knew him by her own response to him—needle-sharp chills—but there was no sign of her lover of three nights ago.

In an atmosphere bristling with tension, with an effort she said, in the coldest and most condescending manner, 'Yes, we are. Good day, Lord Fitzwaring.'

'Miss Cameron.' He bowed, and there was a touch of irony in his mocking tone as he lowered his shining dark head.

Stephen's blood was pumping through his veins. He had not expected Lord Cameron to deliver such a robust lecture on the rules he felt Stephen had broken. As a result Stephen was alert; his consciousness was fine-honed as a sharp blade. The black pinpoints of his dark-blue eyes shot fire.

Delphine had never seen such a look in a man's eyes before. It reminded her of sparks shooting from the glow of a fire. His presence filled the room. He didn't speak. Waiting, Delphine shivered. Silence was a weapon, she realised, and there were men who knew how to use it to deadly effect. Stephen Fitzwaring was one such man. It seemed no one was prepared to speak in his presence unless spoken to. He had the dynamism of a military commander and he was using silence aggressively, to assert his power.

'You are here because my father asked you to come. Is that not so, Lord Fitzwaring?'

'It is. You are well, I trust?'

Delphine actually flinched at the cold, ruthless fury in his eyes as they raked over her. She did not want to disappoint her father now, having decided the moment she'd set eyes on Colonel Fitzwaring to keep her composure, but the effort of holding herself in check in the presence of this arrogant man was too much.

'As you see,' she replied icily, suspecting he would rather face the full might of Napoleon's army than be present at her home today, 'I have survived our last encounter without scars.' This was hardly the truth, but she would not grant him the satisfaction of telling him so.

The impact of his gaze was no less potent for the distance between them. He took a step closer, his powerful, animal-like masculinity assaulting her senses. Melting inwardly, she felt her traitorous body offer itself to this man; in that moment they both acknowledged the forbidden flame that sparked between them, both angered by their inability to control it. He raised one well-defined eyebrow, watching her, a half-smile now playing on his lips. He seemed to know exactly what was going on in her mind.

But Stephen would have none of it. The army was of the utmost importance to him—he had no time for marriage and affairs of the heart. A man who loved too well was vulnerable. Certainly he yielded to the desires of the flesh as much as the next man. Many women had passed through his life—some had faded from memory and a few he had felt affection for, but never doted on, excepting one, a beautiful, callous and treacherous woman, whom he had left with the bitter belief that love was only for the young and idealistic.

He liked mature women, women who understood the rules of the game, women who accepted the fact that affairs ran their course and expected nothing more.

His main aim in life, while the military campaign was ongoing in Spain, was to concentrate on developing his mind and spirit for action on the field of battle—until he'd had the misfortune to encounter this infuriating, if beautiful, young woman. How could he have known that she was the daughter of one of London's elite? His lust had led him into a trap of his own making—now he must pay the price of his passion.

Chapter Three

Lord Cameron looked at his daughter. He had not been made aware of the facts that had drawn Delphine into this man's bed, nor did he wish to be, but unless the Colonel wanted to make a damned fool of himself and create a scandal, he would have to do the honourable thing and marry her. But she should be warned not to anger him overmuch, for, as he had discovered to his cost when he had sought the man out to confront him, the man had a temper and Delphine would do well to heed that.

'Lord Fitzwaring has confirmed that you did indeed have…relations at the Blue Boar three nights past. Since I am a man of honour, I wanted to be sure of the facts before I asked him to do the right thing by you.'

Delphine tilted her head to one side as she considered her seducer coldly. 'And will you, Lord Fitzwaring? Do the right thing by me, I mean,' she said, resenting his effect on her, the masculine assurance of his bearing.

'Of course. Your father and I have discussed the matter and it is our intention to see that you are cared for.'

'Indeed?' She laughed lightly, a laugh laced with bitterness. 'I can vouch for my father's concern, but when I recall your less-than-gentlemanly treatment of me on our previous encounter, you must forgive me if I doubt yours, my lord. Do you think it pleases me to plead for my salvation from the man who stole my virginity? Do what you will. Seek out your own pride and honour, but do no hope to find your conscience clean and laundered at my door, Colonel.'

Stephen's face hardened and his eyes took on a malignant expression. 'I would advise you to have a care,' he ground out, leaning forwards slightly so that his furious eyes were level with hers. 'I did not have to come here today. I could have pleaded ignorance due to my inebriated state at the time and told your father that he was mistaken.'

In no mood to be charitable or diplomatic,

Delphine smiled mockingly into his eyes. 'Your head was sodden with drink—that I do remember—and I also recall you have a rather attractive little mole on your—'

'*Enough,*' he thundered, thoroughly enraged by this chit.

Delphine watched the man's temper fraying—his eyes were dark and strong emotion was choking him.

Bringing himself quickly under control, in a more reasonable tone he said, 'I cannot do more than apologise for my conduct and offer recompense. I have told your father that I am willing to marry you and he has my guarantee that you will be supported in a manner suitable to your upbringing.'

Delphine's lips curved in what resembled a sneer rather than a smile. She could sense the slowly burning anger in him at being manipulated into marrying her. 'How extremely generous of you, Lord Fitzwaring. Where do you propose we start?'

Her father looked at her with cold eyes. 'Enough, Delphine. You are too impertinent. You would do well to watch your manners. It is because of your disobedience and your determination to flout the rules that govern the lives of respectable young ladies that you find yourself in this mess. Can't you get it through your head that you are sullied—damaged goods? By any moral code you are disgraced. If your affair with Lord Fitzwaring comes to light and it becomes known that you are no longer virtuous, every door in London will be slammed in your face.'

Delphine stiffened with indignation. 'Papa, it was not an affair. I—'

'Silence. Your mother and I always said you were a lost cause. This latest in a long line of escapades proves we were right. It is with considerable distaste that I do this, but I must, for your sake, insist that Lord Fitzwaring brings you to the altar.'

Delphine seethed with anger and humiliation. Her father was asking her to enter into a binding contract to change her life, something that would determine her entire future. She had seen so little of the world and knew so little of men. She had attended only a few sedate gatherings with her mother, only a handful of dances and soirées. She had not mixed in society like most girls of her age and all she had to measure Stephen Fitzwaring against were the men who came to call on her twin sisters, Rose and Fern, and the men who had married her older sisters. For the most part she found them boring and not in the least appealing. Stephen Fitzwaring was not like any one of them.

'But I have no desire to wed Lord Fitzwaring.'

'It is not open to discussion. He has agreed, though God knows that if I were a violent man I would take a horsewhip to him. Because of him, if this is not dealt with in the proper manner, you will be subjected to public censure and a scandal that will ruin you and make us a laughing stock. Which is why, two days hence, the two of you will be married by special licence.'

Completely taken aback, Delphine's eyes widened with alarm. 'Why the haste?'

Stephen raised a finely arched brow. 'My duties call me back to Spain immediately,' he informed her coolly.

'Indeed?' She tossed her head imperiously. 'That is no great disappointment to me.'

Stephen's eyes narrowed with irritation. 'You are severely lacking in respect and discretion when you speak to me. When I am your husband, things will be different.'

His words failed to anger her. She gave him

that amused smile, slightly scornful, such as she had seen her father give on occasion, which generally infuriated people.

'When you become my husband, I can only hope the war with France is of long duration and that your military duties will keep you in Spain,' she asserted. 'Until then, if you address me in a civil manner, you will not find me lacking in respect. It is something that comes naturally to me, except when I meet intemperance.'

'Enough,' her father cut in. 'Let us get on with it. There are arrangements to be made.'

'Of course,' Stephen said, speaking precisely. 'Under the circumstances it would be best if Delphine remained here until I return from Spain. I shall then take her to my home in Cornwall.'

'No, sir, you will not,' Lord Cameron asserted forcefully. 'As your wife my daughter's place will be in your house. After the ceremony you will take her there directly. I am sure you will not be delayed too long in rejoining your regiment.'

Stephen turned his frigid gaze upon his future father-in-law. 'And of course you insist upon that?'

His lordship fixed the colonel with an unwavering stare. 'Yes, I do.'

A muscle twitched angrily in Stephen's cheek. 'Very well, although I shall have to leave almost immediately and will have no time to see her settled in.'

'I think I shall manage perfectly well without you,' Delphine said coldly.

Stephen looked at his future wife. 'Marriage to me is what your father wants and marriage to me is what you shall have for the rest of your life.'

'Do you forget there is a war on, my lord? Men are being killed out there. There is every chance you won't return.'

He laughed low in his throat and his eyes were merciless. 'Have no fear, Delphine. I have no desire to leave you too soon.'

'There is the matter of Delphine's dowry to discuss before you go. I am prepared to make a generous settlement.'

'Keep it. I want nothing from you.'

His reply drew a surprised gasp from Delphine. Her father stared at the colonel for a moment, bewildered.

'Did I hear you correctly, sir?'

'You did,' Stephen replied coldly. 'I have no intention of taking payment for marrying my wife.'

'But—it is normal practice.'

'It is not a practice I approve of. I am capable of financing Delphine's needs, Lord Cameron.'

'I will not be a burden to you, Colonel,' Delphine told him, 'socially or financially. At least that way I can manage to retain some shred of self-esteem.'

Stephen looked at her with hard eyes. 'As my wife, you will hardly be in a position to maintain yourself without me. You will find that out soon enough.'

With that he inclined his head to them both and walked to the door. Delphine caught a glimpse of his angry, aristocratic profile as he paused for a moment, then he was gone with only a pledge that he would not be late for the ceremony.

It was over. Delphine was now the wife of Lord Fitzwaring and on the point of leaving London. When they had left the church her face had been ashen. Impatient to dispose of the daughter who had fallen from grace, Lord and Lady Cameron had made it a rushed affair.

There had been no beautiful wedding dress, no

bridesmaids, only a husband who despised her for forcing him into marriage against his will. When they had spoken their vows he had placed the ring on her finger and the traditional kiss on her cold, unresponsive lips. As Stephen raised his head, his taunting smile had seared her and brought a rush of angry colour to her cheeks. He was laughing cruelly at her and her pride was stung. She jutted her chin defiantly and glared at him.

'Were I a man you would not sneer so easily.'

She saw his cheeks crease with a maddeningly slow and mischievous smile, and when he spoke it was for her ears only, low and unmerciful. 'Were you a man you would not be in the situation you are now in, my love.'

Her temper flared and she tried to wrest her arm free from what to everyone present appeared to be a husband's tender hand placed on his wife's arm. To Delphine his grip was like a vice, which tightened as she tried to pull it free.

Lowering his head to hers, his warm breath fanning her cheek, seeming to enjoy her distress, Stephen murmured, 'You cannot escape me, Delphine. I have a very possessive nature.

You are mine, now and for ever, so smile and let everyone see how happy you are.'

Her face burned. She had little left to be proud of. Even her independence had been stripped from her and it goaded her that she must now rely upon this man for her support. 'You must be the vilest of toads that I have ever had the misfortune to meet,' she hissed.

He did not seem surprised or insulted. Undaunted, he lifted his brows quizzically, a twist of humour about his beautifully moulded lips. 'This is a crushing moment, my love. I have been called some unflattering things in my life, but I have never been called a toad,' he murmured, chuckling deep as he walked her back down the aisle.

The wedding feast had been a strained affair and passed quickly. The bride and groom were now about to depart on their journey to Cornwall. Standing in the hall Delphine was indeed living as in a nightmare. Only two of her sisters, Rose and Fern, had been present at the ceremony—although she had seen little of them since the morning of her return following her night with Lord Fitzwaring. She suspected that her mother had purposely kept them away from her lest she contaminate her precious darlings with her loose morals.

Her two older sisters were married and lived too far away to attend the wedding at such short notice. The twins had looked on in bewilderment, with no knowledge of what had transpired between their younger sister and the handsome soldier. They were so perfect, so fragile and dainty, with pale silk hair and rose-tinted skin, both dressed in identical gowns of the palest cream. Their eyes were an incredible bright blue, their mouths soft and tremulous. They were innocent and had perfect manners—in fact, they were everything Delphine was not and they were to marry into the aristocracy a few months hence.

Lord and Lady Cameron doted on their beautiful identical twins. All her life Delphine had longed for her parents to look at her the way they looked at Rose and Fern. Their haste to see her gone from the house was almost too painful to bear.

Now she bade farewell to the servants and family retainers who had gathered to say goodbye and offer their salutations and, unexpectedly, a few tears. She was particularly sad to bid goodbye to her Aunt Celia, who would miss both her and her help at the orphanage terribly. A level-headed woman who was usually in control of herself and any situation, she had been made privy to the circumstances that had brought about this hasty marriage. Aunt Celia's usually stern face broke into a kindly smile and her eyes filled with tears.

'God bless you, my dear,' she said, embracing her tenderly. 'I'm going to miss you for more reasons than you know. I am so proud of you.'

'Proud of me?' Delphine said sadly. 'How can that be when I have disgraced you all?'

Celia smiled at her gently. 'Nonsense. Sometimes a girl cannot help the things that happen to her. She is just a victim of circumstance.'

'Or of a particular soldier,' Delphine murmured sadly.

Celia laughed softly. 'Yes, or of a soldier. But at least your Colonel Fitzwaring is a handsome soldier. When my dear brother told me of your predicament and said a colonel in Wellington's army was to blame, I had cause to worry. I had visions of him being old and ugly and lecherous. I am relieved to find he is none of those things.

I think he is quite magnificent. The donation he made to the orphanage was generous indeed.'

Delphine was genuinely surprised to hear this. When he had offered her payment for her services and she had suggested he make a donation to the orphanage, she had truly thought he would ignore her request. 'I had no idea—although I'm ashamed when I think of the way it came about.'

'Don't be. It is done and life goes on.' Celia gave her a final embrace. 'Now you must go. You have a long journey ahead of you. Promise to write to me as soon as you get to Cornwall. I want to know all about your new home.'

'I will, I promise—and please send me all the news about the children. You will keep a watch over Maisie, won't you, Aunt Celia?'

'I shall.'

'And if anything should happen—if you have cause to feel concern for her safety—you will let me know.'

'Yes. Now go along with you. I'm sure there are some poor souls in Cornwall in need of your care, Delphine.'

Delphine was hard put to restrain herself. Her throat was sore and her chest tight. She said goodbye to her sisters and her stony-faced parents. There was no appeal she could make. They did not touch her or tell her that they loved her. She turned aside hastily and strode away, for her husband awaited her in front of the house.

Inside the confines of the coach she felt miserable and alone. Her eyes stung as they left London behind. So much was bottled up inside her; now it seemed too much. It was choking her. She was a tight bubble of misery being squeezed and ready to burst at any time, but she would remain intact. She would weep no more.

The coach made good speed. Appearing to loathe the prospect of being alone with Delphine in the coach, Stephen, preferring to accompany Mr Oakley on horseback, was mounted on a huge black beast, its glossy black coat gleaming with every ripple of its muscles.

The coach rattled into the cobbled yard of a coaching inn where they were to spend the night. Stephen dismounted and, with an imperious edge to his voice, instructed the driver to be ready to travel at half past eight the next morning before handing the reins of his horse to a groom.

'Dear me,' Delphine remarked to Mr Oakley, who had come to hand her down from the coach, 'my husband does seem most put out. No doubt he blames me for delaying his journey to Portsmouth. What a nuisance I must seem, although,' she uttered drily, casting Mr Oakley a reproachful look, 'if either of us needs somebody to blame for what has transpired, we need look no further than you. Do you not agree, Mr Oakley?'

A man of admirable self-control and discretion and not easily annoyed, Mr Oakley nodded, falling into step beside her as they walked across the inn yard. 'I fear that is so, my lady. Call it a case of mistaken identity, if you like. I misjudged the situation completely and hold myself entirely responsible for the outcome. I can only apologise most sincerely for any distress you may have suffered because of my actions and ask your pardon.'

She smiled at him, finding it impossible to be angry with this good-natured, amiable man. 'You may have it, Mr Oakley. Whether or not I can pardon my husband is a different matter entirely. He does not suffer women gladly, does he?'

'He means you no harm, my lady. Over the years I have learned that women play a small part in his life, even though half of the women he meets fancy themselves in love with so hand-some and dashing a commander.'

'A fancy that is not reciprocated,' Delphine guessed coolly, her eyes fixed on her husband's straight back as he disappeared inside the inn.

'I fear not. My master is a soldier first and foremost, and as a soldier he is too short of pa-tience to be a practised gallant. His emotions are difficult to read—he has learned to guard them well. He thrives most when the country is on a war footing—as it is now with Bonaparte. After long hours in the saddle, he will often inspect his regiment, supervising any improvements he considers necessary. Then he spends long hours writing orders to his commanders, or planning new strategies. Often, he works into the early hours until finally surrendering to an exhausted sleep.'

'Your loyalty to him does you credit, Mr Oakley, although I am not prepared to be lenient quite yet. His exhaustion may explain why he is constantly out of sorts and as ill tempered as a bear with a sore head.' Having reached the inn, she paused and studied her companion. There was an extraordinary warmth and intelligence in his eyes that was reflected in his smile. 'You are very fond of my husband, Mr Oakley. I see that.'

'As I said, my lady, we have been together for many years—through the thick and the thin of it. No matter what is said of him, he is first a man of honour. He has a heart that is all fire and he is possessed of an energy and passion for life— the kind of life he could only find with the army as a soldier. He knew what he wanted from an early age and pursued it single-mindedly.'

'To the exclusion of all else, it would seem, Mr Oakley—including his wife, since he cannot wait to discard her and return to Spain,' Delphine re-marked, tempted to add, *and to be reunited with his Spanish* señorita. She was unable to keep the bitterness from her voice, which was not lost on her companion.

'I'm afraid that is so, my lady, but—' now there was a twinkle in his eyes '—I very much sus-pect that you will be his undoing.'

Delphine was unable to respond to his state-ment, for at that moment Stephen appeared at her side. When she realised she was to share a room with him, her heart began to pound and heat warmed her cheeks. She had given little thought to the fact that she would be ensconced with him for the entire night. But, she reminded herself, it was her wedding night, a night a bride should expect to share with her husband.

She was suddenly nervous, yet she also felt a sense of excitement. A woman was supposed to be terrified of the experience that lay ahead of her, terrified because she was ignorant of what it entailed. But Delphine had already had her first night of passion with Stephen Fitzwaring and knew exactly what to expect. Her traitorous body was already throbbing to experience again what he had done to her. Unable to trust herself when she was around him, she must learn to fight these wanton urges, bring them under control, for she could not, must not, risk her heart.

After sharing a meal with him in the crowded dining room, their conversation limited and stilted, they went up the stairs to their room. Halting before the door, Stephen opened it and ushered her inside.

Feeling less sure of herself by the minute, Delphine glanced at the bed, which was certainly not the biggest bed she had ever seen. Was it really less than a week ago she had spent the entire night with him at the Blue Boar?

Stephen observed the soft flush that sprang to her cheeks as her gaze lingered on the bed and caught the covert glance she then cast his way, which brought a smile to his lips.

'What is the matter, Delphine? Are you remembering the last time you and I shared a bed?'

Delphine held her tongue, not with acquiescence, but with determination not to let her emotions get entangled with being his wife. As he seemed to expect some response from her, she shrugged and said, 'I simply did not expect to be snuggled in so cosily with you, that's all.'

'There were moments at the Blue Boar when you didn't seem to mind being snuggled in so cosily with me. As I recall, you didn't exactly shrink from my attentions.' He stepped close, gently touching her cheek with the tip of his finger, making her quiver with a pleasure so intense it was almost like pain. His eyes held hers in a challenging stare. 'You look pale, my love. Does the idea of sharing a bed with me strike you as distasteful? It is customary, you know, for a bride and groom to spend their wedding night in the same bed.'

Delphine almost retreated from those suddenly fierce eyes, but she steeled herself and held her ground. 'I am quite aware of that, sir,' she replied stiffly. 'But I am not yet ready for a repeat performance,' she lied, for her body was telling her that she was, but her pride and her diffidence would not allow her to admit it. 'At the present moment I do not feel like your wife. The wedding ceremony was a miserable affair, one I shall not look back on with affection. I have never given any thought to getting married, since I have not met anyone I wanted to marry. But one thing I have always known is that when I did marry, my wedding would be a happy occasion—to begin favourably, in a blaze of joy, instead of darkness.'

Stephen's face was inscrutable as he moved past her, languidly loosening the collar of his jacket. Her words pricked at his conscience, since it was what every woman dreamed of—a wedding day to remember. And yet it seemed that she would play the reluctant virgin to the hilt, when they both knew she had no cause.

'I was aware of your reluctance to be married and I assure you that I shall behave with more dignity than you seem concerned about.'

'I objected to the groom,' Delphine told him coldly. 'Had I been given any other choice, my behaviour would be different. By your actions and my parents' eagerness to rid themselves of me, I was left with no other alternative.'

'Worry not, my love. I have no intention of making love to you tonight or any other night in the near future—unless, of course, I find I cannot resist you and am unable to help myself,' he retorted sarcastically. 'When I take my pleasure of you it will be at my convenience. Your father has got what he wanted, so be content with that.'

'What do you mean?' she asked, bewildered.

'Don't play the innocent. I'm not proud of myself for what I did to you that night, Delphine. I ravaged and ruined an innocent young woman. Had I known who you were, that you were the daughter of a highly respected nobleman, I would have sought you out and apologised to your family—even though your father would have been within his rights to call me out. But for you to tell them what had transpired between us, to have your father hunt me out and threaten me, was a very unwise thing for you to do. I cannot believe you didn't know what he planned to do if I refused to marry you.'

Slowly shaking her head, she stared at him in

confusion. 'No. I really do not know what you're talking about.'

He laughed bitterly. 'No—I don't believe you do.' His eyes settled on her face and he ran his finger down the tantalising curve of her cheek. He was certain she was ignorant of his frustration and rage engendered by the threats Lord Cameron had used to force him into marrying his daughter.

She had dressed with care for the journey, in a gown of mulberry silk. The décolletage was quite daring, revealing the swell of her breasts, yet it would be considered modest compare to the fashions of the women who followed the regiment. Her hair was parted down the middle with clusters of ringlets falling over her ears. Two curls had escaped their pins during the journey and rested tantalisingly against her neck.

'You truly are innocent, are you not, Delphine?' he asked softly. 'You are also a beautiful and fascinating woman. You really are as lovely as I remember.' He bent his head and his lips touched where his finger had preceded them.

Delphine allowed his mouth to caress her face. It was gentle, and as long as nothing would follow, she would not take the chance to stir his anger by refusing him this much. 'Tell me what my father did to make you marry me,' she asked softly, feeling foolish at the quiver in her voice.

His lips trailed from her cheek to her ear and, like tinder to a paper, his touch set her blood afire, his mouth a living flame as it nuzzled the hollow of her neck. She shivered involuntarily at its burning intensity. Nervously she drew back, fearing he would not keep his word.

'Please tell me.'

His mood when he drew back was once more cool and harsh. 'If it matters so much to you, then I shall tell you. Your father was going to expose me for a rapist if I did not agree to wed you. Such an accusation from a man of your father's standing would have caused the biggest scandal—not only in London but among the English contingent in Spain. It would have brought disrepute to my family name, ruined my career and your reputation. I would have been drummed out of the army and sent to prison.'

Delphine stared at him, appalled that her father had threatened him with such an ultimatum. 'That is truly awful. I—I did not know. You must believe that.'

He looked at her hard, then nodded and cupped

her chin in his palm. 'Why is it I want to believe you?' His thumb stroked her lips. 'And what is it about the night I spent with you that makes me feel like someone punched me in the gut? What I have an aversion to is being forced. It goes against the grain. Your father had no thought for you when he threatened me, of how such an accusation would affect you, which told me you do not rank highly in his affections.'

'No,' she whispered, 'I know that. It is something I have always known. My—my happiness never came first with my parents.'

Hearing the catch in her voice, Stephen considered her a moment. 'I did get the impression that you were not their favourite child,' he remarked quietly, dropping his hand.

Furious with herself that she should show such weakness, Delphine lifted her chin and found the deep-blue eyes resting on her with something akin to compassion or pity. She smiled wryly. 'You must have seen my twin sisters. Indeed, I'm sure you were unable to tear your eyes away from them. I am the youngest of five girls. The eldest two are married with children. Rose and Fern are to be married shortly. You must have seen how perfect they are—fragile, lovely and as demure as the names by which they are known. They are everything I am not.'

'You do not resemble them in looks, but you do yourself an injustice. You are far more beautiful than your sisters. They lack your vibrancy and spirit, which are traits I admire in a woman.'

Delphine raised her brows mockingly. 'I confess I am not used to such compliments and, coming from you, I cannot be sure of their faithfulness.'

'I may be many things, Delphine, but I am always honest.'

Her cheeks suffused to a delightful pink, Delphine lowered her eyes. 'Aunt—Aunt Celia told me about the large donation you made to the orphanage,' she said hesitantly, changing the subject to cover her confusion, 'for which I thank you. I hope I was worth it,' she added drily, 'since I am not proud of the manner in which it was acquired.'

His eyes narrowed and he nodded. 'Oh, yes, Delphine. You were worth every penny—and more. A lady who prefers to involve herself in charitable works instead of useless activities—I can only extend my sincerest admiration.'

'I am no saint—far from it, just the reverse—

and you more than anyone else should know that. My parents tell me I am not ladylike, for I have this awful habit of doing the opposite of what I am told to do and arguing when I should be agreeing.'

On a sigh and suddenly feeling very tired, she turned from him and unpinned her hair, shaking it loose with her fingers. Stephen's mouth went bone-dry as he watched it ripple down her back. The lamp and the moonlight shining in through the open window brought out all the glorious, vibrant, fiery shades. Ten years as a soldier had conditioned him to react to any situation with lightning reflexes, yet now he didn't move, didn't think—and damn if his traitorous heart didn't beat faster and a spear of lust pass through him. The sensations spreading through him were like nothing he'd ever experienced before. They came in waves, each faster and stronger than the last.

Pleasure rolled over his body, pleasure turning to desire. He wanted to taste her, to run his fingers through the silken mass of her hair. Within seconds his loins stirred and his manhood hardened. He was not sure he could wait until he'd returned from Spain to have her. Then, just when the erotic sensations grew so intense they verged on pain, she turned her head and looked at him over her shoulder, her eyes large and warm in her flushed face.

Delphine's senses were similarly enhanced. She wondered if he had any idea how attractive he looked in his uniform jacket, his white trousers moulding his muscled legs, his black hair gleaming and curling about his handsome face. She felt heat suffuse her cheeks and her stomach lurched. The desire she'd experienced on that other night returned with a vengeance.

Immediately, to hide his embarrassment, with an angry oath Stephen spun on his heel and strode to the door. 'I'll leave you to prepare for bed. I have to speak to Oakley. Go to sleep. I won't bother you.'

A small frown touched her brow as she looked at him. 'Where will you sleep?'

He glanced back at the large leather chair by the hearth. 'In the chair.'

'I am not unaccustomed to discomfort,' she informed him, thinking of the late nights she had spent trying to sleep on the most basic of furniture at the orphanage. 'I will be content sleeping in the chair if you like.'

Stephen glanced at her, his lips twisted sardon-

ically. 'I am happy to know I have a most agreeable and considerate wife, but it is I who make
the decisions. I am a soldier. The chair will be
more than adequate for my needs. Believe me,
it is a luxury compared to some of the places
in which I have slept. I shall return shortly,' he
said, opening the door. Then he was gone, leaving Delphine alone at last.

Delphine had never seen the sea before. When
the coach crested a hill and it came into view,
the sight took her breath away. They had set off
from the inn in brilliant sunshine and travelled
at a less arduous pace than the day previous.
Stephen wanted to give Delphine the opportunity
to admire the lovely countryside as they travelled
through Devon and into Cornwall, and this last
leg of their journey offered a spectacular taste of
the countryside and the sea at its most dramatic.
As they drew closer to this never-ending expanse of water, Delphine leaned out of the window and asked Stephen if they might stop. Happy
to indulge her, he instructed the driver to pull
over. In her eagerness to get a closer look, she
climbed out and almost ran to the edge of a high

headland sloping out to sea. Stephen dismounted and went to stand beside her.

The breath caught in Delphine's throat with a gasp as she stared around her. Her eyes shone and her cheeks were flushed with an unfamiliar excitement. It was as though she had just been deposited in a wonderland. 'Oh, what a beautiful sight,' she enthused. Looking up at Stephen, her eyes wide and round, she laughed like a child. 'I suppose you think I'm quite mad, but I've never seen the sea before.' She turned her attention back to the view. 'Oh, Stephen,' she exclaimed, unaware that she had addressed him by his given name for the first time, 'I have never seen anything quite so beautiful.'

There was something about the sea that touched her deeply. The day had all the drowsy beauty and heady scents of midsummer, which drifted into her senses. She stood spellbound, though the sun was hot and the glare hurt her eyes. Trees, rustling with the summer breeze, grew thick to the edge of the pale sand, and moss, succulent and green, clung to the rocks. The sea was deep blue and green and shining, with silver glints darting like quicksilver over its gently rippling surface. It was untroubled and calm, with little waves lapping and foaming gently on the shore, only to retreat. Gulls flew overhead, wheeling and crying above the foam, diving now and then in search of food.

She turned and looked up at her husband. Having discarded his uniform for the time being, he was clothed in dark blue, the high, stiff collar of his coat embroidered with gold thread. His stock was pristine white and held only the lightest cologne. He was impeccably groomed and so handsome that she felt weak just looking at him. She could not forgive him for forcing her into their marriage, but knew it would be foolish to live at loggerheads with him. She must at least make life as bearable as possible. Carelessly his hand brushed her arm. She felt a sudden stillness envelop them. Vividly aware of the heat of the sun and the scent of the trees and the grass, she was overwhelmingly conscious of him. Confused, she looked away. Despite all the irritation he roused in her, the magnetic attraction remained.

Stephen was no less struck by the intimacy of the moment. Studying her profile as she stared ahead, his gaze lingered on the dainty ringlets that curled around her ears, the astonishing length of her black lashes and the soft fullness of her lips. She wore a fetching gown in a pastel shade of green, with tiny puffed sleeves and a scooped neck. In the softest of materials it failed to conceal all the delicious lines and curves of her body. Stephen was not surprised to discover that, having sampled them once, he was anxious to reacquaint himself with those curves.

'Is—is your house near the sea?' she asked haltingly.

'Very close. Does that please you?'

'Oh, yes. This is a million miles away from London and the orphanage. How I wish I could bring every one of those children to a place like this. Some of them have never ventured further than the dingy streets where they were born.'

'Your caring nature does you credit. I hope those children know the value of such kindness.'

His remark brought a smile to her lips. 'Your donation will be appreciated much more than anything I do. Be assured it will be put to good use. Our work, what we do for the children, is the only hope they have. They depend on us. They have no one else. If we did not help the boys to obtain respectable occupations, they would roam the streets and become members of some brutish gang. A worse fate, too awful to contemplate, awaits the girls. Establishments like the one in which Mr Oakley found me are waiting to snatch them up—although I know not why I am telling you this. How can someone like you possibly understand if you've never been inside an orphanage? You cannot have the faintest idea of what it is like.'

'I cannot. You told me you were at the brothel looking for a missing child. Did you find her?'

She nodded. 'A girl called Maisie. Her mother works at the brothel.'

'Which is probably where the child will end up.'

Delphine swung her head round and looked at him fiercely. 'She will not. I will do everything within my power to prevent it. Maisie is a very pretty girl. Unfortunately, she has already drawn the attention of a man who is determined that she will follow her mother into the profession—a vile man who is constantly on the lookout for girls like Maisie to fill the brothel. He is known for his excesses and is one of the very worst examples of bullies, reared in the belief that because he instils fear in those weaker than he, he is entitled to do anything he likes. In the corrupt world he inhabits, he commands a great deal of influence and power.'

'And his name?'

'Will Kelly.' She turned her gaze back to the sea. 'I hate him,' she said quietly.

He gave her a dubious glance. 'And you left the child at the brothel? Was that wise?'

'Her mother promised me she would see she was returned to the orphanage the next morning. I trusted she would keep her word. I met your Mr Oakley when I was leaving.'

'I had arrived in the city that very day. It was my intention to spend no more than three days in London before travelling on to Portsmouth to take ship for Lisbon—which I will do when I have introduced you to Tamara, your new home. I was on short leave from the fighting in Spain and military duties kept me for the past month at the Woolwich Military Academy, which was where I trained to be an officer for the Artillery. On the night we met, I was feeling restless, so I had Oakley find me a little diversion. His choice was surprising—a virgin with a very influential father. I was amazed by his haste to have me do the right thing by you. I suspect the fact that I am going back to rejoin my regiment in Spain might have had something to do with that.'

'Along with the fact that he wanted me off his hands,' Delphine uttered with more than a little sadness. 'My rebelliousness and my refusal to bow to protocol was the cause of much strife in our otherwise peaceful household. I do not care for society in general, but this makes me all the fonder of being with Aunt Celia and those I meet through the charities I'm involved with. I enjoy working among the poor and hungry and destitute—helping, in my own small way. I felt wanted—a sense of purpose. I take delight in the society of children, to see the joy light up their faces when they are given a treat or a toy of some kind.'

'What you do, being friend and mother to waifs and strays, is commendable. Did your parents resent your charitable work?'

'Oh, no. Mama has charities of her own she supports—most ladies in her position do the same. After all it's a very noble thing to do— to be seen to do good to the underprivileged. It was the way I involved myself in the practical sense they resented. My parents had long since decided to marry me off to the first man who offered for me—which seemed most unlikely since I refused to attend the balls and soirées my sisters take such delight in. My mother has been heard to say on several occasions that it would take a brave gentleman to take me on.'

'Then you are in luck, for I am no coward. It is obvious that you enjoy what you do at the orphanage.'

'Yes, I find it most rewarding. I am not completely lacking in social skills or domestic management, but I do tend to neglect the way I look. Poor Mama finds it extremely tiresome and rebukes me about it all the time. I can embroider and play a tune and hold my own in dinner-party conversation like the best of them, but I enjoy my charity work most of all. I like what I do—like you enjoy being a soldier. The difference being I don't kill people.'

He looked at her earnestly. 'Killing is necessary in war,' he said quietly. 'I do not like doing it. When it is over I shall set aside violence and settle down to a different existence.'

'If you can. You will miss being a soldier.'

'As you will miss your work at the orphanage.' She looked at him. 'Yes, of course I will. Those

children were important to me. My work was
my life.'

Stephen was smiling no longer. Delphine saw
before her the firm, tanned face and hard eyes,
which the sunlight had turned to steel. A frown
darkened his attractive face and his eyes locked
on hers with a cool cynicism she did not understand.

'You had to marry one day. It has simply happened sooner rather than later. You will find
plenty to occupy your time at Tamara.'

'Yes, but it shall never be the same,' she said,
turning away and slowly walking back to the
coach.

Chapter Four

The sun was setting behind the trees when they reached their destination. Tamara—so named, Stephen explained to Delphine, after a nymph of folklore who had given her name to the River Tamar—was situated in a peaceful valley facing the sea and rugged cliffs rose on either side. One of Stephen's ancestors had built Tamara during the fifteenth century in the days of his prosperity. He was a tough professional soldier living in a tough part of the world—there was little or no law in Cornwall at that time and people had had to look after themselves—and he had built a tough house of Cornish granite. It had not been altered since it was built.

From a distance Delphine thought the house looked cold, strong and commanding rather than mellow and welcoming, but her opinion began to change as they followed a cobbled drive through an archway into the main courtyard around which the house was built. Here the house suggested gentler times. There were gables over the handsome Tudor windows with diamond-shaped panes cut through thick granite, which, Stephen told Delphine, lit the parlour and the great chamber on the first floor. There was also a charming little bell tower on a small chapel. Delphine gazed about her with awe, noting the overgrown lawns in the main courtyard and the creepers growing in profusion up the house's mellow walls, badly in need of trimming, but nevertheless she thought Tamara quite beautiful in its neglect.

The coach drew to a halt at the bottom of a shallow flight of stone steps. They had sent word ahead for the staff to expect them, but when no one came out of the house to greet them, Mr Oakley went inside to summon the servants' attention. Taking Delphine's arm, Stephen led her inside. When he released her, she looked about her in awe. Delphine stood in the centre of a long, dark oak-panelled hall, which had a table running its entire length. She made a slow, full circle, taking in every aspect with wide, disbelieving eyes. Her heart plummeted and a cold shiver of disappointment travelled down her spine.

'Dear Lord, would you just look at this place.' The words fell from her mouth before she could stop them.

The hall was lofty, with a fine timbered roof, and huge cobwebs hung from the ceiling. Despite the heat outside, it was cold—not a biting cold, but a dank chill that sank through the skin and gnawed at the bones. It smelled damp and fusty and would have benefitted from a fire being lit in the huge fireplace, she noted.

Whether it was chagrin or irritation Delphine saw in Stephen's face, she could not rightfully determine, but the muscles in his cheek flexed tensely as if he bit back a reply. 'Permit me to apologise for the state of the house, Delphine. I have not been home for some time—almost two years, in fact, and I can see the servants have let things slip.'

'Slip? That is putting it mildly,' she remarked, running her finger through a film of thick dust on the surface of the table. 'It is clear that you have not been spending money on follies and the house and a coach and four. This place smells like a tomb.'

'Wait here. Chambers, the caretaker, cannot be far away. I shall go and see what's happening.'

Stephen strode towards a door, the sharp sound of his boots reverberating around the walls. Delphine turned when a woman appeared from a room across the hall, perhaps in her thirties. Untidy brown hair escaped the confines of a white cap and a soiled apron tied about her ample waist covered a black dress. She looked at Delphine through suspicious eyes.

'And who might you be?' she asked rudely.

'I am Lady Fitzwaring—your new mistress,' she informed the woman.

The servant blinked at her and a grumbling sound came from her mouth. She sounded unfriendly and her eyes were narrowed in suspicion, not knowing how to refer to Delphine.

'What is your name?' Delphine asked sharply.

'Alice Duncan—my lady,' she added grudgingly.

'Where is the caretaker my husband left to look after the house? A Mr Chambers, I believe his name was. Lord Fitzwaring sent word for you to expect our arrival. Where is he?'

'Dead and in his grave these past six weeks— my lady.'

'Oh, I see. Well—I am sorry to hear that. Would you be so kind as to fetch the house-keeper, if you please,' Delphine said.

'Mrs Crouch's gone into the village to visit her sister. She's not expected back 'til later. There's just me and Davy.'

'Davy?'

'Me brother—and he's seein' to the wood for the fire.'

Delphine hadn't expected obstruction and was inclined to reply sharply, but reined herself in. 'My husband expected the house to be fully staffed. I fear our arrival will cause a good deal of trouble—opening up the house after so long.' She indicated the door through which Stephen had disappeared. 'Lord Fitzwaring went that way. We have come a long way and would appreciate something to eat—and a fire would be agreeable,' she said, rubbing her hands along her arms to ward off the chill that permeated the house. 'Would you see to it?'

Delphine had been raised to show respect and restraint when dealing with servants, but she suddenly knew that she was going to have to assert herself if she was to survive in this house.

Slowly she moved about the hall, glancing about her. The sunlight slanting through the high, lead-paned windows did little to erase the shadows and lighten the mood of the hall. A wide, ornately carved oak staircase clung to the wall at one end.

Returning to the hall, Stephen smiled ruefully. 'The message I sent informing the servants of our impending arrival failed to get here—and sadly old Chambers has passed on.' His wife's distaste for the house was apparent. 'The house is not what you are accustomed to, Delphine, but you'll get used to it in time.'

She sighed deeply. 'I sincerely hope so—but at this moment it feels neither warm nor welcoming.'

Her husband came to stand in front of her and stared at her dubiously. 'I know how disappointed you must be and I respect your frankness—if nothing else. Will you give the place the benefit of the doubt and compromise your standards?'

Delphine's spine stiffened at his mockery and her tone was brittle as she lashed out with a stinging reply. 'Whatever standards I might have had have been so completely tarnished of late that they bear no resemblance to the shining values of my youth.' More gently, she conceded, 'I fear it is part of growing up. To give up those values and dreams for reality is the cost, it would seem—if the condition of your house is anything to go by—I must pay.'

Stephen smiled without a trace of rancour. 'Well said, Delphine. I have sent someone to the village to fetch Mrs Crouch. She will soon have some food on the table. In the meantime I will show you around—although if the hall is representative of the rest of the house, I cannot imagine it pleasing you.'

It did not. But despite the neglect, the furnishings were tasteful and Flemish tapestries depicting folklore and scenes from Greek mythology, many of them faded with age, hung in every room. The floors were all on different levels, which made a tour of the house a curiously up-and-down affair. The rooms and the great chamber all had big windows overlooking the courtyard.

Arriving back in the hall, Stephen shot his wife a questioning glance. 'Well, what is your opinion of the house, Delphine? Do you think you will be happy living here?'

Without replying immediately, she crossed to the hearth where the elusive Davy had lit a fire. Already it was taking hold and its heat went a little way to thawing her heart.

'This is a fine house, that I cannot deny, but there is much to be done. Everything has been badly neglected—and the beds must be aired before we retire.'

'Mrs Crouch will take care of that,' Stephen said, standing beside her with his back to the heat. 'Apparently most of the staff left after my last visit.'

'Was there a reason?'

He glanced at her, a mysterious smile playing on his lips. 'Oh, yes—ghosts.'

Delphine's eyes opened wide. 'Ghosts? Are you joking?'

'I never joke about something as serious as ghosts,' he said teasingly.

'Are you telling me the house is haunted?'

He nodded. 'So they say—many who have stayed here have heard strange sounds on occasion. In these parts, people have a firm belief in the wandering spirits that are supposed to inhabit the region, often occupying themselves with the same objects and pursuits as before they passed into the world of shadows. Every dwelling place in Cornwall, in particular the old houses, has its ghost—not that I've experienced any hauntings myself. Do you mind?'

Unable to repress a smile, she shook her head. 'Not really—although I am reminded of All-Hallows Eve, when some of the older children at the orphanage would frighten the little ones with tales of goblins, ghosts and spirits until they refused to sleep alone. I have never experienced any myself. I know not whether I believe in such things—not that I've given it much thought—but I always think the living cause more trouble than dead.'

'Those are my thoughts exactly. I strongly suspect that the peculiar noises heard are more to do with the caves that run beneath the house and the sea that fills them when the tide comes in. Strong winds blowing in from the sea might also have something to do with it. After the servants left, Mrs Crouch was hard put to get anyone else. Alice Duncan and her young brother Davy stayed on. They were born here; their parents worked for my father and they look upon

Tamara as their home. Ghosts do not frighten them. When it becomes known that Tamara has a new mistress, I doubt we shall have any trouble recruiting staff, since every man and woman in the vicinity will want to take a look at you.'

'I sincerely hope not, since there is clearly so much to be done. Are there any mines in the area?'

'Several.'

'And do you own any of them?'

He nodded. 'Three—all productive and profitable, one extending under the sea. Most of the people hereabouts depend upon the tin and copper mines for a living. Of course, another of the major industries in Cornwall is smuggling. It's as well you know about this clandestine trade. The smugglers use the cove here at Tamara to bring in their contraband, so if you should wake in the night and hear horses' hooves, turn over and go back to sleep. Ask no questions. Let them get on with it and they will leave you alone.'

'Even though what they are doing is wrong?'

'Absolutely. Interfere at your peril. Many inns and houses along every stretch of coast have deep cellars and passageways that provide a secure store for their contraband—even the caves

I spoke of are used from time to time if the conditions or the Excise men prevent it being transported over the moor. It's part of the fabric of their lives.'

'But what they are doing is criminal.'

'Government taxes on imports and exports are to blame. Far from being reviled, the smugglers are celebrated as local heroes. It is not limited to the poor. Priests, doctors, gentry to the local magistrate—even the Customs men frequently take part in it. They are all involved in one way or another, happy to turn a blind eye in return for the odd keg of brandy.'

'Goodness! I begin to wonder about this extraordinary turn my life has taken. Smugglers and ghosts! Dear me! Cornwall suddenly makes London seem extremely dull.'

He grinned. 'You shall soon get used to it—and the house.'

'I had no idea it would be so big or that it would need so much work.'

'Mrs Crouch and Alice Duncan could not manage it alone.'

The competent Mrs Crouch impressed Delphine the moment she laid eyes on her. She was a tall woman, tall and thin, yet as solid as a tree. Perhaps in her mid-fifties, her skin was flawless. Most startling of all were her eyes, which were deep and dark, in strange contrast to her snow-white hair. She was wearing a black gown with a plain white-linen collar and cuffs and her voice was soft, clipped and businesslike. Delphine liked her immediately. She could deal with someone like Mrs Crouch, whose authority was quietly impressive.

Stephen and Delphine sat on either side of the large stone fireplace enjoying a glass of wine while Mrs Crouch prepared their evening meal. Stephen was the first to break the silence that had fallen between them.

'I have decided to leave Tamara the day after tomorrow, Delphine. It is imperative I leave for Portsmouth. I have delayed my departure too long as it is. Had your father done as I asked and kept you in London until my return from Spain, things would have been different. As it is, you must make the best of it. You will find plenty to occupy your time and, when the local gentry get to know about you, you shall have no shortage of visitors. Mrs Crouch and Alice understand that you have governance of the entire household.'

Delphine sighed, a frown puckering her brow. 'That in itself is daunting to me. When I was growing up my mother worked hard to encourage interests beyond my charity work, but sadly I am no housekeeper.'

'Mrs Crouch will help you. She has formidable organisational skills and is willing to roll up her sleeves and lend a skilled hand with any task you ask of her. It is important to me that you are happy here. Tamara is a beautiful house—your home, now—and while I am gone you have my permission to make it truly yours.'

'Indeed?' she said, looking around the gloomy hall. 'In what way?'

'In whatever way you wish. You may transform its Puritan austerity with brightness and comfort and anything else that takes your fancy.'

'Am I allowed to hang new curtains at the windows,' she asked, tentative at first, then growing bolder as fresh plans rushed through her brain, 'and have the sofas and chairs re-upholstered in a colour and fabric of my own choosing?'

Stephen grinned, enchanted by her enthusiasm. 'Absolutely.'

'And light the rooms with chandeliers and replace the floor coverings with Oriental carpets?'

'Anything.'

Suddenly she looked concerned. 'I must con-

fess that arithmetic was never my best subject
and I have no experience of book keeping. Are
you not afraid that I might ruin you?'

'I think I can stand it.'

'And you can afford to trust me with such a
mammoth task? Can you really afford all that?'

'Of course I can. I am a wealthy land-and-
mine owner, Delphine. Money is no object; besides, nothing has been done to the house since
long before my mother died. It's time new life
was breathed into it. You need not concern yourself with matters other than the house. The land,
the mines and the people who depend on the
Fitzwarings for their living are in the hands of
capable agents.'

'And what if something should happen to you
in Spain? It is possible, considering the dangers
you face on a daily basis.'

'It is possible. In the event of my death, without issue the estate will pass into the hands of a
cousin.'

'And if I should have a child?'

'Boy or girl, the child will inherit Tamara.
Unlike most big estates, Tamara is not entailed
to the male line. If there is no child, then you
needn't worry. You will be well taken care of.

I have written to my lawyer in Falmouth to advise you in my absence and to instruct the bank to have money made available to you.'

'I see,' she said stiffly, avoiding his piercing gaze, wondering why she should feel this immense disappointment. Why should his leaving affect her so? She reminded herself sternly that he had not married her by choice.

Stephen frowned, eyeing his wife curiously. 'You seem put out. Why, Delphine? While the war in Spain goes on it is my duty to be out there with my regiment. You know that. It is important to me.'

'So was my own work,' she reminded him dejectedly. 'Everything I have known—my life— my work—lies in ashes at my feet, all because of a brief moment of madness. I shall miss it dreadfully.'

'I know. For what it's worth I am sorry, but you always knew I had to return to my regiment.' Content and relaxed, he joined his fingers in his lap and stretched his long legs out in front of him, crossing them at the ankles. 'Are you upset because you will miss me?' His eyes narrowed on her speculatively, feeling a sudden reluctance to leave her behind. 'If that is the case, then you could always follow the drum and join the other women who do not wish to be parted from their men even in war.'

Brushing her hair away from her face, Delphine looked across at him, her eyes suddenly alight with laughter. 'What? Be a camp follower trailing after you? Oh, no, Stephen. I think not.'

'Why not? That way we should see each other often.'

'Thank you for the suggestion, but I would not wish to be an encumbrance. Besides, why would I wish to drag myself off to Spain when I have a lovely new home to take care of and spend all your money on?' she teased, suddenly tempted to take him up on his offer, shake off her cares and take to the open roads of the Peninsula.

'Then I won't waste words trying to convince you to abandon your mission.'

'And I will have to go to London at some point for my sisters' weddings. You would not object to that?'

'Of course you must go. Your *beautiful* twin sisters would not take kindly to your being absent?'

'Precisely,' she said, unable to conceal the hint of bitterness in her tone, for she knew full well that she wouldn't be missed if she didn't go, not by her sisters and certainly not by her parents. 'When I was born my parents couldn't forgive me for not being the much-wanted son, and to be less beautiful than any of my sisters only added to their disappointment.'

'You are far more beautiful than your sisters, Delphine,' Stephen said softly. 'I have not yet met your two older sisters, but in my opinion you possess a radiance and vitality that the twins lack.'

Delphine forced a smile, touched by his attempt to make her feel better about herself. She was fully aware that any compliments he gave her were empty ones. He simply wanted to make her feel happier about herself and at home in these new and strange surroundings, and, if compliments might do that, he would no doubt tell her she was as alluring and captivating as Cleopatra herself.

'I never thought short-sightedness to be one of your afflictions, Stephen,' she chided. 'My mouth is too big and my cheekbones too high. My eyes are not the fashionable blue—and the colour of my hair is certainly not in vogue these days.'

'You do yourself an injustice—and there is certainly nothing wrong with my eyesight. True, you are not the blue-eyed blonde with soft, pretty features, not beautiful in the vapid, traditional way, no. There's too much character in that lovely face of yours, too much intelligence in those pensive eyes.'

'There you are, then, you agree with me,' she said, a little hurt by his unflattering description of her face.

'Allow me to finish. For a start, your mouth is not too big. It is a full, sensuous mouth, beautifully shaped. Your cheekbones are divine. They give you a cool patrician look few patrician women ever attain, and your eyes and the striking colour of your hair are incredibly arresting. So you see, on the whole, you are very beautiful.'

Slightly embarrassed, she flushed. 'I am surprised at your sudden propensity to flatter me.'

'I am no flatterer, Delphine. I give my opinions honestly.' Stephen's expression was serious. A lock of dark hair had fallen over his angular face and there was an intensity in his eyes that surprised Delphine. More attracted to her by the moment, Stephen studied her closely, curious as to the reason for her particular allure. It was more than just her face or her body that attracted him. She had a glowing gentleness that warmed him, a fiery spirit that challenged him and a radiance that drew him towards her with increasing power. His lips curved into a smile and when he spoke his voice was low and husky. 'But what chance has a common soldier with a lovely young woman so in love with her charity work?'

Because of her previous experiences with people and the many times she had been hurt, Delphine refused to take him seriously. 'My charity work has nothing to do with it. I love being involved—and you are far from a common soldier. You are a colonel in Wellington's army, fighting for your country. You should be proud of that.'

Stephen looked at her long and silently, which surprised her, for he was not usually at a loss for words. His expression was unreadable, until gradually his stare became admiring. 'You are a strange creature, Delphine. Just when I think I'm getting to know you, some new trait shows itself.'

She laughed lightly. 'Goodness! May the good Lord save me from being predictable.'

'I doubt you shall ever be that. And therein lies

your charm,' he responded. 'You don't mind my
going away?'

'You have to, I know that. I do not expect you
to desert your post because you married me—
and I imagine you shall have plenty of accom-
modating female company,' she ventured quietly.

His jaw hardened. 'You are determined to
think me a libertine.'

She flushed. 'And you must understand why.'

'And upon that you condemn me?'

'I do not condemn you. Everything has happened so quickly. We have scarcely known each
other a week. All this is new to us both. I am
sure you enjoy the ladies—and they must adore
you—although stealing your heart away from the
army would be a difficult task for any woman
to accomplish.'

'That may have been true once, but now I have
a wife it no longer applies.'

At that precise moment Delphine became convinced that there were no eyes in all the world
bluer than the ones that settled on hers. Staring
into those darkly translucent depths now, she
found it easy to imagine a woman being swept
away by admiration for him without a single
word being uttered.

'Thank you, Stephen. It is important to me to know that.' Seeing his expression darken, Delphine regretted her blunder about other women. She so wanted to believe him, to trust him, but how could she when there was so much about him, about his life, that she didn't know? She laughed to dispel the seriousness of the moment and looked across at him through lowered lashes.

'Now, I believe our meal is ready—and I am ravenous. I shall join you when I have changed my gown.'

Stephen seemed reluctant to end their conversation, his countenance appearing aggrieved, prompting a mischievous response. Rising to her feet, Delphine sank into a deep, playful curtsey. 'I shall take my leave of you now, my lord,' she quipped.

His gaze was drawn to her bodice, which displayed a generous view of her breasts. Seeing his eyes flame, she put up a hand to cover her décolletage. His composure slipped.

'Devil take it, Delphine! Don't tempt me. You will soon come to know that I am not made of stone. Indeed, I can foresee our relationship coming down to a simple test of endurance, with one or both of us being pressed to the limit.'

'Restrain yourself.' She laughed. 'They say it is good for the soul.' And with that she went to change.

When they finally settled down to eat, Delphine was delighted to discover Mrs Crouch was also a wonderful cook. With few ingredients to hand, she managed to prepare a mouthwatering dish of mutton and vegetables, followed by delicious baked apples and thick cream.

They sat on either side of the long table in the hall and, as they ate, Delphine was conscious of Stephen's presence, of his long fingers as he held his knife and fork. For most of the time he maintained an easy conversation, regaling her with tales of his life as a boy at Tamara and his exploits in Spain, but Delphine was aware of the ever-present tension inside her as she endured his disturbingly intimate, lazy gaze. Silence prevailed between them as they ate their main course, for Stephen's appetite for food had waned with the blunt realisation of his own craving for carnal appeasement. His wife looked unbearably lovely, her rich hair a vibrant cloud in the candle-light, so very young and so vulnerable.

Unable to stay silent any longer, Delphine put down her knife and looked across at him. 'Kindly say what is on your mind, Stephen,' she urged, 'for it appears you are more interested in watching me than in eating this delicious food Mrs Crouch has prepared for us. Come, I am listening.'

Stephen's mouth quirked thoughtfully as he continued to stare at her in silence. If he were to do as she asked and make her privy to his thoughts, he would likely shock her senses and send her fleeing back to London.

As the recipient of that intense, midnight gaze, Delphine grew increasingly uneasy. She could only believe that whatever he was about to say would not be to her liking and he was reluctant to tell her. 'I really wish you would not do that.'

'Do what?'

'Stare at me so intently. It makes me feel I am being dissected.'

Stephen looked at her, grinning wickedly. 'Then I shall strive most heartily to improve my manners and not stare at you—difficult as that will be. You are extremely lovely to look at with your hair tumbling about your shoulders.'

Delphine's heart slammed into her ribs. 'I cannot imagine why something as trivial as my hair piques your interest so.'

As he leaned back in his chair, Stephen's attention never strayed from her. She really was quite lovely in her finery, a simple gown of saffron and gold that brought out the lights in her hair, and his gaze feasted eagerly on her face. 'To a man, a woman's hair is never trivial. Imagining how it feels in one's hands can become a man's obsession.' He paused to imagine curling a loose tendril of her hair around his finger. 'I well remember the occasion when it was spread across my pillow.'

Waves of heat flooded through Delphine's body at his words as the image of her hair spread across his pillow flashed across her mind, pursued immediately by what had followed. She reminded herself of his callous indifference to her feelings at the time, and of her own pain, throwing the ice-cold water of reality on the hot, inexplicable hunger flaring inside her, a hunger she could see reflected in the intensity of his gaze.

She forced herself not to look away. 'Is it the

priority of all men to concentrate on what a woman is like on the outside? Are they not concerned with what we are like on the inside?'

Her question brought a leisurely smile to his lips, showing incredibly white teeth. 'Where women are concerned, not all men look very deeply.'

She arched a lovely brow, giving him a look of disdain. 'You do not have a very high opinion of the character of your own sex, Stephen.'

He grinned, a mocking gleam in his eyes. 'True. Love turns some of them into complete idiots.'

'Why do you speak of love in so derogatory a manner?'

'Do I? I apologise, Delphine, but discussions of this sort bring out the worst in me.'

'Then let us not discuss it.' She stood. 'I think I shall retire to bed. It has been a long day and I am tired after the journey.'

Stephen sighed in exaggerated disappointment. 'What a shame. I was enjoying our conversation.'

'There is always tomorrow,' she murmured as he rose to his feet. 'I am surprised you find conversing with me enjoyable.'

'You can hardly fault me there.' His tone was

equally soft as his eyes caressed her warmly.
'You sorely test my restraint, Delphine.'

'Restraint?' She raised a delicate brow in disbelief. 'I have seen no evidence of such.'

He grinned roguishly. 'If you really knew, you'd think me a scoundrel.'

'I already do.'

Meeting his gaze, she paused a moment. Her heart was troubled, the heart that she had thought stone cold, incapable of ever being warm and loving. It would be wonderful to let this strong husband of hers take her in his arms, his life—his bed. How well she remembered her response to the hard demands of his body—so wanton she had been ashamed. He had awakened some warm and sweet thing that had been satisfying.

Afraid of the way he was looking at her and the path her thoughts were wandering along, she almost danced away as he approached her and with a toss of her head made her way up the stairs.

After a fitful night's sleep and a busy day making a list of all that needed doing in the house, feeling restless and in the need of some fresh air, Delphine walked down to the rocky cove, uplifted by the smell of the sea. Perching on a large flat rock, she looked around, relieved to find the beach deserted.

The cove was secluded and cut deep into the craggy cliffs, the sandy beach scattered with boulders. At high tide the waves crashed against the rocks with an explosion of white foam, filling the caves with water, but the tide was low now and the sea was calm and gleaming like glass. Gulls wheeled and squawked overhead, their white wings bright and shining, and two herons foraged among the reeds higher up the beach.

She heard soft footfalls on the shingle behind her, but did not dare to turn round and face her husband. After a moment she turned her head slightly and watched him approach. A smile curved her lips, inviting him to share the moment. His face remained expressionless as he came to stand beside her. His feet were bare, his trousers rolled up to his knees and his white shirt open at the throat billowed in the gentle breeze.

'I saw you leave the house and thought you were heading here,' he said good-humouredly.

She gave him a sidelong smile. 'I couldn't resist taking a closer look at the sea—and it's such a lovely day.' Her gaze drifted back to the horizon, to the play of light—pink, mauve, gold and saffron—above the deep indigo of the sea.

Stephen's gaze did not follow. Instead he looked down at her, watching the bright rays of the evening sun strike gleams from her hair—the play of the light on her face and lips, the soft lustre of her dark eyes, held him in thrall. In repose, her chest rose and fell; her hands were clasped round her drawn-up knees. The picture she presented held an innocence, a sparkling freshness he was not too jaded to see.

'You looked deep in thought,' he remarked softly, leaning casually against her rock. 'I hope I am not intruding.'

She sighed and shook her head. 'No, not really, and you are right, I was thinking. I was thinking that if ever I feel a need for peace and quiet, to put everything into perspective, this is the place to come.'

'And is that how you feel at this present time?'

She nodded. 'Yes. Marrying you has changed my life so much—more than I could ever have imagined.'

'I hope it will turn out to be for the better.'

'As to that, we shall have to wait and see.' She glanced up at him and smiled. 'I am sorry,

Stephen. I cannot blame you if you think me odd. I have always found something wanting in my life, whilst having an absolute sense of knowing there was so much there I could not see. It's a certainty that should make the whole world shine. I am not very good at obedience and accepting poverty—my parents can attest to that— not when I have always had so much. Everything I do—whether at home or in my charity work— presents some kind of conflict.'

Stephen grinned. 'You sound like a mystic.'

'I don't mean to. I'm not a very practical person, but I am realistic. I have such a sense of duty for what I do, yet I long to be free and want to rebel at every turn. I wanted to help and care for people—for the children at the orphanage—but whatever I did was never enough. I also want beauty in my life, and passion, but it eludes me. And yet I sense there is another world around me—and I can never express how I feel—not to anyone.'

'You have just done so—to me.'

'I know and it is strange—unless it's because that is what you are, a stranger, and it is easier to talk to someone you do not know.'

'Perhaps you are right; I will remember what you have said today.'

'Will you? I wonder,' Delphine murmured, stretching out her legs on the rock. 'I saw you taking a swim earlier.'

'At Tamara I take an early swim every day, whatever the weather. As a boy I would watch the ships sail by and dream of being a sailor, sailing across the Atlantic, round Cape Horn and up into the China Seas.'

'But in the end you became a soldier. Did you deliberately pursue such an adventurous life?'

'My father was a soldier. I was commissioned into the same regiment.'

'Are you like him?'

He nodded. 'In many ways. With a parent's concern for his only offspring, he sought to share the wisdom he had gleaned from his own experiences. He taught me not just with words, but by example, showing me the true meaning of duty and honour. He taught me that compassion, fairness and integrity were some of the characteristics a man could lay claim to both as a soldier and a gentleman, and that the weight of responsibility had to be carried gallantly, no matter how it might weigh heavily upon a man at times.'

'He must have been a fine man.'

'He was—the best.'

'And it is obvious to me that you enjoy being a soldier. You are almost married to the army,' Delphine said wistfully.

'Not really,' Stephen answered. 'I enjoy the adventure and the excitement, but it has its downside—when bullets begin flying. When the war in Spain is over I want to settle down with a family just like the next man and live out my days at Tamara in contentment.'

'And love?' she dared to ask.

'Is for fools,' he replied quietly.

'Not everyone would agree with you. My sisters fell in love with their beaux at first sight and after a month declared they wanted to marry them.'

'Then I hope they will be happy, but this affliction of the heart, which is claimed to be love, is mere lust parading in moral guise—a trap to snare a man into the bonds of marriage.'

'And you do not believe love has anything to do with marriage,' Delphine returned, deriding his cynicism. 'I agree that love is a contract based on bartering oneself for security. Where love is concerned, it must have the foundations of trust and fidelity and should be fettered.'

'Love is inconsistent, a contradiction of emotions, whereas desire and lust are honest emotions.'

Delphine shook her head. 'Desire and passion do not last. True love is to give oneself unselfishly and unconditionally. But I forget, you are a soldier—tough and invulnerable. No doubt your training has taught you that a man need trust none but himself—and use women for naught but pleasure.'

He grinned. 'Well, it would seem I have married a romantic,' he declared. 'I agree that desire, lust, passion—call it what you will—is good while it lasts. But it is fleeting; doused by the boredom of familiarity.'

It took Delphine a moment to answer, for he could not have made his feelings clearer, which only made her more determined to guard her heart. There had been a warning in his words, telling her not to expect more than he was prepared to give. If she had not known exactly how he felt before, she did now. She did not want him to feel like that about her. She did not wish to be a burden, endured but unwanted. Swallowing the pain his words had caused her and concealing her thoughts, she met his gaze calmly.

'You have an uncommon honesty about such matters, Stephen,' she said quietly. 'Those are the words of either a confirmed bachelor, or a man who has been hurt by love—who finds love itself frightening.' The darkening of his eyes and the tightening of his jaw told her she might have hit upon the truth. 'Forgive me. I do not mean to pry.'

His tone was mocking when he eventually spoke. 'Have you no more questions? Is there nothing further you wish to know?'

'If you want to tell me, you will.'

'I do not always find it easy to say what I think and feel, Delphine. I am not accustomed to baring my soul—not yet. No doubt that shall come with time.'

Whatever had befallen him had left scars and hardened his heart. Delphine felt she had revived painful memories for him and she regretted her curiosity. She wondered about the woman Mr Oakley had mentioned before, but although she would have liked to ask him outright, she found it difficult to ask him directly, fearing his displeasure.

'Have a care,' she warned softly. 'One day you may venture too close to love's flames and be burnt.'

'I doubt it.'

'Will you teach me to swim?' she asked suddenly on an eager note, considering it wise to change the subject.

He looked at her with surprise, then laughed at the very idea. 'You should freeze to death.'

She turned her face up to his, which was framed by his dishevelled raven curls. '*You* don't—why should I? I learn very quickly how to do things. I'm sure I should soon learn how to swim.'

'I have every faith that you would. But it can be dangerous. The currents in the bay are strong, especially when the tide turns.'

'I am not afraid of danger.'

'No,' he murmured, gazing at her. 'I don't believe you are. Are you not afraid that a wave might come and carry you away?'

She gave a shake of her head. 'Not in the slightest.'

'Why do you want to swim?'

'For no other reason than I want to. Do you disapprove?'

'Not at all.' Turning his head, he looked at the

sea in silence. After a moment, having made a decision, he said, 'Very well, Delphine. When I return from Spain I will teach you how to swim.'

'Do you promise?'

'I promise—although I'm not sure how successful I will be.'

The wind had dropped and the dying sun was warm. Soon that glowing orb would sink below the horizon and darkness would shroud the land, but for the moment it was a lovely time of day and they were both disposed to enjoy it. By unspoken consent, they put aside all disagreeable matters and talked of nothing in particular, only enjoying each other's company.

'Lord, I'm hungry,' Stephen said suddenly. 'Come, it is time for dinner.'

Delphine could see hunger in those deep-blue eyes of his well enough, but she doubted very much that it was the kind of hunger anything in the larder could satisfy. She gave him her hand and he helped her down from her rock. Only then, standing directly before him, did she meet his gaze. His lids were half-lowered, his eyes dark. Delphine felt the breath catch in her throat; she hesitated, then, calmly, her lips gently curving, she turned her head in the direction of the house.

'Yes, it is perhaps time we made our way back.'

Stephen hesitated, watching her intently, then gently turned her towards him and cupped her face in his hands.

'Do you know how difficult it is to hide the strain you are putting on me, Delphine?'

'Strain? I cannot for the life of me think what you mean,' she murmured, unable to look away from his lips only inches from her own.

'It is true. I am exerting a great deal of gentlemanly effort not to capitulate on my marital rights.'

She laughed lightly, nervously, feeling the heat warm her face. 'I do not see why it should be such an effort. I am not fighting you, Stephen—and trapping a woman on the beach in an attempt to seduce her into a kiss is hardly gentlemanly.'

He met her gaze, the tone of her voice telling him she was not rebuking him, that she did not mind being held thus. 'Trapped? You are in no such position. If you wish to walk away, then you are free to do so. I will not stop you.'

Delphine held his gaze, unaware that she was holding her breath. She was acutely aware of the contours of her body, her breasts and nipples hardened by the cool wind, and by a desire that descended on her like the mist over the sea, banishing her senses, blocking out all save his handsome face, his black curls, and the soft, velvety richness of his voice.

'Is that what you want?' she whispered.

'No, because if you did, I would be unable to do this.'

He kissed her then, not forcefully but confidently, as one sure of his welcome. His lips were feather-light, his tongue ran along the crease of her lips. 'Kiss me back.'

Her lips parted beneath his, inviting him to taste. She closed her eyes, groaning into his mouth. His tongue slipped inside, teasing and tantalising, sampling her softness, laying claim to all she offered with a possessive, consummate skill. Delphine pressed herself closer.

For the duration of the kiss, the fire burned between them, flames leapt and a gentle magic held sway. Then very slowly, very deliberately, Stephen drew back a little, his lips barely an inch from hers as he waited until her lids fluttered open. For a long moment his eyes held hers with penetrating intensity. The dark-blue depths were as enigmatic as they were challenging and Delphine felt an answering *frisson* of excitement. The darkening in Stephen's eyes warned her he was aware of her brief response. Holding tight on to his control, he released her; when he spoke, his voice was harsh.

'Go back to the house, Delphine. I shall follow in a moment.'

Her eyes searched his. She was slightly bemused by the sudden change in him. Then she backed away. 'As you wish.'

Her soft reply reached him as she turned away. He watched her go. She did not glance back. Drawing in a deep breath, Stephen turned towards the sea, watching the orange ball of the sun until it had slipped below the horizon. He sighed, running the tip of his tongue over his lips. Delphine's kiss had been as erotic as he remembered.

He did not often feel ashamed of his actions, but some devil had goaded him to speak sharply to her. He had begun to feel drawn to her, protective towards her, and he did not like the feeling. His present mode of life suited him and before Delphine had become his wife he'd had no ties, no regrets. And most importantly, no emotional involvements. A familiar ache returned to strike at his heart. He crushed the memories he had thought long buried. He had sworn never again to trust a woman. Once he had been capable of love, the kind of love Delphine had spoken of so passionately. There had been no doubting her sincerity and he had been wrong to mock her opinions, to judge her by the standards of another woman.

Delphine was nothing like that scheming bitch Maria. Angrily he thrust away the memory of the beautiful, perfidious *señorita* he had fallen in love with in Spain. The mere thought of her brought a bitter taste to his mouth. He deliberately banished Maria from his thoughts, as he had banished her from his life. He knew the folly of placing his trust in womankind.

Chapter Five

Delphine's head had been in a whirl as she had walked back to the house. Somehow, despite all her efforts to hold herself aloof from Stephen, there were times, like now, when a gentle camaraderie sprang up between them and she found him impossible to resist. Yet his sudden change of attitude had confused her.

She was disappointed when he did not come to share their evening meal; although she lingered, hoping he would make an appearance, he failed to do so. Feeling deeply hurt, for she was acutely aware that he would be leaving for Portsmouth in the morning, it was with reluctance that she sought her bed. She curled up tightly under the quilt, hoping she could find oblivion in sleep, for only in sleep would she find a release from the pain and confusion Stephen had implanted in her heart.

* * *

She hadn't been in bed ten minutes when suddenly the door swung open. Turning her head towards it, she was startled by the sudden brightness. Stephen was standing in the doorway, a lighted candle in his raised hand. It cast harsh shadows on the strong planes of his face. He entered the room, closing the door softly. A heavy lock of hair dipped carelessly over his forehead. His shirt was open at the throat, his black trousers clung to his well-muscled legs. His expression was hard with barely controlled emotion and he loomed over the bed, large and dangerous.

Delphine's heart leapt with fear, yet her breath quickened with excitement. Gasping with surprise, she sat up, her hair tumbling about her shoulders. The lace at the neck of her nightdress was stark in the dim light. Hot blood stained her cheeks and her eyes fixed on his face were almost black.

'Stephen,' she whispered, 'please leave.'

Ignoring her request, without speaking, he placed the candle on the table beside the bed and in seconds he'd divested himself of his clothes, lifted the bedcovers and slipped in beside her. Taking hold of her shoulders, he pulled her down beside him. Pushing her nightdress aside so that it clung to the crests of her breasts, the heat of his lips laid siege to her senses and her head rolled back. The scent of him was intoxicating, musky, a lingering trace of horses and leather, but above all eternally male.

'Stephen,' she repeated, unable to believe what he was doing. She felt the surging thrill of danger in her veins. What had happened to put him in such a state?

'Damn you, temptress,' he uttered hoarsely, cupping her face and looking deep into her eyes. 'With your hair all adrift and your beautiful eyes so wide—you look like an angel,' he whispered, his mouth against hers.

'But—I…'

'Not now.' His mouth covered hers in a stormy, demanding kiss, silencing any protest she might make, his passion overriding his self-control. Releasing her lips, Stephen slid his hands to the ribbons on her nightdress. Her skin was warm and silky smooth against him and the intoxicating scent of her encircled him.

Delphine trembled as she eased back to let him divest her of her nightdress; the harsh intake of his breath as he gazed at her nakedness was the sweetest accolade she had ever heard. When his lips left her mouth to kiss the pulse beating below her ear, a moan rose from her throat.

'Hush, Delphine, my angel,' he murmured, pausing and looking down at her lovely face, her eyes large and melting with desire. 'I know you want this as much as I.'

She knew what he was doing, casting that spell of his again with the dark velvet voice and magnetic eyes. She could feel her strength to resist him draining away. The blood pounded in her head. As her eyes remained locked with his, she forgot where she was and some kind of madness seized her. The magnetism of their glances made the air between them shimmer.

Delphine pressed herself closer as he kissed her forehead, her throat, her cheeks. There were no protests, only Stephen's lips on hers, on her body, both dominant and tender. Her senses were besieged by the feel of him, the power, the strong beat of his heart beneath her palms when she tangled her fingers in the thick curling hair on his chest. She moaned softly under his exploring, practised hands, his fierce, fevered kisses, his tongue teasing her breast, moving across her ribs and down across her hips and stomach, until she was writhing from the pleasure they evoked. She cried out as his kisses gathered intensity, fanning a fire that seared her very soul. Fervent ardour possessed them and Delphine clung to him, giving herself wholly to his passion, becoming enmeshed in its intensity. Sliding her arms about his neck, she pressed her soft breasts against him, feeling his manhood against her, gently searching.

Stephen tilted her hips and the thrusting heat of him entered and filled her. Guiding her legs so that they locked about him, he took what he wanted mindlessly, driven by a violent compulsion to have her. He took her with urgency, with a hunger that stunned and aroused him.

Delphine matched his rhythm, her body moving in mindless, shameless pleasure, every nerve in her body screaming for release, but he held himself back, driving deeply into her, refusing to deprive her of the same pleasure she was affording him. Her eyes were closed and she was moaning softly with desire, desperate for something she didn't understand, afraid to have it, afraid to lose it. And then she went up in flames as their release exploded simultaneously between them, groaning with the extravagant splendour she was making him feel.

Whatever had driven Stephen to bed her was forgotten as he wrapped his arms around her and pulled her with him on to his side. Loath to draw apart from that heavenly sanctuary, his throbbing heat remained inside her. A fine film of sweat glistened on their bodies as they lay entwined. She was magnificent, exquisitely soft in his arms, and her pleasure had been as great as his.

'Have you changed your mind about me, Delphine?' he asked softly, turning his face into the luxuriant curls of fragrant hair that spilled across his shoulder, inhaling the delicious scent of her.

'In what way?' she murmured, sighing deeply with contentment as she ran her hands over the muscles of his back.

'About hating me?' He laughed softly, his breath warm on her face.

'I don't hate you, Stephen. I never said that.'

'Then has my lovemaking given you reason to like me a little more?'

She smiled, snuggling into him. 'I'll tell you tomorrow,' she whispered. 'Morning is a long way off, so you have ample time to redeem yourself.'

He chuckled softly and, with a twist of his body, brought her up astride him. As she bent her lips to place them on his, she saw that his expression was as guarded as ever, except that the tension had gone from his face and there was a softening in his eyes. No words of affection had been spoken, nor had she expected them or uttered any herself. But as she moved her hips and took one of his nipples between her teeth, she felt the leap of his response within her and gloried in her power to bring pleasure to this enigmatic man.

Night still shrouded the land when Stephen opened his eyes. The candle flame flickered in the draughts that sneaked into the room and bounced eerie shadows across the ceiling as it illuminated the figures within the bed. Delphine was curled up against him, her head resting in the curve of his shoulder, her arm flung across his chest. Her hair was spread across the pillows and his shoulder. He gazed down at her in wonder and his heart turned over at the sight of her lovely face. She was deliciously warm, soft and rosy in slumber, her dark curling lashes sweeping her cheeks, her face serene.

He had been driven by lust when he had sought her out in her room. Now he felt a protectiveness so profound that it shook him to the depths of his being and looking back, the sweet memory of her response to him touched him deeply. She was as open and generous in her lovemaking as she was in every aspect of her life.

He could succumb to the temptation of a beautiful woman as easily as the average man, but he had never experienced anything like what he was beginning to feel for his wife. He had never experienced anything of a woman's love that had nothing to do with sex—not from his mother, nor the devotion of a nurse or nanny—and certainly not from Maria. In this moment of calm he realised that there had always been an unidentified, repressed hunger within him for female contact—physical, mental and spiritual.

He was stunned. He had thought life had given him compensation of immunity because of his yearning all his life to make the military his life. Now it appeared that he was instead the victim of an insidious affliction. He felt like a man dying of thirst, given his first taste of water. He had vowed not to touch Delphine until he returned from Spain. But just a short while in her presence and gone was the reserve, the restraint he exercised over all aspects of his life. He shook himself in irritation, ashamed of his thoughts. What was it about him that a beautiful woman such as Delphine should bring out every wicked, shameful trait he possessed?

And now here he was. All his self-esteem had been set aside; he had been trapped by a guileless girl like a green lad barely old enough to control his urges. Every minute he remained with her, her hold on him would grow stronger, and before he knew it he would be hard pressed to withhold his amorous attentions. He would become enslaved, then destroyed. It was a situation he could not even begin to contemplate at a time when his mind was occupied with returning to his regiment.

But suddenly returning to the army had lost its appeal. He knew Delphine played a part in his disillusionment and in a way he blamed her for it. He would delay in leaving for Portsmouth no longer, where he would embark for Lisbon.

* * *

Delphine awoke in the big bed. Opening her eyes, she stretched luxuriantly, a sleepy smile curving her lips. Reaching out her arm to the right of her, her fingers encountered soft linen and the edge of the mattress, nothing else. She was alone. Stephen had gone, leaving her body feeling cold and exposed. Desire stirred within her, her body flushing as memories of the previous night coursed through her. Her lips still felt bruised by his kisses. She could still taste him, could feel his body imprinted against her own. Any moment he would return, she would see his smiling face and again they would make love.

But he did not return. Delphine rose from her bed and dressed, her mind preoccupied with conflicting emotions. At home in London her maid would have brought her breakfast, pulled the curtains back and prepared her bath. At Tamara, devoid of servants, she would have to do all that for herself until the house was fully staffed.

Encountering Alice in the hall, she enquired after her husband.

Alice shrugged. 'He's gone, my lady—went early, he did.'

'Gone? Gone where?' Delphine demanded, though she'd heard the servant plain enough.

'Back to Spain.'

'Spain!'

The news hit her like a physical blow. He had not simply gone to call on his neighbours or journeyed back to London to visit friends, which would have been bad enough. No—he had abandoned his wife as soon as he had taken what he wanted from her. Without notice, he had left her here alone, and gone to a foreign country to fight a war.

She stood frozen in the draughty old hall for a moment, trying to get her feelings under control. He lacked even the most basic decency to say goodbye to her, to assure her he'd be back—after how long?

'Of all the self-centred blackguards,' she muttered, unable to find a satisfying word with which to complete the sentence. If he walked in now, she would be tempted to hit him over the head with a blunt instrument.

However, forcing her mind to travel along more rational lines, she was forced to concede that he had done no wrong. Had he not told her he would have to leave before dawn for Portsmouth?

Concerned for her welfare, initially he had wanted her to remain in London with her family and friends until his return. It was her father's refusal to comply with this suggestion that had led to her abandonment here in a cold, draughty house surrounded by strangers.

Wandering through the empty rooms and eerily echoing passageways of her new home, desolation seized her and she was pierced by an unfamiliar sense of loss. She did not *want* to want him, but she did. She couldn't help it. How could he have done this to her? Why had he left her? And why should she care? What did it mean? She really didn't know him at all, but his leaving had left her feeling bereft and strangely empty.

That day Delphine did the most courageous thing she had ever done in her life—she faced up to her new life at Tamara, concentrating on the realities of her future. Stephen was a soldier and she could not, did not expect him to give it all up for her, not when there was a war to fight. She was not the only woman whose husband was away from home fighting in the Peninsula, so she would have to make the best of things until he came home, and then… She could not think beyond that.

* * *

This had been a time to forget the old and seek out the better moments of whatever life had to give. With this attitude she had concentrated on the practicalities of adjusting to her new position and duties. Until the servants came back, there had been work to be done.

And so it was that after many weeks, with every floorboard and every stick of furniture polished, Delphine found herself becoming a part of Tamara. New friends began to claim her time, inviting her to this and that, and on the whole she liked them very well. She always presented the calm and untroubled face of a lady of the manor who had nothing more to worry her than the ordering of her servants, the making and receiving of calls, the ordering of gowns from her dressmaker and the entertainments and charity events at which she wore them.

Tamara, this private place, became a world unto itself, a haven against the battle being fought against Napoleon across the sea. Though she sat at her desk and composed letters telling Stephen of day-to-day matters, his sporadic replies were stilted. In one of his early letters he told her not to be offended or think badly of him for not writing more often, since his regiment was always on the move. At least she knew that he was well and he always wished her well, but there was nothing in his brief letters to indicate the passion, the desire, the need he had demonstrated on his last night at Tamara.

At night she fought the loneliness of her big bed, surprised by how much she missed having him beside her. The pleasure and the intensity she had experienced on the night he left were now too painful to contemplate, but however hard she tried not to think of him at all, the very act of trying not to brought him more swiftly and powerfully to mind.

She had been at Tamara for three months when she realised she was pregnant, putting the whole household in a state of excitement. After the initial shock subsided, excitement raced through her and she laughed deep in her throat, feeling wonderful. A baby! She was going to have Stephen's baby! Her pregnancy also gave her the perfect excuse—along with the wet and blustery winter weather—not to travel to London for Rose's and

Fern's weddings, which were set to be a truly grand double affair according to her mother's letters.

As soon as her daughter was born, the world began to glow with the soft radiance of light and colour. Delphine was exhilarated by her strange, fiercely possessive feelings towards the small, helpless infant. Her baby was perfect, with skin as soft as a rose petal, a mouth as soft and pouting as a pink rosebud and her eyes a dark midnight blue.

She looked exactly like Stephen.

Delphine felt such complete devotion, such overwhelming love that was without condition, without reserve, without demands. She named her daughter Lowenna, which Alice informed her was the Cornish for joy.

She had written to Stephen, informing him of the birth of their daughter, and sent a letter to her family. Within two weeks her mother had replied, insisting that as soon as she was fit enough to travel, she must come to London for a visit. Delphine had no objection, for she was very keen to see Aunt Celia. Since her arrival at Tamara, her aunt had written often about the progress of the charities, keeping her up to date about what was happening at the orphanage, and in one of her letters her aunt had informed her that young Maisie's mother, Meg, was dead. Unfortunately her aunt did not give any details as to how this had come about, but it was plain that her aunt was worried about Maisie, who was coping with the loss, but only just—and most worrying was that Will Kelly was constantly hanging about, trying to lure Maisie away from the orphanage.

Delphine prayed this would not happen. She wished fervently to help Maisie and had written to her aunt offering to remove Maisie from the orphanage and bring her to Tamara, where a position would be found for her in the house.

During the months following her birth, Lowenna was embraced into the rhythm of the house. Her smile was a little ray of sunshine. She gurgled and cooed and was quite happy to submit herself to the mass adoration of everyone. A bold, fearless little thing, she walked at ten months, talking her baby talk as she staggered recklessly about the house on her sturdy little legs.

The only dampener on these happy days was

the fact that, having received Stephen's letter telling her of his intense joy on the birth of their
daughter, she heard nothing else. She tried to
excuse his tardiness by telling herself that com-
munications in Spain, with regiments constantly
on the move, were bound to be confusing. When
sixteen months had passed and still there was no
word, she was no longer able to ignore the con-
stant, stabbing unease. She was dismayed at the
depth of fear she felt for her husband, the idea of
him coming to harm was intolerable.

She had had no time to get to know Stephen,
and yet, as the weeks and months passed, he
seemed no stranger to her at all, but someone
whose image she carried in her heart, held in her
imagination like a promise of something more,
something better.

Never in the rest of his life was Stephen able
to determine precisely what he did and where he
went in the aftermath of the Battle of Badajoz
on the seventh day of April. The fighting had
been ferocious, the battle one of the bloodiest
in the Peninsular War. The town, held by the
French, was taken by the Allied troops. When
dawn came, it revealed the horror of the slaugh-

ter around the curtain walls. Bodies of British soldiers were piled high and blood flowed like rivers through the trenches.

But then came slaughter of a different kind. British troops had burst out from the discipline of their firm commanders and let their emotions rule their actions, behaving with sickening savagery to the Spanish inhabitants. The town was subjected to two days of pillage, murder, rape and drunkenness—as many as four thousand Spanish civilians, mostly women and children, were massacred.

It was something that Stephen had not foreseen, therefore he had not calculated the effect that it would have on him. For it is one thing to lead soldiers into battle and fight honourably; it is quite another to see those same soldiers—well organised, brave, disciplined and obedient— turn into a pack of hounds, all military discipline gone, and attack the Spanish civilians they had been fighting to liberate. Blood was everywhere—the whole world seemed to be drowning in blood.

It appeared to him afterwards that he had escaped being killed many times over, for he had wandered, half-dazed with fatigue, through the streets of Badajoz, as musket fire and the screams of women and children echoed around him, buildings blazing on either side, without getting so much as a scratch.

Returning to camp, he sat with his head in his hands, loyal Oakley standing close beside him.

'By the eyes of God, Oakley, things like this age a man twenty years in as many minutes. I've had enough. A musket ball through the head would be a kindness.' Raising his head, he looked at Oakley. His face was hard and smeared with powder, shadows of exhaustion from what he had seen that day, his mouth twisted with bitter mockery. 'Do you know what day it is today, Oakley? It is my daughter's first birthday. She is one year old and I have never laid eyes on her. And now, every birthday of her life, I shall remember this day.'

From Badajoz Stephen had gone on to Salamanca and fought in the hills around Arapiles, south of Salamanca. It was here that he received an almost fatal wound to the chest. Had it not been for the care of Oakley and a local woman, he would not have survived.

The battle had been fought in choking dust and heat. The French forces could not recover and the broken remnants of their army straggled back towards the Pyrenees and France.

As a consequence of Wellington's victory here, his army had been able to advance on Madrid for two months, but then retreated back to Portugal, where Stephen had embarked for England.

Now Stephen stood at the prow of the ship, unafraid of the dangers as the vessel pitched and rolled through the storm. He was returning to England with no sense of triumph, only the leaden sickness of mounting disillusionment.

All the years of his life, the only thing he had invested with real importance had been the army. It had always given a meaning to his life, to everything he did. Now that the war was over, he had every intention of settling down to a more sedentary existence with his wife, whose absence from his life was the main cause of his disillusionment. And his child?

He blinked his eyes in an attempt to clear his fogged senses. Delphine—a young woman he had made his wife—a young woman he hadn't had the time to get to know. A dim vision of a girl with deep-red hair glaring at him with open defiance—of that same girl gazing up at him with warm, passion-filled dark eyes after they had made love—drifted into his mind.

'Delphine,' he whispered in pained regret, re-calling the night he had taken her in a drunken stupor. His actions that night had culminated in his whimsical, impulsive marriage to that same bewitching girl with whom he had truly shared a bed only twice. 'My wife.'

The thought of seeing her again brought a thrill of anticipation racing through him and his heart gave a leap of excitement in his chest. He had re-buked himself many times over the way he had left her, creeping away like a thief in the night because he couldn't bring himself to face her, to say goodbye. The feelings she evoked in him had brought bitter memories of his relationship with a callous, treacherous woman that had left painful scars, as yet unhealed. And yet when he'd looked down at Delphine's sleeping face, her wonderful mane of deep-red hair spread out over the pillows, he'd seen something in her that was in himself and something had stirred in his hardened heart.

Seeing the Cornish coastline on the horizon, he felt suddenly uplifted, a smile lightening his intense dark features. He looked forward to the moment when he would hold his daughter for the first time. He contemplated what his homecoming would mean to Delphine. Would she welcome him home, or would she have become so independent in his absence that she would resent his return? Hoping for the former, he drew in one last deep, satisfying breath and went to find Oakley.

The sea was high and the wind loud in his ears. He was unable to hear the shouted warning given by one of the crew, warning him of the boom that had worked its way loose from the securing ropes and was swinging about precariously. When it hit him, he experienced an explosion of white hot pain that seared inside his head.

Darkness had fallen when Delphine went upstairs to her bed. Sensing something was not quite right, she went to the window and looked out. The moon cast its light through the barren limbs of the trees, creating dark, tangled images on the ground. She eyed the shadows carefully, half-expecting some movement to startle her, and did not realise how tense she was when it did.

There were horses, two of them, and instinctively she knew that one of them carried Stephen.

Picking up her skirts, she hurried down the stairs and out into the courtyard, Mrs Crouch hurrying in her wake. One of the riders, whom she recognised as Mr Oakley, had dismounted. Her gaze went to the other rider. He sat slumped in the saddle, sagging weakly forwards; his head lolled forwards on to his chest. He looked like he had fallen asleep. Delphine was aware in that instant of a sudden pang in her breast and an unfamiliar, wild, uncontrollable beating. The suddenness of recognition made her body feel weak. It was Stephen. She ran towards him, alarmed by the sight of blood running down his face from beneath a crude dressing wrapped around his head. His eyes were closed and, beneath the black curling hair and sun-bronzed face, his skin seemed bloodless.

'Stephen?'

When there was no response, she turned to Mr Oakley, her face similarly drained of colour. 'What is wrong with him?'

'He lost consciousness some miles back,' he told her, going to his master. 'I'm amazed he managed to stay in the saddle.'

'But—is he ill—wounded? What?'

'Wounded.'

'How bad is it?'

'I cannot say. He suffered a wound to his head caused by a heavy blow from a loose boom on the vessel bringing us back to England. He did not lose consciousness and allowed me to dress the wound—such as it is. He didn't want a fuss.'

'Have you ridden far?'

'We left the ship at Plymouth.'

Delphine turned to one of the grooms, her eyes blazing urgently. 'Go to the village for Dr Jenkinson. Have him come at once.' Further instructions sent two of the maids running ahead to prepare the master's chambers and have hot water and towels sent up. She was relieved when Davy came hurrying out of the house.

'Quickly,' she said, sick with dread. 'Get him inside. One of the grooms will take care of the horses.'

Together Mr Oakley and Davy dragged Stephen from his horse and between them managed to carry him up to his room, where they laid him on the bed.

Delphine had recovered somewhat from the initial shock and now stood over him. Every line and curve of his face was etched indelibly on her mind: the sweep of his long lashes as they rested against his cheeks, the little creases at the corners of his mouth, the black curls flecked with silver around his temples, the silver more pronounced than she remembered. She had memorised every detail of that strong, bronzed face and she now felt that she could go on looking at it for a life-time and never have enough of looking.

His eyes flickered open and, as if the effort sapped his strength, instantly closed again. Something in those dark-blue depths so briefly seen made her catch her breath. Once more she felt her body blaze with emotion and for once she did not care. She had so long been denied intimacy with her husband, had so determinedly kept her mind from any such feelings, that she now recklessly welcomed them.

Mr Oakley opened Stephen's coat. His eyes remained closed, but he groaned when Mr Oakley raised him slightly and removed the coat completely.

'How serious do you think his wound is?' Delphine asked, not taking her eyes from her husband's face. 'Please tell me the truth. Do—do you think he will die?'

Mr Oakley looked at her gravely. 'I honestly do

not know the answer. I've known many men receive such a blow and recover without any after-effects. Your husband acquired several wounds in battle, one when his chest stopped a French bullet at Salamanca, the last battle he fought. The surgeon considered it serious at the time but mercifully, he was tenderly nursed and ultimately recovered. I fear, however, it weakened him. His request to be discharged of his duties was immediate upon his recovery.'

Delphine stared at him in disbelief. 'He requested to be discharged of his duties?'

Sombre-faced, Mr Oakley nodded. 'He was not recovering as quickly as he should. It was as if something was holding him back—as if he were fighting something. It wasn't just infection of his wound. He seemed to sink deeper and deeper into what the doctor called depression.'

'And what was your opinion, Mr Oakley? You know my husband better than anyone. If, as the doctor said, it was depression, what was the cause?'

Oakley shrugged wearily. 'A combination of many things. Personally I think it was what he witnessed at Badajoz. It was a dreadful time for soldiers and civilians—a time for looking into one's soul and asking what the war was all about. That, and the loss of will, was what decided him to leave the army. But in addition, Lady Fitzwaring, I believe he was missing his home and family. He could certainly have done without further injury.'

With a single-minded purpose and a tenderness she had shown no other man, Delphine tended her husband, cherishing the hope that Stephen had indeed been eager to return home to her and their child. After removing the dressing from around his head, stroking back the black, glossy curls from his brow and wiping away some of the blood, she placed a cool, wet cloth against his forehead. She sat beside the bed to await the doctor.

Delphine was seriously concerned by Stephen's condition. He was still unconscious. Beneath the loose dressing she had applied, the wound still bled profusely. A thin trickle of blood ran down his forehead and over his cheeks as far as the corner of his tightly closed lips. His face was impassive, the eyelids tight closed over his dark-blue eyes. Occasionally his features tightened in a spasm of pain.

* * *

When Mrs Crouch ushered Dr Jenkinson into the room, Delphine rose to greet him. 'Doctor Jenkinson! I am obliged to you for coming so soon. My husband requires urgent attention. He has received a blow to his head and the wound still bleeds. I am most concerned that he has not recovered consciousness.'

Doctor Jenkinson lost no time in examining the wound. 'There's no fracture,' he said at length. 'But there is a ruptured blood vessel.'

'What are you going to do?'

'I am going to cauterise the wound and seal the vein.'

'Will it leave a scar?'

'The wound is small despite the severity of the blow. I shall barely touch it so as not to leave too large a burn. Besides, his hair will cover it.'

Removing his coat, he rummaged in his bag and brought out some shining instruments, selecting one in particular. After wiping it carefully with a small piece of cloth on which he had poured a few drops of acrid-smelling liquid, he placed it in a small metal pot containing hot coals, which Davy had just brought in. After a moment, with a steady hand and Mr Oakley and

Davy holding Stephen down, he applied the red-hot metal tip of the instrument to the wound.

Delphine stayed near as the doctor tended the wound. She closed her eyes and clenched her hands when Stephen's body jerked, but she could not shut out his cry of pain and the smell of burnt flesh and singed hair.

'There,' Dr Jenkinson said, standing back to survey his handiwork, 'the vessel is sealed. I shall apply some salve and a dressing. In a few days the wound should have healed.' When he had bound the wound, lifting Stephen's eye-lids and feeling his pulse, he seemed to be sat-isfied. 'Let him sleep,' he advised, thrusting his arms into his coat. 'He will need every ounce of strength when he comes round.'

Silently Delphine was thankful for the time she had spent at the orphanage. It was thanks to her aunt's tuition that she was not ignorant of balms and medicinal cures and of caring for the sick or injured.

She refused the pleas of both Mrs Crouch and Mr Oakley to go to her own chambers and rest, stating resolutely, 'I will sit with him. A room will have been prepared for you, Mr Oakley.

You look exhausted. You can go to bed knowing Stephen is in safe hands.'

Seeing no opening for argument, Mr Oakley
finally relented.

Left alone with her husband, Delphine stretched
the covers over him and touched her hand to
his fevered brow. She found her eyes irresist-
ibly drawn to a loose black curl that shaped itself round his ear and lay softly coiled against
his neck. Reaching out her hand, she touched it,
feeling its softness. With a wistful sigh she sat
beside the bed and remembered how it had been
between them before he went away.

Despite the manner in which they had come together and the often angry and bitter words they
had exchanged, they had been unable to fight
what they felt for each other, which was not just
desire, but lust. How could it be anything else
when they barely knew each other? In fact, the
length of time they had been together was less
than one week. But there it was, and there was
no use denying it or fighting it. Nor could she
regret it. How could she ever regret what they
had done? How could she regret having known,
even for such a short time, the feel of Stephen's

body in union with her own, never having known what it felt like to have a fire inside her soul, never having known that such a dark, wild passion could exist? And the outcome of all that passion was the beautiful child they had created together, the child he had yet to meet.

And now he was home.

In his delirium he muttered softly, rolling his head slowly from side to side. When he grew feverish and his brow felt hot to the touch, she bathed him with cool water. When he became restless and muttered incoherently, she murmured soothingly, tenderly, stroking his brow until he calmed. Apart from these small comforts, there was little else she could do but sit and wait, praying that he would soon regain consciousness.

Suddenly he cried out, his voice hoarse and fierce as if something troubled him, and his long fingers clutched at the covers. Delphine leaned over him, trying to catch what he was saying. A grimace of pain contorted his face and his eyes flew open. They were blank and staring. Sunk into fevered delirium, he didn't see her.

'Dammit! What do I have to do to put you from my mind?' Suffering dragged at his mouth.

'Count the days, count the months,' he muttered quickly, squeezing his eyes tight shut. His words trailed off into an incoherent mumble.

Delphine thought he must be in pain, for he seemed so tormented. She was alert, listening to the low, disconcerted murmurings that now and then escaped his lips. She bathed his forehead and tried to soothe him, gently shushing his ravings, but she could not seem to penetrate the barrier behind which his mind wandered. Every movement he made, every whimper or whispered word he uttered, she was aware of it. When the words started again, sharp and angry and louder, and his head began to thrash against the pillows, when she tried to quieten him and soothe him, he gave a sudden jolt and strained away from her as if she were the very devil. She realised he was locked in a nightmarish torment.

'Damn you—damn your fickle heart! God in heaven, Oakley—so much blood and death—the wench has blinded me. Her face is branded on my soul. She taunts me, seduces and torments me, and the more I have her the more she leaves me wanting.' He groaned, turning his head from side to side as he raved and tossed, plagued by some unavenged demon.

'I thought I could take my freedom and flee—but not even battle and death can stop me wanting her so that I have no more will of my own.' His voice broke and he flung his arm across his eyes, hiding his face, and when he next spoke his words were barely above a whisper. 'Aye, Oakley, when I think of her I think of softness, of warmth. I see her eyes aglow, tender in a moment, then dark with an anger I know I have caused—may God forgive me—and Angelet.'

That last word was said on a breath, and then he fell silent, the moment over. When he lowered his arm, the pain of longing marked his face with a momentary sadness.

Delphine's heart wrenched and her throat tightened. His words had penetrated her very soul and with tears gathering in her eyes she bowed her head in abject misery. Who was this woman he spoke of, the woman who made him suffer so, the woman who had woven her web about him with such intricate care and skill and entrapped him among the silken threads—this Angelet?

Her vision remained blurred with tears as an overwhelming sense of despair sank its merciless talons into her, damaging her hope and confidence. Stephen had never spoken of the women he had known before her, he had not had occasion to, but she had the impression there had been many. It was inconceivable that a virile man like Stephen would spend so many years as a soldier without knowing women. She had never thought herself a possessive woman, nor had occasion to be, but the jealous pangs she now endured were more searing than she could ever have imagined.

She wondered just how deeply Stephen had become enmeshed with the woman in Spain. Mr Oakley had told her that her husband had been tenderly nursed following his injury. Was it she who had cared for him, this mysterious Spanish woman, and was she still confidently expecting his favours, despite the distance between them, and even though he had a wife?

She had waited day after day for news of him since that night two years ago when he had left her. She had spent the time fearing he might have been wounded in battle—or worse—but she could not have foreseen this end: that this wrenching anguish was a suffering of the heart wrought by his love for another woman—a woman she remembered Mr Oakley had once called a beautiful *señorita*.

Tears fell on her hands, lying clenched in her lap, as she relented to this fresh sorrow. She was grateful that her husband slept, that he would not see firsthand how he had hurt her. Stephen was the only man she had known intimately, the only man she had ever hated after he had forced himself on her. And now that her feelings had altered so very much, now that she had begun to look forward to a shared future, she could only envy and despise the woman who occupied the place in his heart where she wished so desperately to be.

Unfortunately, she could not control her feelings, but she could control how she acted upon them, and she vowed that while this Angelet held sway over his heart, she, Delphine, would not share his bed—and yet, she thought, annoyed by the sudden weakness that crept over her, he was her husband. How could she deny him? How could she resist him?

As the night wore on and the moon crept stealthily across the sky, for Delphine the hours ran together, and when Stephen rested in the quieter states of fevered sleep, limp and unresponsive to her presence, she curled in a chair beside the bed, dozing fitfully, her mind skimming the troubled fringe of sleep. Then she would wake, and watch him intently again. So the night continued.

She kept her vigil until dawn, at which time the door opened and Mrs Crouch came to stand over her.

'Go to your room and rest, my lady. You'll be no good to him, or yourself, if you don't. Go. I will see to him,' she insisted. 'Come back later when you've bathed and tidied yourself.'

Delphine could do little but obey. Exhausted, she went to her bed, and still clothed, she stretched her weary body across the covers and tumbled into the deep vortex of slumber.

After several hours sleep, when Delphine awoke she was surprised to find she was no longer in the throes of wrenching heartache, although a vestige of pain still lingered. She tried to understand herself and realised she had spent the last two years trying to be what Stephen would expect and hope for when he returned, trying to anticipate his every need, working to make Tamara a home to be proud of, desperate to please him, and now she was left with a man lovesick for another woman.

She called herself a fool for her unrealistic illusions. Most of all she grieved for the painful destruction of the hope in her heart for Stephen's affections, hope that she had not even acknowledged to herself until knowledge of this other woman had shattered it. She told herself, more with defiance than sincerity, that the Spanish woman, whoever she might be, was welcome to him. But he was not free to go to her—and Delphine would never be free of him.

But at least this sorry state of affairs had made her understand something about herself she had never seen before. Being the youngest of a large family and for the most part ignored by her parents and sisters, all her life she had felt the need to be needed, trying to fill the void in her life with her work at the orphanage and other charities. Here at Tamara she had tried to do the same, deep down desperately wanting to feel needed, valued and appreciated. And now, just when she hoped everything would work out right for her, this Angelet had stolen him from her. She could not ask him about his love for another. Her pride forbade it. She now knew that he would never return her love and therefore she would not risk her heart.

But what now? What did the future hold for her? Pouring some water from the ewer into a bowl, she swilled her face. The piercing chill of the water was calculated; from it grew a renewed and resolute strength. Going back to London for good was not an option. She had severed all ties there, and whatever rebuilding was needed must begin here at Tamara. She had married Stephen and was determined to hold her course. But, she thought, straightening determinedly and wiping her face, he would never make her weep again.

Chapter Six

Stephen lay in his bed with his eyes closed, in a blissful lassitude of surrender to his weakness, in the unexpected luxury of complete absence of pain. Perhaps he slept; when he fought his way upwards into light again, he was in his own room, in his own bed. Moments earlier, he had drifted upwards through a cloud of haunting impressions and entered the realm of full awareness with a strange sense of well-being.

Almost immediately, he realised he had been ill, which made the contentment he now felt all the more puzzling. He could not ascertain the cause. Hovering on the fringe of consciousness, he had listened to the drone of voices around him without hearing the words. His hazy recollections seemed detached from reality, yet he was beset by glimpses of Delphine tending him and an awareness of her soothing his brow, her soft breasts lightly brushing his arm, her slender thighs pressed against the bed.

Gingerly he raised his hand and fingered the bindings around his head as if to ease the dull ache of his wound. Though the curtains were drawn—bright golden-fringed ones in place of the dull dark blue he remembered—the light was far too bright for his dry, aching eyes. He blinked several times and gradually things began to take shape.

What struck him first was the quiet. It seemed he was alone, but then, sensing he was not alone, he turned his head from side to side, despite the pain this caused him. Not seeing anyone, he lowered his sights, his eyes lighting on a little face surrounded by a glossy mop of ebony black curls.

The child stared up at him with interest in her wide eyes. She was a bright, strong-willed child and afraid of nothing, loved and cherished and indulged every day of her short life. Inquisitive, she loved anything out of the ordinary and had been drawn to the room by her mama's comings and goings, sensing this man promised to be something of that nature.

Unable to tear his gaze away from the child,

Stephen lay quite still in those first moments, his eyes seeking the truth, which in his heart he knew already. There was a silence, a stillness. The moment seemed like for ever, though it lasted not five seconds. The little girl, the most beautiful little girl he had ever seen, peered into his face with the greatest curiosity. Her lips were rosy and her eyes were blue, long black lashes framing their vibrant depths and fanning her honey-gold cheeks—eyes of such a distinctive midnight shade that it was impossible to deny this child was his daughter.

He looked up as a woman entered the room and came to stand behind the child. For the first time in two years he came face to face with his wife. He studied her, moving his eyes up and down her slender body in undisguised familiarity. Her hair was drawn back from her face and she was modestly dressed, though the smooth brown wool did not detract from the beauty of her face but, rather, threw it into relief like a perfect cameo.

He'd noted as she walked across the room that she moved with a natural grace and poise that evaded most other women. Her skin glowed clear and healthy and she still exuded a gentle inno-

cence that drew him to her. But he remembered
her well enough to know that beneath this she
was a passionate woman. Fragments of a sensual nature flitted through his mind. They were
neither far-fetched nor illusory, but true, for this
was the same young woman who had knelt on
the bed with her gown falling down around her
and her soft, lustrous breasts gleaming with a
rosy hue—breasts full enough to fill his hands
and about as perfect as any man could possibly
envision—who had lain beneath him with her
nails clawing at his back as he had poured his
love into her, had heard her rapturous panting as
she soared to the lofty pinnacle of ecstasy.

When he spoke his expression gave no indication of the road upon which his thoughts travelled. 'This has to be Lowenna,' he murmured
softly.

Even if she had wanted to, Delphine could
not deny it, for two almost identical faces now
looked at her, their expressions the same: auda-
cious, fearless, compelling and yet with a quirk
of humour at the corner of each upturned mouth.
Lowenna even had the same arrogant jut to her
baby jaw as her father, the same determined
scowl. She knew by Stephen's expression that

he was not shocked or stunned now he had come face to face with his daughter and that he would love her.

He was watching his wife calmly; Delphine felt she had been struck dumb, felt unable to move, unable to breathe, unable to form any sort of coherent thought. The blue of his eyes had not faded. If anything, two years of hardship in Spain had made him more attractive, rather than less, had made him even more compelling to her. She was an inanimate object and might have remained this way for ever, had she not felt her daughter's little hand tugging on her skirt to claim her attention. She scooped Lowenna into her arms and rested her on her hip, then turned back to her husband.

'Yes, Stephen, this is Lowenna—your daughter.'

'*Our* daughter,' he corrected. 'It takes two to make a child, Delphine. You and I made this one.'

The way he looked at her, the sound of his voice, made her want to run from the room, but at the same time her treacherous body longed to put the child down and fling herself into the space beside him. She wanted him to take her in his arms and hold her tight, wanted to bury her face in his neck, wanted him to love her with such passion that she forgot all else. She had lived for the day when he would come home to her. But the knowledge that another had claimed his heart shielded her from the onslaught of desire.

Without taking his eyes off the child, Stephen struggled to sit up, wincing when a sharp stab of pain shot through his head. Propping himself up with the pillows, he held out his arms.

'Give her to me. Let me hold my daughter.'

Delphine handed the child to him, relieved when Lowenna went trustingly and gladly into his arms. He was careful not to clasp her too tight when he embraced her and Lowenna, who was afraid of nothing and no one, settled down with him most amicably.

The child gazed up at him, her eyes wide open. 'Are you Papa?' she asked in her baby voice.

'I am, sweetheart,' he replied, his voice hoarse with emotion, hugging his daughter to him and gently kissing her rosy cheeks. Lowenna put her arms about his neck and hugged him back, then began to wriggle, for the attention span of such a young child was limited. She scrambled off the bed and tottered about the room. Stephen watched her, his expression conveying a rare softness and pleasure.

It was very quiet inside the room and the silence began to bite keenly into Delphine's nerves. After a moment he looked at her, admiration and a growing respect in his gaze, a look he had never given any other woman.

'You have done well, Delphine. Lowenna is a credit to you. I congratulate you for having the courage to face what you have done alone. It cannot have been easy. Everything that has happened to you over the past two years was caused by me. And you have pierced me in the weakest spot—by giving me a lovely daughter.'

Delphine stared at him, aware of a startling triumph that she had hardly dared to expect, but also aware of how everything trembled in the balance.

'Do you mind not having a son?'

'Good Lord, no. Lowenna is perfect,' he said, casting his daughter a look of wonder, of love, approval and pride.

'Well, I am very glad to see you awake at last. We thought you'd taken leave of us. Do you have any recollection of what happened to you?'

'I remember something hitting me and the pain in my head, then nothing.'

'According to Mr Oakley, you were struck on the head when some of the rigging on the ship became loose in the storm.'

'How long have I been unconscious?'

'Two days. Doctor Jenkinson is confident you will make a full recovery. Mr Oakley has been extremely worried about you—he told us you were only recently wounded in Spain and that you are still suffering the after-effects. He'll be relieved to know you've come round at last.'

Stephen's brow cocked at an inquisitive angle as he looked at her narrowly. 'And you, Delphine? Were you worried about me?'

Delphine kept her face carefully averted, but Stephen noted her primly elevated profile as she responded with strained dignity. 'Of course—as I would be for anyone who had been knocked unconscious,' she answered evasively.

He frowned. 'Anyone? But I am not just anyone, Delphine. I am your husband and I might have hoped for a warmer welcome.'

'From me? To be frank, Stephen, I'm surprised you remember me,' she replied, unable to keep the sarcasm from her tone. 'It was such a long time ago and your letters were so few and far between, you must forgive me if I thought you had forgotten I exist.'

His lips came up at one side in a sweetly lop-sided smile. 'I'm hardly likely to forget that I have a wife. You must forgive my lack of communication. I have always been undependable. But not for one moment did I forget you.'

'Mr Oakley informed me you have resigned your commission, Stephen,' she said, trying to ignore the warm, penetrating look in his eyes.

'Indeed. I'm not going back. Now the war in the Peninsula is over I have decided that it's over for me, too. I still have some loose ends to tie up—which I can only do by going up to London—but as far as I am concerned my fighting days are over.'

'I see. I must confess I am surprised, knowing how important the army is to you. Will you not miss it?'

He sighed, moving his head into a more comfortable position. 'It was indeed always an important part of my life, but I've had plenty of time to think about the future and to put things into perspective. I have an estate to run, along with the mines. And now that Lowenna has come

along, I have other responsibilities. I'm quite resigned to settling down at Tamara with you and
our daughter. So you shall have to get used to
having your husband around all the time. I'm
sure you'll be more than happy for me to take
the reins.'

Delphine stiffened at once. 'I hope you don't
mean to start ordering me about, Stephen. I've
been on my own, making my own decisions for
too long to stop now you are back.'

'Dear God, are we never to—?' He clamped
his lips together and looked at his young wife,
the mother of his child. He had imagined their
first meeting a hundred times and rehearsed the
words he would say to her. But nothing had followed his plans. He wanted to tell her how much
he regretted the circumstances that had brought
them together, but he had merely ended up looking—at least in his own eyes—a monster.

'Are we never to what?'

'It doesn't matter.' He looked at her with those
lovely, deep-blue eyes. 'At least I will be here to
protect you and take the burden of Tamara from
your shoulders.'

It was spoken with an attempt at nonchalance
and ardent chivalry, with the charming confi-

dence in which Delphine knew him to be so proficient, but he did not quite manage to pitch it right this time. At that precise moment he did not look capable of protecting anyone, looked, indeed, to be in far more need of protection himself. He looked so tired, his eyelids almost too heavy for him to hold open, and some of her defiance began to melt away in the face of his vulnerability.

But Stephen was not so tired that he could not admire his wife. His mind was filled with thoughts of bedding her, of undressing her, of running his hands over her bare flesh, of plunging inside her, feeling release as he emptied his seed. But he had already decided to take things slowly, to tread carefully, not to rush things. He wanted to take her hand, which was within his reach, but his nerve failed him, for he had no wish to send her back into the stubbornness, the mutinous obstinacy she had shown on the day he had married her.

'Do not misjudge me,' he said softly. 'Doubtless you think me the most abominable cur for seducing you. But I swear that at the time I did not know you were a respectable young lady—and you were so damned lovely I could not help it. I despise myself for it. I am tortured by guilt for what I did to you.'

Unable to doubt the sincerity of his words she managed a little smile. 'I could never think you a cur. And all that is in the past, Stephen.'

'I will try to control my urges in the future, Delphine.' He gave her a most gentle, contrite smile. 'But it will be no easy matter.' For a moment neither of them spoke. Then he said, 'I promise you I will not take advantage of you. For now, you are quite safe from me.'

God help her, she did not wish to be safe from him. As he turned his head away she wanted to beg him to kiss her like he had before he went away, to make her his, to ignore all his good intentions. The man she had married had been a libertine, careless of his life and in love with danger. There was a change in him now, which she assumed was caused by the horrors he had seen in Spain and his experiences of war. In the beginning they had hidden their feelings, had fought and argued—and made love. And now here they were, at a place where both of them longed to be, and yet they were strangers once more, both of them tongue tied.

'I am relieved to hear it,' she replied. 'You've

been away a long time. We need a while to get to know each other. I think we should take each day as it comes; see what each day brings.' She met his gaze levelly. 'For the time being I wish to be left alone—to go to my bed alone. I think you know what I mean.'

Stephen looked at her hard. Whatever ebullience he had briefly relished upon waking and languishing in erotic thoughts of his wife swiftly darkened into a sour irascibility. So, he thought, that's the way she would have it. She could not have spoken plainer. It had not occurred to him that the beautiful, innocent temptress who had surrendered in his arms before he'd left for Spain, who'd returned his passion with such intoxicating sweetness, might no longer be quite so easily won over.

His wife had erected a high, sturdy barrier around herself, but not for one minute did he believe it was impregnable. Delphine was a warm and passionate woman; he was confident that he could succeed in luring her into bed any time he chose. But for the time being, with his head throbbing like hell and feeling as weak as a kitten, seducing his wife would have to wait.

Scooping Lowenna into her arms, Delphine

crossed to the door. 'Now you're back with us I'll have some food brought in to you. I'll send Mr Oakley. He will continue to take care of all your personal needs while you remain in bed. What a loyal servant you have there, Stephen. I hope you appreciate him. He's hardly left your side for a minute.'

After spending a further feverish three days in his room, driven to desperation by Mrs Crouch and Oakley fawning over him—but not his wife, who seemed to make a point of keeping away—Stephen made up his mind to rise from his sickbed.

As he strode about the house, becoming stronger by the day, Delphine watched his gradual improvement with admiration and pride, despite herself. Though thinner than she remembered, he looked healthy and bronzed, and his deep-blue eyes were clear and calm.

With each new day the bond between father and daughter grew stronger. Utterly enchanted by his beautiful child, Stephen doted on Lowenna; when he was with her, his eyes came truly to life. Delphine often found them asleep together in a chair, Lowenna curled up happily against his chest. At times the charming sight brought tears to Delphine's eyes and she felt a tiny twinge of shameful envy, wishing she was the one resting her head on Stephen's chest. Stephen was so gentle and patient with Lowenna that the child joyfully accepted this stranger as her papa.

Where Delphine was concerned, his eyes were always guarded. They were polite with one another, pleasant even, both of them doing their best to begin the process of making something of their lives together and to make a secure and happy home for Lowenna, but it wasn't easy. Neither of them mentioned the couple of times they had spent in bed together before he'd left for Spain. Delphine didn't wish him to see how desperately she wanted him. Her heart yearned for a two-way affection, not this one-sided affair, where all the emotion seemed to be on her side, and where all his tenderness was simply born out of natural lust.

The day was fine, the sea a sparkling sheet of light when Stephen returned from his ride over the moors. He entered the house so suddenly that Delphine, arranging flowers in a large vase, was put into a state of utter confusion. He paused in the open doorway, the light behind him, his shadow stretching across the hall. He wore a black jacket and white shirt and neckcloth, and it was strange seeing him out of his military attire. There was a brief silence, then he was striding forwards, his shining black hair, tousled from the ride, curling into his neck and outlining his tanned cheeks, the same magnetism she remembered of old in his midnight-blue eyes. The hall jumped to life about him as his presence filled it, infusing it with his own energy and vigour. There was not a trace now of his vulnerability when he'd lain wounded in bed.

'They look nice,' he said, indicating the golden blooms.

Stephen was almost bowled over when her face broke into a sudden dazzling smile. She was dressed in a powder-blue confection, her deep-red hair tied back with a ribbon of a darker hue, and he wanted to fold her into the embrace he'd craved since recovering consciousness. He felt the pain in his heart ease somewhat as his strange young wife began to fit tidily into an empty spot in his heart he hadn't known was there.

'Yes, I thought they'd brighten up the hall.

There,' she said, placing the last flower in the middle of the display and standing back to admire her handiwork.

'Where is Lowenna?' he asked, looking around, as if expecting his daughter to pop up out of nowhere.

'Having her nap.'

'I swear she grows prettier every day.' He smiled. 'She is as lovely as her mother,' he said, meeting her gaze warmly. 'Pretty as a princess, in fact.'

Flustered by the soft intimacy of his remark, Delphine could feel her face grow warm beneath his intense gaze. 'Lowenna is certainly that—but she doesn't resemble me in the slightest. She is the mirror image of you.'

'I have the most beautiful wife and the most beautiful daughter in the kingdom. Any man would envy me.'

Stephen went and sat by the hearth, his long legs stretched out in front of him, tall shiny boots up on the fender, watching her. He was unable to believe what she had done to the house. Plasterwork and paintwork so obviously nearing the end of its life in the original stone-flagged medieval great hall, and the long gallery lined with an impressive array of Fitzwaring ancestral portraits, had been restored by master craftsmen. The carved-oak staircase rising majestically from the hall, in dire need of repair for years, had been put right, and the chimneys that smoked had been cleaned and repaired.

There was warmth, comfort, luxury even, in every room: the windows exquisitely draped with the finest fabrics and Chinese carpets in lovely shades covering the floors, their textures like velvet—all this without changing the nature of the beautiful old house. Even outside there was evidence of the time his wife had spent with the gardeners, discussing the care of the overgrown gardens that now pleased the eye wherever one looked.

'I feel I must congratulate you, Delphine,' he remarked as she took a seat opposite, the light from the flames reflected in his eyes. 'You've worked wonders on the old place in my absence—and the gardeners have excelled themselves.'

'I'm glad you approve of what I've done. You did give me *carte blanche* to spend whatever I wanted.'

'I did, and after taking a look at the accounts I see you have spent wisely.'

'What conclusions do you draw from my choice of furnishings?'

'That you have excellent taste and that you are fond of colours—though delicate, not garish.'

Despite herself, Delphine laughed at the diplomacy of his answer.

'You see, I am not so dull, am I? All women are fond of colours.'

His gaze lingered on her mouth. 'I like hearing you laugh,' he murmured. 'You should laugh often.'

Her stomach lurched and she turned her head aside to hide her blush. She did not want him to be courtly and romantic, for if he did, she might succumb. She might start to believe he truly cared for her, when it was only a façade to get her into bed and satisfy his lusts. He did not love her, but she knew from the hurt in her heart that she was in great danger of loving him.

'Tamara has not looked so fine in years—not since my mother was alive.'

'Thank you,' Delphine replied, touched and gratified by his praise of the changes she'd made. 'But I cannot take all the credit. None of the changes could have been achieved without Mrs Crouch—and Alice, of course. It was a relief when the servants returned, otherwise we could never have done so much.'

'And you never left to visit your parents in London?'

'No. I couldn't—not with Lowenna on the way, and afterwards there always seemed to be so much to do. But—I have arranged to go.'

'When?'

'Next month—in three weeks. My parents are keen to meet Lowenna. I thought I should go while the roads are suitable for travelling. Do you mind?'

'Would it matter if I did?'

'Yes, of course it would. You've only just arrived home. I would understand perfectly if you objected to my going.' She frowned, giving him a questioning glance. 'Do you?'

'Rest assured, Delphine, I have no objections. It's understandable that your parents should want to see you and to meet their granddaughter. I expect you are looking forward to the prospect after two years of enforced rustication. I told you I have several military matters to take care of myself in London, so I shall accompany you.'

'Oh,' she gasped, 'I hadn't thought…'

'What? That I wouldn't want to go?' He smiled. 'Naturally I wish to accompany my wife. I never had the chance to woo you before our marriage; now the perfect opportunity presents itself. No doubt we can attend a ball or two and take Lowenna sightseeing—although I suppose she's still a little young for that. I shall take you shopping—for new gowns, material and jewels and anything else you might fancy.'

Delphine laughed at his exuberance. 'Shopping?' she asked, somewhat bemused.

'Why not? Surely a man can be forgiven for giving his wife jewels and wanting to have her beautifully dressed.' He waited for her to say, *Do you think you can buy me…?*, but instead she simply laughed again.

'If you want to throw money at the goldsmiths and mercers in London, then do so—but please don't expect me to wear them all at once. Anyway, I have more than enough of everything.'

'Ah, but not chosen by me.'

She gave him a look of mock offence. 'Are you saying my taste displeases you?'

'No, you have excellent taste—if leaning somewhat towards the practical—and I have noted that you do tend to favour browns and greys and other unexciting shades. You have spent too long championing the poor and needy and neglecting yourself, Delphine. Now I think it is time for a little pampering.'

Delphine stared at him with disdain. 'I have never been pampered in my life; I am sure I would not like it if I were. And jewels I have no need for. Everyone knows that jewels are displayed as a symbol of status, of wealth, which is meaningless to me.'

'Nevertheless, I insist.'

'Very well. If you want to indulge in wanton extravagance, then who am I to discourage it?'

'Would you have everyone pity you for having a miser for a husband?'

'I do not seek the approval of strangers.'

'No.' He laughed. 'I don't believe you do.' And then on a more tender note that made Delphine's heart flutter and brought her head up, he said, 'There is nothing ordinary about you, is there, Delphine?'

'I hope not. Do you mind?'

'Most certainly not. I applaud the wildness and

individuality I first saw in you. I would not have you any other way.'

The warmth of his voice brought a soft flush to Delphine's cheeks. 'I'm sure you won't be bored in London. No doubt you are familiar with all the gentlemen's clubs and have done your fair share of gambling.'

He grinned. 'I confess I am not averse to a spot of gambling now and then, and have done so in most of London's polite and impolite gaming houses. Now tell me what you have arranged by way of accommodation.'

'I—I have arranged to stay with my parents, naturally. I shall understand perfectly if you wish to stay elsewhere.'

'I confess that I do not relish the idea. On the other hand, I have no wish to be parted so soon from you and Lowenna. I shall send Oakley on ahead to look for a property to rent. That way we can be together and you can still see your parents. Is that agreeable to you?'

'Not really. Rose and Fern are to be in London and Mama was so looking forward to having us all to stay.'

Stephen brooded for several moments, then took a deep breath. 'Then I'm sorry to have to disappoint her. The manner in which your father forced my hand into marrying you still rankles. I am not yet ready to begin playing happy families, so you will abandon this idea, if you please, Delphine.'

He said it reasonably enough, quietly enough, but the space around them was hushed, waiting for something that would not be pleasant when it came.

'I do not please, Stephen,' she answered, her own voice quiet. 'Since you have an aversion to staying with my parents, *you* can stay in rented accommodation and Lowenna and I will stay with them.' Having made her own decisions during his absence, without having to answer to anyone, she deeply resented his high-handed attitude.

Stephen's face hardened and his eyes darkened to indigo. Anger flared in them, as sudden and as bright as quicksilver. 'I think not.'

Delphine felt her heart sink, but she ploughed on regardless. 'How are we to discuss this terrible dilemma if every time my parents are mentioned you refuse to put behind you the threats my father made at the beginning?'

'Can you?'

'Yes, I must,' she answered, determined to be truthful, wondering if she would ever be able to speak to him of her father without him freezing up. 'Can you not see how awkward this situation is for me? What am I to do? It is natural that in time my parents will wish to come to Tamara—to see where their daughter lives.'

'Even though their treatment of you through-out your life has bordered on neglect.'

She nodded, the memories still painful. 'I have to, Stephen. I know that you and my father can never be friends, but what you did to me does not endear you to him, either.'

'Really!' he drawled. 'You astonish me. I meant what I said, Delphine. When we go to London, we will live together—in accommodation of my choosing. Is that understood?'

Slowly but deliberately, Delphine said, 'Are you asking, or ordering me?'

'Does it make any difference?'

'Yes, it does.'

'I am your husband. You vowed to obey me. But in this instance I am asking you. Your first allegiance is to me—your husband. Remember that. It is I who make the decisions. A house of our own will be more suitable to our needs.'

She stood up and when she spoke her voice was icy. 'You speak to me as if I were one of your soldiers, Stephen, and the way you use that word allegiance—why, anyone would assume we were about to go into battle, when it is nothing of the sort. Very well. It will be as you wish. I will go and write to my mother at once to inform her of my change of plans.'

The household at Tamara functioned with a smoothness Stephen found satisfying. Delphine saw so little of her husband. When he wasn't working in his study on all sorts of unfathomable business transactions, meeting with his agents and bailiff, he spent his days at the mines and riding about the estate. When they were together, they did not quarrel or disagree on anything of importance, but there were tense undercurrents running between them that each was aware of.

In all this time Stephen did not step any closer to his wife. He did not fool himself into thinking that she loved him—he had known the truth of her feelings before he married her and, if he was perfectly honest with himself, knew she would not have married him had she not been forced into it. He had apologised for ravishing her—an apology ludicrously inadequate considering the seriousness of the crime.

And to add insult to that already injurious crime, after spending the most passionate, erotic night of his life in her bed, he had left her without the common courtesy of a goodbye. Little wonder she was unwilling to want him in her bed. As every minute, every hour of every day they had been apart had passed, Delphine's hurt and anger had hardened her heart against him.

Just thinking of that time infuriated him for, by God, he wanted her. He wanted to go to her and pull her into his arms, to carry her to bed and lose himself in her. During his absence she had become a complete woman, content in her own life at Tamara, shaping their life and that of their child in a way that pleased him. All he prayed for was that one day she would look on him with softness and come to feel some affection for him.

More than that he could not hope for at present, but he was not a man to give up. Not for a moment did he ever doubt that Delphine would yield to him either willingly or unwillingly. It was just a question of when. In the latter case, the balance of their coming together and combat would have to take place in his bed.

In an attempt to bolster his wife's drooping spirits following their disagreement about their London accommodation, Stephen had proposed they went riding together.

Delphine had been about to refuse, but the words died on her lips when she looked at the lazy, relaxed man with the slightly smiling mouth and eyes like deep-blue velvet. Suddenly a ride across the moor or wherever he chose to take her had seemed immensely appealing. It would be precisely what she needed to shake her wits into place.

'Yes—I would like that.'

'Excellent. We'll lunch at the Saracen's Head some few miles from Penryn. It provides the best food this side of the Tamar.'

It was a mild morning, carrying the promise of a lovely summer's day on the faint sea breeze. Faced with the tall roan she always favoured on her rides, Stephen came to lift her into the saddle. She placed her hands on his shoulders as he placed his own firmly about her waist. Wide-eyed, she met his gaze, and saw his brows lift, a quizzical expression in his eyes.

'I've never seen you ride. Do you ride well?'

'As well as most. You can judge for yourself.'

They rode side by side across the rolling countryside. Fresh, cool breezes were fragranced with an invigorating scent of the sea. Casting a sidelong glance at her husband, Delphine admired the way his body flowed easily with the big gelding's stride, both horse and master strong, a picture of combined, harnessed power.

Stephen was no less admiring of her. Gracefully perched side-saddle, when she soared over a wide ditch, he grinned approvingly. Delphine was light and lovely on horseback, managing her horse with expert skill. She urged it into a gallop, her hair and skirts flying out behind her. She let the horse have its head as she charged full pelt laughingly along the rutted track. Soon the speed and the air revived Delphine's flagging spirits, making her feel more alive than she had in days.

After riding for several miles, Stephen drew up on the cliff top overlooking the sea and dismounted, then walked over to lift Delphine down from her horse.

'The ride has done you good,' he said, noting the blooming colour in her cheeks and sparkling eyes.

'I enjoy riding. I often ride along the coast—this way, in fact, and sometimes inland over the moor.'

'It has been good for you to explore by yourself. It's important you get to know your new home, to learn to see it through your own eyes. I am biased about the charms of Cornwall, but I've no doubt you shall fall in love with it, too.'

'I think I've already done that,' she told him, perching on a large rock and smiling up at him, and realising to her surprise that it was true. 'I found no difficulty at all in falling in love with Tamara and the surrounding countryside. And I like the people. They're hardworking and friendly and—when I ceased to be a local curiosity—they made me feel very welcome.'

'And have you found any waifs and strays to look after?'

She frowned, tilting her head to look up at him. 'There are plenty of children in need wherever you go. Some of the families—especially those among the mining community—find living hard. I still find it difficult to take in that children actually work alongside women at the mines. I do what I can to make their lives easier.'

'Yes, I'm sure you do. But whether you agree with it or not, having children working alongside their parents at the mines is a way of life. Only time will change that.'

Turning from her as if distracted, Stephen went to the edge of the cliff and stood looking out to sea. A small frown touched Delphine's brow. He was already lost to his thoughts. As easily as he had dismissed her from his life when he went away, so on his return could he dismiss her from his mind. He had honoured her wish that for the present there was to be no intimacy between them. The fact that being a virile, passionate male he had not tried to change the situation surprised her, leaving her relieved and dismayed at the same time—and more than a little hurt, which confused her.

Without moving, she studied him. For a man of such imposing herculean stature, he had an elegant way of moving in his casual clothes. Wearing a tan coat, his long legs were encased in biscuit-coloured trousers and highly polished dark-brown riding boots. His hair was dishevelled from the ride, the black curls brushing the edge of his collar. The sun illuminated his bold, lean profile and that aquiline nose that gave him a look of such stark, brooding intensity. His mouth seemed hard and grim. She watched him lift his hand and, as he absently rubbed the muscles at the back of his neck, her treacherous mind suddenly recalled how skilfully those long fingers had caressed her own body and the exquisite pleasure he had made her feel.

Her heart suddenly swelled—with what? Admiration? Affection? Love? No, not that. She could never love a man who was in love with another woman. Could she? Even if that man was her husband? However hard she tried, she couldn't help but want him. But then, hadn't Aunt Celia once told her that the heart wasn't always wise when one's body was driven by base desires?

Recollecting herself, she shook away such thoughts angrily. She was being an utter fool romanticising Stephen, simply because he was a beautiful man, sleek and fierce as a bird of prey, with his raven-black hair threaded with white, and incredibly skilled in arousing her desire— and because she was a spineless idiot who was disgustingly and helplessly attracted to him.

But there it was and there was no use denying it or fighting it. Nor could she regret it. How could she regret having known, for such a short time, the feel of his lips on hers, his naked body pressed close? Until then her heart and body had been dormant, waiting for the spark that would make it explode into life. And if Stephen had not ignited it, she would have spent her whole existence not knowing what it felt like to have a fire inside her soul, would never have known that such a wild, sweet passion could exist. Better by far to experience that passion for such a short time, than never to have known it at all, even if it brought such pain and heartache, or to die not knowing such joy was possible. But it was unfortunate that now she had had a taste of the intoxicating sweetness of his lovemaking, she realised it was completely separate from what she really yearned for—an intimacy of the heart.

She took a few steps to stand by his side. Looking up at him, she wondered what he was thinking. There were times when he would become preoccupied, his thoughts far away—especially the times when correspondence arrived from Spain. At these times she would often catch him unawares. He never spoke of the war; in fact, he always seemed reluctant to do so. Was it because he was pining for the woman who had stolen his heart, or because of the terrible memories of war doing so would evoke?

When he'd returned to Tamara and she had seen the ugly red scar on his chest, her heart had twisted with pain at the suffering he must have endured. Mr Oakley had told her how he had been so badly wounded at Salamanca that the surgeon who had treated him had feared that he might die. He had been fortunate, but his mind clearly remained troubled.

Every morning he would leave the warmth of his bed for the cold of the sea, as if some unnamed nightmare could be banished only with an early-morning dunking in the sea. Delphine tried not to dwell on what it was that he felt the need to wash away, what he needed to exorcise, but it did not seem to have worked because the dark, troubled shadow in his eyes since his return from Spain was still there. He always returned to the house before breakfast, but she feared that one morning he might not come back. What if he swam out too far, or was not as alert to the currents and the undertow? She tried not to think of how he could be dragged out to sea, or his body hurled against the rocks in a sudden storm.

'What are you thinking?' she asked softly.

As if he hadn't heard her, Stephen continued to look straight ahead, seeing faces of men he had known—men who'd been blown to pieces by French cannon or mutilated beyond recognition, men he had known intimately, good friends, commanders and regular soldiers alike. When Delphine's voice penetrated his thoughts, he looked down at her and then fixed his gaze on the distant horizon once more.

Something hard flared in his eyes for a moment, but then he shrugged resignedly. 'I was thinking of Spain.'

'About—the war?' Delphine asked tentatively—or about Angelet? she wondered, too afraid of his possible response, too unable to bear the rejection to ask.

He was silent for a moment, then he said, 'What else could there be?'

Delphine wanted to tell him, but instead she said, 'Why do you never speak about what happened in Spain?'

Stephen looked straight ahead. His eyes had grown distant as the horizon, as if he had withdrawn into himself, into his painful past. Delphine wanted to reach for him and bring him back, but she was almost afraid to.

Stephen didn't want to talk about Spain, of how he'd come to be wounded many times, some wounds more serious than others, of how he'd wanted to die of his wound at Salamanca, cursing the fate that had spared him when so many of his fellow soldiers had died. He had a tidy, well-ordered mind and his worries were all rational ones: whether or not his battle strategies would work out, how to deal with the times of inaction, defective equipment and lack of sleep, the discomforts of sleeping on wet ground and waking with an empty belly because rations were short.

With all these everyday anxieties and discomforts of war, he had always been assured that the men he led, so valiant in the field, with military discipline instilled into them, would deal with whatever was thrown at them. But what he had witnessed at Badajoz—the mindless slaughter of innocents by these same men, this terrible lapse in human nature—had shocked and horrified him to the core of his being. But that was another life, another time—those last terrible last months in Spain were to be forgotten. But he could not imagine forgetting. What he had seen would continue to haunt him for evermore.

'I will not speak of it,' he said through clenched teeth, trying to keep his voice as free of emotion as possible. 'You were not there. You would not understand.'

'That's nonsensical. Perhaps if you were to speak of it, the pain would ease. I am persuaded that you must talk about it. Why have you closed your mind to it?'

'Out of necessity,' he retorted.

Something about the way he looked stirred Delphine's sympathy. 'I would like to think you could talk to me. I do wish to know what happened to you in Spain,' she said quietly, suddenly needing to know more than she had ever needed to know anything else. Her eyes were full of concern. 'How else can I understand?'

Instantly she cursed herself and her confounded curiosity. Never had she seen those little indentations above his nose and at the corners of his mouth appear so defined, or the warning flash in his eyes, like lightning in a summer sky, swift and searing, a charge of angry power that suddenly made her feel afraid.

'I do not ask for your understanding.'

His eyebrows rose in frustration, then dipped swiftly and ferociously into a frown, a look that had become so familiar to Delphine that she felt her heart wrench agonisingly, but her face remained smooth and concerned as she said, 'Forgive me. I should not be so inquisitive. I suppose if you must vent your spleen at someone, it ought to be me—your wife.'

'I apologise, Delphine,' he uttered, glancing at her. 'I did not intend to cause you distress.'

Offended and deeply hurt by his superior, condescending attitude, the weeks of tension and aggravation that had built beneath Delphine's supposedly serene exterior began to surface. Convinced he had been thinking of the Spanish woman, she managed to make her voice sound light and cool, as though it was of no importance to her. Stepping away from him, her carefully held control beginning to slip a notch, she said with impatience, 'I am not distressed in the slightest. It doesn't matter—I only enquired out of concern. It was kindly meant. I shall not waste any more words on asking.'

'I would appreciate that. As I said, I do not wish to discuss it.'

'Then I shall not aggravate you further by doing so. But this I will say,' she said, straightening her shoulders and meeting his gaze with a hard look. 'Clearly your sufferings in Spain were great—as were the sufferings of others who went to fight—and I am deeply sorry. But do not forget that you went there by choice. No one forced you to take up a commission.'

Apart from a hardening of his jaw, Stephen's face remained expressionless. 'I know that,' he said icily.

'You may be an officer in the British army and a lord, but you are not the sun around which the world revolves—quite the opposite, in fact,' she continued haughtily.

His eyes became penetrating and locked on to hers. 'Clearly I am not the sun around which *you* revolve, Delphine. Had I not come back from Spain, how deeply would you have grieved for my demise? Would you have managed a tear or two, missed me, mourned for me and said prayers for my eternal soul—or would you have moved on to wed someone else?'

That was so far from the truth that Delphine's voice shook with quiet anger. 'Stop it. I had no intention of doing anything of the sort, you arrogant hypocrite.' She saw him flinch, but, un-deterred, drawing a deep breath, she went on, 'In fact, you are quite the most selfish man I have ever known. Inconsiderate, too, for you care nothing about the feelings of others and are con-ceited enough to believe your rank entitles you to behave that way.'

Stephen was astonished by her outburst and felt more than a little put out. He was angry, too, not only because she had dared to speak to him in such a way, but also because it was the first display of real emotion she had shown since his return. As for being a hypocrite—what the devil had she meant by that? Frowning like thunder, he opened his mouth to dress her down for her unprovoked impudence and to insist that she ex-plain herself, but she had turned on her heel and was striding indignantly to her horse before he had a chance to do so.

'Delphine, wait,' he commanded.

'Why should I?' she said, with an angry toss of her head, while telling herself she was being ab-surd. Why was she doing this? Why was she try-ing to provoke him? It was not what she meant, not what she intended, but she seemed unable to stop. 'You are not required to tell me anything.

After all, why should you? I am only your wife and your life is your own. You have my word that I will not speak of that wretched war again. In fact it would please me enormously if I never had to hear of Spain ever again. Come, the Saracen's Head cannot be far from here. The ride has given me an appetite.'

Chapter Seven

Delphine was in the saddle before Stephen could assist her, spurring her horse forwards. She rode ahead of her husband, but she could feel his burning, angry gaze on her back all the way. Having vented all her pent-up resentment and anger on him—without seeing a single gratifying scrap of reaction from him, but knowing that her words had hit their target—she felt exultant.

When they dismounted in front of the Saracen's Head, Stephen had not recovered from his wife's outburst and his face was as black as thunder, but before he had the chance to speak to her, an open carriage pulled up alongside them.

A middle-aged man and woman, Christopher Fielding and his wife, Mary, climbed out. They were Stephen's good friends from St Austell.

Having met them on several occasions, Delphine always enjoyed their easy company. Mr Fielding was a jovial sort and he smiled at Delphine in the most engaging manner, complimenting her on how well she looked and that she was as pretty as ever.

Shrugging off his heated altercation with his wife for the present, though it was in no way forgotten, Stephen laughed, slapping his friend good-humouredly on the back as they went inside the inn. 'I see you're as silken tongued as ever, Christopher. Save your compliments for your own wife and leave mine alone. We are here to partake of the Saracen's hospitality. You and your lady wife will join us, I hope.'

'Why, we'd be delighted. It's such a splendid day Mary and I thought we'd take the carriage and journey to Helston to visit our daughter and her family. Not wishing to put them to any trouble, we thought we'd stop off at the Saracen's Head for a spot of lunch.'

The Saracen's Head was a respectable establishment. It was a busy coaching inn, frequented by ship's masters, owners and brokers of merchant vessels based in nearby Falmouth. Carriages were drawn up outside. Inside it was plain from the bustling clientele that business was good. The landlord was a genial sort. He had a round, sunburnt face and a grey beard, and looked more like a sea captain than an innkeeper. On recognising Lord Fitzwaring, honoured that one of the most important gentlemen in the district should visit his hostelry, he ushered the four of them to a quiet alcove that offered them a degree of privacy.

'Might I suggest that you aid the digestion of your food with fine wine and brandy brought in from France?'

'It surprises me that such luxuries are available, when Britain and France have been at war for so many years,' Delphine remarked, making herself comfortable beside Mrs Fielding, careful to avoid her husband's dark-blue gaze.

'A war fought by soldiers on behalf of politicians,' the landlord replied.

'And we Cornish have never allowed such considerations to stand in the way of trade, have we, landlord?' Stephen remarked with a knowing wink.

'By God, never! It benefits us all.'

Mrs Fielding leaned towards Delphine. 'Have you seen anything untoward at Tamara, Lady

Fitzwaring?' she asked quietly. 'You know—smugglers, that sort of thing?'

'Oh, yes,' Delphine replied in a low voice. 'There have often been nights when I've been awakened in the early hours by strange sounds and, peering from behind my bedroom curtains, I have seen pack-laden ponies heading off across the moor.'

'And what do you do?'

'What can I do? Not that I would wish to do anything. One thing I have learned since coming to Cornwall is that the gentlemen are not openly discussed. The country people give nothing away. The men involved in the illicit trade have a reputation for brutality and it would be most unwise to apprehend them.'

'Not without foundation,' Stephen said, his eyes narrowing on his wife. 'They have no respect for anyone—be it man or woman—who gets in their way. They are quite unscrupulous.'

'Then I will take the greatest of care not to get in their way,' she replied coolly. 'Are they, do you think, so savage that they would harm children also? Lowenna is not yet two.'

Mrs Fielding gave a little shriek of mock horror and began fanning herself rapidly. Stephen's lips curved in a half-smile.

'Calm yourself, Mary,' he said, picking up his glass of deep-red wine. 'My wife was jesting, of course. I would assure you, though,' he added, looking at Delphine once again, 'that the matter of smugglers must not be treated with levity. I feel responsible for the safety of the people who live on my land, especially for my own family. Rest assured that where Lowenna is concerned there is no need for anxiety. The same applies to you.'

'I am gratified to hear it.' She looked at the serving girl as she placed dishes of steaming vegetables in the centre of the table. 'Being a gullible, foolish female, it makes me wonder how on earth I have managed without a man to protect me for the past two years.'

'You managed admirably,' Stephen said in an ominously calm tone that belied the simmering anger in his eyes.

'And there is nothing foolish about you, my dear,' Christopher Fielding remarked, scooping a generous helping of potatoes on to his plate. 'Although we all do foolish things at one time or another. Is that not so, Stephen?'

'Do we?' Stephen countered repressively. 'The fact has escaped me.'

'Then you either have a very poor memory,' Delphine challenged softly, looking down at the succulent roast beef on her plate and nudging it with her fork, 'or a very convenient one.'

Stephen carefully placed his wine glass on the table. 'Precisely what is your meaning, madam?' he demanded.

Delphine withered before the blast of those deep-blue eyes, glad that Mr and Mrs Fielding were preoccupied with helping each other to the vegetables. 'Why, nothing at all,' she lied softly.

Over the clink of cutlery, no more was said on the subject of smugglers as the four of them ate their meal, speaking instead of the ending of the war in the Peninsula and other matters closer to home. But as Delphine watched Stephen's hand flexing on his wine glass, clenching it and loosening it, she suspected he was wishing that her neck, not his wine glass, were in his grip.

His mood appeared to mellow as the meal progressed and more wine was consumed. When one of the serving girls came to clear the table, Stephen leaned back in his chair, his lashes lowered as his gaze raked over her with the leisure of a well-fed wolf.

An answering sparkle twinkled in the girl's eyes. She tossed her brown curls and her wide green eyes touched him everywhere. Boldly, she reached out and slowly removed his empty plate, intentionally brushing his hand. A piece of cutlery dropped on to the table.

'Allow me.' Stephen was quick to retrieve the knife and place it on the pile of plates in the girl's hands. He continued to smile and, looking at his wife, caught her brittle regard of them. She sat stiffly on her chair, considering the serving girl with anything but friendliness.

Picking up Delphine's plate, raising her big eyes, the girl found herself beneath Delphine's glare, which was cold enough to freeze her on the spot. Unabashed, the girl's smile broadened as she turned away and sauntered across the room, hips swaying, the sound of her shoes brushing the wooden floor, leaving a smell of cheap perfume behind.

When the same girl returned to remove the empty vegetable dishes, Delphine saw her look deep into Stephen's eyes, her red, pouting lips in her painted face smiling a blatant invitation, her green eyes flashing, her voluptuous breasts heaving against the fabric that strained to contain them. In the spirit of the moment, completely at ease and confident of himself, Stephen winked and chuckled, watching as she twirled away, swaying her hips provocatively.

Observing the exchange in a state of angry, humiliated pain, Delphine was torn between a desire to rush after her and scratch her eyes out and the need to turn away, to pretend she was not affected by the incident in the slightest.

'My word, Stephen,' Christopher Fielding remarked, laughing jovially, 'you've charmed that serving wench all right. Would that I were thirty years younger.'

'You mustn't take it seriously, Lord Fitzwaring,' Mrs Fielding said with a smile. 'It's all part of the act with these girls. The landlord insists that if they keep the customers happy they'll return. At the next influx of customers, some other fortunate gentleman will be getting the favours.'

Stephen glanced toward Delphine, who had been sitting silent and stunned at the serving girl's blatant flaunting of herself. It was madness to feel such keen jealousy rip through her, but she had felt it and still did—full bodied, sick jealousy. She had never thought herself a possessive woman, nor had occasion to be. But Stephen was her husband, she thought, with a quite irrational primitive feeling of possession, and no other woman was permitted to touch him in any way.

Stephen chuckled softly, leaning towards her. 'Perhaps I should have warned you about the girls at the Saracen's Head,' he said lightly, seeing her frozen look. 'But they are friendly enough and mean no offence.'

Delphine forced herself to laugh. 'Good heavens, Stephen, it's no matter to me,' she said, as carelessly as she could, considering the way she was seething inside. 'I can see for myself that the girl is friendly, but there are no circumstances I can imagine that would make acquaintance or even contact with her necessary. Please do not think for one minute that I'm jealous of a mere serving girl.'

As soon as she had spoken, she felt colour stain her cheeks. She had sounded appallingly haughty, and if their companions didn't notice it, Stephen certainly did. His look was as insulting as her own words had been.

'You need not be so patronising, Delphine,' he said quietly. 'When I recall your involvement with those less fortunate than yourself in London, *you*, of all people, should understand what an insult it is.'

She bridled at what he must think of her. She knew very well it had been searing jealousy at the sexual invitation from the serving girl that had made her speak the way she had. But that wasn't something she was going to admit, especially to this hard-faced man who had left his true love behind in Spain. She was aware of Mr and Mrs Fielding glancing awkwardly at one another, suspecting that all was not right between Lord Fitzwaring and his wife. Knowing that she had better draw back, at least for the time being, if she didn't want the meal to end in an embarrassing scene, Delphine gave an acquiescent sigh.

'You are quite right, my love. It's an unfortunate trait of mine I will have to watch very closely and no one can deny that the young women the landlord employs are extremely fetching. I am sure his business booms every time he opens his doors. And the food is of excellent quality. Don't you agree, Mrs Fielding?' She turned to the older lady, not wanting to linger on Stephen's sardonic look at her endearment. It was the first time she had ever called him her love, though it hadn't been said with any loving intent and they both knew it.

She could not see why her casual remark should have mattered to Stephen at all. Why had he not defended her instead of reproaching her in front of their companions? Why could he not have dismissed it with a shrug or even applauded her wildness and individuality he had remarked about the previous day? But because something had soured between them since his return, he had taken against her. It was almost as if their current predicament was somehow her fault.

Delphine could see Mrs Fielding was thankful the awkward moment had passed. She was even more thankful when they rose to leave. They bade farewell to their companions and Stephen escorted her outside to their horses.

'It isn't like you to be pompous, Delphine,' he remarked as they walked across the yard to their waiting horses. 'I hope it isn't a true indication of your character and that you've been playing me false.'

Delphine drew her breath in sharply. Any softening of her attitude and the vain hope that the incident would pass vanished immediately.

'How dare you say such a thing to me?' she

flared. 'You didn't have to make it quite so obvious that you were so displeased with me. I know I was foolish in saying what I did—if you must know, I deeply regret it—but did you have to reproach me in front of Mr and Mrs Fielding?'

'I am not displeased with you. And I am the one with the regrets, not you.'

She looked at him sharply. The sun was not as strong as it had been earlier, but she still had to shield her eyes from the glare to look at him.'You mean you regret marrying me, don't you?' Her heart was breaking, but she had to ask.

'I regret hurting you.'

'That wasn't what I asked.'

'How could I regret marrying you when you have given me the gift of Lowenna?'

'Prevaricate all you like, Stephen,' she said coldly, 'but it makes no difference whether you say it or not, if it is what you think.'

He hadn't answered her question, but, too afraid to delve deeper lest she didn't like the answer, she left it at that. How could he not regret marrying her when her very presence in his life barred him from being with the woman he really wanted? How could he be so cruel, condemning her to a life with a man who had so little regard for her feelings that he would openly flirt with another woman in her presence?

The one small salve to her pride was the fact that she had never told him how deeply she had come to care for him. Thank God he didn't know, for that would be the final humiliation.

'I have always been completely honest with you.' She gave him a pointed look. 'Can you boast the same? Are there not things you keep hidden from me?'

If she had hoped to goad him into betraying some unease at her words, she was unlucky.

'This is not about me, Delphine.'

'Yes, it is,' she said, trembling with hurt fury as she faced him. 'How dare you look at that serving girl in that way? I hope I never have to endure such humiliation again.'

His gaze flicked to her. 'I did not realise you cared sufficiently to mind it,' he drawled cruelly.

Her eyes blazed with indignation. 'Well, I do care. I understand perfectly that when soldiers are away from their wives for some considerable time, they have—paramours. Naturally they are expected to be discreet about such matters. But when you flaunt your interest in other women in front of your wife, it's profoundly humiliating and it—it hurts. I have no doubt that should you return alone, you will find her waiting and willing. Do you not always get what you want?'

The dark-blue eyes chilled as they met hers squarely. 'Usually,' he answered irately. 'Perhaps because I am arrogant, inconsiderate and self-ish—or so I have been told.'

Delphine didn't like having her own words quoted back at her. She raised her chin obstinately. 'If you hope for an apology, you hope in vain.'

'Hell and damnation!' he barked. 'I don't want an apology—nor do I intend on becoming closer acquainted with the serving girl. And another thing that I would like you to take note of, *my dear wife*: I am not going to let this situation between us continue. Know this, Delphine. As long as you live under my roof, you will come to share my bed.'

'You would force me?' she retorted with disgust. 'How easily you forget the conditions set forth for our marriage when you came back from Spain. You agreed then to give me time…'

Stephen threw up his hands impatiently. 'Damn it, Delphine, I'm not going to rape you—*if* indeed it can be classed as such a thing between a husband and his wife. But I've given you long enough.' What he said was true. His patience had run out. He'd been willing to indulge her until she was used to having him back at home, using the time to savour the anticipation of what was to come. Now, however, he was no longer interested in anticipation.

'Just tell me one thing,' he went on with irate frustration. 'What am I to you? Your plaything? Your puppet—that I should dance at your bidding, tossed aside when you become bored or vexed, where I must wait until the mood strikes your fancy and I am brought back to perform for your pleasure? Be damned, I'll not be at any woman's beck and call. I kowtow to no one. You shall conform to this marriage, so get used to it.'

'Not until I am ready,' she stubbornly declared.

An icy hardness came into those midnight eyes, making Delphine draw back slightly.

'Yes, you will,' he rejoined tersely. 'Two years we have been married. How much longer do you need? I consider myself a married man, not a monk. We have one child and I mean for her to have a sibling before long, so we will settle our differences and have done with it. Perhaps if you

were to itemise your grievances we could talk
about them and come to an understanding.'

She looked at him coldly, still smarting over
his disgraceful flirtation with the serving girl.
When she spoke her tone was cutting.

'I was left alone for a long time, Stephen—so
long that I almost forgot what the father of my
child looked like. When I married you I knew
little about marriage—even less about being a
wife and mother. I was denied the opportunity
to experience the former two—as for the latter,
I have done my best. All I asked when you returned was that you give me time to get used to
having you home. Surely there is nothing un-
usual in that. If you want us to live in harmony
it is something you will have to agree to.'

'For how long?' he retorted sarcastically. 'A
month—six? A year?'

'You're angry, Stephen. I think we should let
the matter drop.'

'Angry is hardly the word for it. Furious would
be more appropriate to describe the way I am
feeling—and yet I doubt I'll ever be too angry to
ignore your presence. Were you ugly then I could
ignore you as you wish. But of all the women in
London, Oakley had to choose a precious vir-

gin—the queen of all virgins, who sits upon her throne surrounded by a sea of purity.'

'Curse virgins all you like,' she flared, 'but it met your mood to take me when there was no one else.'

Delphine turned from him, but immediately found her arm seized in Stephen's hand. He spun her about and caught her by the shoulders, his fingers digging into her soft flesh, his face dark with rage. There was scorn in his eyes and a contemptuous curl to his strong mouth. 'Be warned, Delphine,' he stated icily. 'You are my wife. I wronged you, true, so wreak your vengeance upon me if you must, but then be done with it and let me hear no more. You tempt and taunt me every time I lay eyes on you, then you deny me my right as your husband.'

Delphine's anger was increasing by the second and she felt anything but calm. Tearing herself from his grip, she glared at him. 'If you're feeling so badly done by, perhaps you should revert to type and take to the streets to purchase a paramour lively enough to meet your taste,' she hissed, displaying her anger and sarcasm without fear of retribution. 'You have only ever turned to me in the absence of anyone else. What do you expect of me, Stephen—that I should humbly wait and when you snap your fingers, jump into bed like a well-trained bitch? Do you think I should dote on you and spend my life pandering to your fancy when you're feeling bored with no other female around to tempt you?'

Raking his hand through his hair in angry disgust, he half-turned from her. 'I'm beginning to think you enjoy baiting me, for you do it better than anyone I've ever known.' He frowned as a thought suddenly occurred to him and cocked his head. 'You're not afraid of me, are you, Delphine?'

'No,' she replied, whirling from him, 'just cautious. I am a woman—my own woman—and I do have some pride.'

Stephen watched her as she walked away, admiring the sight of her body moving with unconscious grace. He felt the familiar burning need for her rise in his loins. He didn't know how much longer he could stand this living arrangement. He didn't follow her to their horses immediately. Whatever she felt for him, her words just now had confused him. She seemed to suggest that it was all right for him to have a paramour when he was away from home, to satisfy his lust, but her pride was piqued at the idea of him making up to any other woman in public.

Unable to understand the logic of this, shaking his head, Stephen followed her. He had never imagined he would return to Tamara to find himself confronted with this apparently insurmountable barrier—the barrier Delphine had erected around herself like a wall of ice. But if she thought to continue withholding herself from him indefinitely, then she was mistaken. Because of the time they had been apart, he had respected her wishes and had not touched her in any way. But she was still his wife and he did not intend living a celibate life for much longer.

They rode home in silence, a silence that pierced Delphine's heart. She told herself that it didn't matter, that there had been no love between them when they married. But if so, why did the images of him with another woman cause her such agony? Why did the thought of him kissing this other woman tear her heart in two? Why did the thought of them in bed together fill her with an empty loneliness and despair that made her feel as if she wanted to die?

* * *

The house Mr Oakley had arranged for them to rent during their time in London belonged to Sir John Kiligrew, a widower, who held an important position with the East India Company and was currently in India. Conveniently placed in the heart of Mayfair, the house was white with ornamental wrought-iron gates at the front. Inside, it displayed an awe-inspiring opulence reflecting Sir John's personal tastes. It was fully staffed and ready to receive them, and just a few streets away from Delphine's parents.

It was late when they arrived. After Delphine had settled a sleepy Lowenna in the nursery, her nursemaid in the next room, she was too tired to eat and retired to bed.

Stephen went to one of the exclusive gentlemen's clubs in St James's that he habitually frequented when in London. After catching up with friends over a few brandies and engaging in a game of cards, he returned to his lonely bed in the rented house.

He and Delphine had been virtual strangers since that day at the Saracen's Head. During the uneventful journey to London, the strained atmosphere between them had relaxed somewhat.

It seemed to Delphine that perhaps if they both made the effort to be civilised to one another, the following days could be endured without too much acrimony—even with a degree of common courtesy—as long as he didn't attempt to get too close. She didn't trust herself around her husband, and that, she knew, rather than anger, was at the root of her resistance.

The day following their arrival, Delphine settled into their new quarters and took Lowenna to visit her parents in the afternoon. Their delight on seeing her surprised her; they accepted her explanation that Stephen had gone to Woolwich to settle some military matters and was not expected back until the following day.

Rose had given birth to a son, Thomas, who was three months old, and Fern was enceinte. Both her sisters looked blooming and were full of their usual empty chatter. Lowenna immediately wanted to see the nursery, which had housed two generations of Cameron children, and Thomas's nursemaid was happy to oblige her. The moment they were gone, Delphine asked Fern how she liked living in Hertfordshire and her sister went into raptures about the magnificent house she lived in and its many luxuries, and the grand estate owned by her aristocratic husband, Viscount Falkener.

Delphine had been introduced to the young man before her own marriage; in her opinion the viscount was a weak, rather uninteresting—though good-natured—individual with curls the colour of golden guineas and a high colour in his cheeks. It was clear that Fern could command him to any whim or fancy she thought up. As long as he was allowed to shoot and fish and hunt in season, he was content to allow his pretty young wife to do exactly as she pleased.

As Delphine was driven home from the visit, an excited Lowenna chattering on about all the toys she'd been allowed to play with in the nursery and the beautiful baby asleep in the crib, she asked herself if she would exchange her compellingly vigorous, exacting, exciting and incredibly handsome husband for the easy-going young viscount to whom Fern was married.

No, she would not! Despite the strained and often intolerable atmosphere that existed between them, she knew she would not. Her husband was a complex man, a strong man who allowed few to see the real Stephen Fitzwaring, and as a consequence she could honestly say she did not know him very well at all. When they'd met he had made love to her with such passion he could not have faked it. But she did not fool herself into believing he could possibly have had feelings for her since he'd had no idea who she was, and when lying beside a willing female body of personable appearance, any man would make love to her regardless of feelings.

Stephen was a man with his feet planted firmly on the ground of reality and she knew now that her life would be empty without him. They had lived as man and wife for such a short time, yet she could not bear the pain if they should part. She did not know how she was going to get through the empty days ahead, but somehow she would find a way. She would have to be circumspect; the reason for this was buried deep inside her where even she had not dared to look too closely, concerning the feeling she had for her own husband. It was something hidden, something deep, too deep to have a name, but it had awoken and stirred on the night before Stephen had gone to Spain, and increased a thousandfold since he had come home. It had blazed into life, burning her, scorching her and she didn't know what to do with it, or about it.

Remembering the times when they had lain together, when she had pressed herself wordlessly against him, wrapped her long legs about him, welcoming his warm mouth, deliciously sweet on her tongue, his hard body capturing hers, his kisses on her mouth, her neck, her ears, racing her and himself towards an explosion of pleasure that left them both breathless with the joy of it, she desperately wanted to experience it once more.

Despite the bitter words they exchanged, there were times when she knew he wanted her. She saw it in his eyes when he looked at her, in his expression, and she so wanted to relent, to set aside her jealous feelings for this other woman, for him to take her in his arms and hold her fast. She supposed she was feeling self-pitying, but she was tired of it, tired of the awful half-life she led, and knew that if she wanted to make her marriage happy and solid, she must do something about it.

Instead of withholding herself, perhaps she should do the opposite. It was up to her to make him want her more than he had ever wanted any other woman. Did she have the power to make him forget the Spanish woman? Did she have the power to hold him so that he would never want to leave her?

The following day had been spent amusing Lowenna, and Delphine had been in bed when Stephen returned, so they did not meet until the next morning. They encountered each other in the hall. He had just returned from an early ride in the park and Delphine was on her way out, having ordered the carriage to take her to the orphanage. She had hoped to be gone before he returned to avoid a confrontation about where she was going, but it was not to be.

Taken unawares, she paused in the act of putting on her gloves. 'Stephen, you're home.'

His eyes were drawn to the sound of her voice. He looked at her, expecting defiance, that head-held-high hauteur she flaunted whenever she thought she was in the right, but today there was a slight droop to her shoulders and a brooding sadness in her eyes. His heart was moved to something he knew was not pity and he wanted to ask her what the matter was, but when he saw her straighten her shoulders and raise her chin, he silenced his enquiry.

'As you see.'

Striding into the hall, he threw his top hat on the table and drew off his gloves, tossing them on the table as well. He proceeded to take off his excellently tailored riding coat and draped it over a chair, shrugging the tension out of his wide shoulders. Delphine felt her gaze travel over the sinuous curve of his strong back. His snug waistcoat accentuated the sweeping breadth of his shoulders and the tapered leanness of his waist and hips.

'H-have you enjoyed your ride?'

'I have—although give me the countryside and the cliffs of Cornwall to ride over any day. It's a fine day though. You should be out of doors.'

'Yes, I would like that.'

He ran his eye over her plainer-than-usual day dress and the little hat perched atop her neatly coiffured hair. Giving her a pointed look, he said, 'You're going out.'

'Yes—I was just…'

'Yes?' His tone was sharp, his eyes penetrating as they fastened to her face. 'If you are going to visit your parents, I shall get changed and accompany you. I suppose I shall have to confront your father sooner or later.'

'I am not going to see my parents today. I visited them while you were at Woolwich and I shall go again tomorrow. I—thought I might pay Aunt Celia a call,' she said tentatively.

The true nature of her visit to Aunt Celia didn't register with Stephen immediately. 'Pity. I thought I would take you shopping—or perhaps we could take Lowenna on a picnic to Hampstead Heath. It would be nice for the three of us to go on an outing together.'

Delphine's heart warmed at the thought that her husband wished to spend some time with her and Lowenna and she broke into a smile. 'I would like that—and I know I can speak for our daughter. A picnic would be nice before the weather turns too cold.' She looked into Stephen's face, a face that smiled with satisfaction, for it seemed she was willing to allow him to do something for her.

With an inner resignation he finally faced the fact that he could no longer ignore: the throbbing desire he felt for her was as insistent as ever. She had struggled for two years to make Tamara a home, had borne him a child. It would give him immense delight to do something for her, to shower her with all the things his wife deserved, all the things he thought she should have and wanted her to have. He would even visit her parents and put the hostility he still felt towards her father behind him.

But he did not care for the new expression on her face. It was an expression he did not like; she looked perturbed and impatient.

'What is it, Delphine? Is something I said not to your liking?' he asked as he crossed to the stairs.

His voice was harsh with disappointment. Just when he thought that everything would come right between them now that they were in London where he could spoil her, she had turned truculent and he couldn't see why.

'No—not at all—but...'

At the bottom of the stairs he stopped and slowly turned to face her, his expression unreadable. 'But what?' Suddenly his look became suspicious. 'Aunt Celia, you said? That wouldn't be the same Aunt Celia who runs the orphanage, by any chance?'

Her spirits sank, for if he knew the true reason

of her outing, she thought that he might forbid her to go. Although perhaps she was being too harsh on him, for Stephen had never expressed any objection to her charity work.

'Why—yes, it is. I thought I would go over there to see how things are, that's all.'

'Why do you not invite your aunt here? Then she can give you an update as to how things are at the orphanage and see Lowenna at the same time. We are in London for such a short period, I would like us to spend the most part of it together as a family. I shall make a donation to the orphanage, if that sets your mind at rest, but there is hardly time for you to resume working there before we have to return to Cornwall.'

'Please do not forbid me to go. I don't intend being long. Perhaps we could have the picnic this afternoon. I'll ask the housekeeper to prepare us a picnic basket, if you like.' She said it pleadingly, hoping he wasn't about to argue.

Stephen didn't, for when her eyes gazed at him so large, soft and pleading, the protective tenderness in which he longed to enfold her burned within him and he didn't give a damn what she wanted, if only she would go on looking at him like that. But he wasn't to be taken in so easily.

He closed the space between them, looking down at her darkly. 'And if I did forbid you to go?'

She stiffened, the softness melting from her eyes. 'I hope you won't.'

'Because?'

'I would have to disobey you,' she answered quietly, looking at him directly. She would never respect herself if she cowered before him. 'I will not be intimidated by you, Stephen.'

His dark eyes narrowed to slits of wrathful warning. 'It is not my intention to intimidate you. Quite the opposite, in fact.'

'I'm glad to hear it.' Quickly she finished pulling on her gloves and straightened her hat. 'I cannot understand your objection to my visiting my aunt.'

'I didn't say that.'

No, she thought, to be fair to him he hadn't. 'I shall return forthwith, I promise. A footman will accompany me, along with the driver, so I will be quite safe, if that's what worries you.'

Knowing how much this meant to her and seeing no reason to deny her, he nodded, although he was apprehensive, for he would never forget the harm that had befallen her at his own hands the last time she had been in the vicinity of Water Lane.

Leaving the safety of the well-populated Covent Garden, the carriage entered the shadowy labyrinth of airless narrow streets and alleyways. The familiar stench from the reeking gutters in this twilight world was overpowering and touched like cold fingers upon Delphine's deepest fears. It was the stench of poverty—the foul, unacceptable smell of humanity at its lowest.

The alley opened out into the more hospitable Water Lane, a congested thoroughfare through which the driver expertly manoeuvred the carriage, passing a jumble of vehicles, animals and pedestrians. As they passed the Blue Boar, Delphine's eyes were drawn reluctantly to the building where she had lost her virginity; she gazed at it for a moment, remembering what had taken place there. The memories of her own wanton behaviour made her face burn, for it was the shame of this wantonness that had been at the root of her resistance to her husband since his return from Spain.

When the carriage stopped at the bottom of the steep steps leading up to the orphanage door, she climbed out.

'I shan't be long. Half an hour at the most,' she told the footman, who was uneasy about taking his mistress to such a place abounding, as it did, with every kind of miscreant imaginable.

Pausing to look around before she climbed the steps, her eyes lighted on a man slouched against the wall of the orphanage. His hat was pulled down over his face, concealing his features, but there was something familiar about him. A sense of foreboding stole over her. As if sensing her scrutiny, he lifted his face in her direction, and although Delphine could not see his features, she felt his stare. There was a stillness about him that was entirely menacing. And then, when their eyes met in chilly recognition, she felt the hairs stand up on the back of her neck.

Shoving himself away from the wall, he swaggered towards her. Stopping in front of her, he casually tipped his hat back on his untidy fair hair and grinned. With the certainty that he was savouring the moment, Delphine's sense of foreboding grew.

'Well, well,' he grinned, his voice mocking.

'So we meet again. If it isn't Miss Cameron—or should I say Lady Fitzwaring? Very grand, I'm sure! Come to hobnob with the beggars in your fancy clothes, I see. It's been a long time.'

'Not long enough where you are concerned, Will Kelly,' she returned, her voice as hostile as her manner.

She turned away with the intention of climbing the steps, but he moved forwards, barring her path. Their combined movements brought them close together. He stared at her with impudent admiration, his gaze travelling insolently over her body, lingering on the swell of her breasts. She felt sick and more than a little afraid of this repulsive man, but her anger and indignation were much stronger.

'Be so kind as to step aside.'

'I'll be happy to—for the price of a kiss from your luscious lips.'

'I'd as soon kiss a rattlesnake. Move out of my way.'

Out of the corner of his eye Will saw the footman climbing down from the coach. Reluctantly he stepped aside.

Delphine swept by him and, raising her skirts, climbed up to the door.

Chapter Eight

Life inside the orphanage had evidently carried on just as before. The only difference was that more children were crammed inside, most of them scrawny, stunted and bowed from malnutrition. Little faces looked at her curiously. She was touched to find some of the children still remembered her.

Her Aunt Celia had spent most of her life in Water Lane. Delphine noticed how tired her aunt looked as she came down the wooden stairs, carrying a small child, whom she handed to one of the older girls. The flesh had left her aunt's slender frame and her face was contorted with a permanent anxiety, but she greeted her niece warmly.

'My dear Delphine.' She smiled, holding out both her hands. 'I am truly delighted to see you again.'

'And I am happy to be here.'

'How pretty you look,' her aunt murmured approvingly, looking Delphine up and down and marvelling at the pink softness of her niece's complexion. 'Married life and motherhood must agree with you.'

'Yes—although Stephen has only recently returned from Spain, as you know. Lowenna, our daughter, is such a treasure—you must come to the house and see her.'

'I will do that, I promise.'

Delphine sighed, looking around her. 'It's been so long since I left, Aunt Celia, but I've thought about you and the orphanage constantly. How are you?'

'Not without my little discomforts,' the older woman replied, gently ushering two small boys out of their path, 'but I am well enough. Nothing has changed at the orphanage—except that we are hopelessly overcrowded. So many of the abandoned children who come here are either ill or have been ill treated. There is always so much to be done.'

'How I wish I could help. Cornwall is so far away—and I am in London for such a short time.'

'Do not concern yourself, my dear. One way or

another we'll manage. There are plenty of willing hands—but I shudder to think what will happen when we can take no more children. This place is full to capacity. The children are so dependent on us—they have no one else, poor mites. The charity schools take some of them, and there are other Foundling Houses, but what we really need is bigger and better accommodation. This has preoccupied my mind and the majority of my time since you left. I have been lobbying all those who contribute to the charity.'

'And have you seen anything suitable?'

'Oh, yes. There's an ideal property—an old boys' school at Islington—that could house the orphanage and more children besides. It also has some land, which would mean we could keep some animals and grow our own vegetables, but it requires a vast amount more money. But enough of this. You haven't come to hear my woes. Come and see Maisie. She's been in a state of high excitement ever since I told her you were coming to London.'

'Aunt Celia,' Delphine began, pulling her aunt aside so they were not overheard, 'I saw Will Kelly hanging about outside. Is he still determined to get his hands on Maisie?'

'Oh, that reprobate. What I wouldn't give to have the constables take him away and lock him up for good. I hardly dare let that girl out of my sight. She even sleeps in one of the warders' rooms in case he forces his way in and tries to take her. Maisie is a darling girl and her help is much needed. I do my best to keep her here, but I'm afraid I can't keep her indoors indefinitely. Will Kelly is determined to have her.'

Delphine looked away, reminding herself that, considering all the time the girl had spent with her unfortunate mother in Mrs Cox's bordello, there wasn't much that Maisie hadn't seen.

'What's to be done about her I don't know, but I won't see her end up like her mother.'

'But, my dear aunt, I wrote and told you that I can take her away. She can come back to Cornwall with me—far enough away to be out of his reach.'

'Would you really do that? I imagined your hands would be quite full once Lowenna was born.'

'If Maisie is happy to leave London, she will always be welcome at Tamara.'

'Oh, Delphine, I can't tell you what a weight off my mind that would be.' Delphine smiled at her aunt's obvious relief, but her expression darkened as an unpleasant question occurred to her.

'Aunt Celia, how did Meg die?'

'She fell down the stairs and broke her neck. I think she was pushed, but no one can prove it. The constables have more important things to do than investigate the death of a prostitute in a brothel.'

'I suppose you're right, but poor Meg—she deserved better than that. You don't think Will Kelly was behind her death?' Her aunt looked grim.

'Yes, I do. He plagued Meg night and day to have Maisie taken from the orphanage to Mrs Cox's. Of course she wouldn't hear of it.' Celia sighed, shaking her head wearily. 'I don't suppose we'll ever know the truth of what happened. But what we can do is take care of Meg's daughter and make sure he doesn't get his hands on her. Come and see her.'

The moment she set eyes on the familiar child, the effect of her mother's death was all too evident to Delphine. Maisie had such a tragic, woebegone face and such enormous, wistful eyes as would break anybody's heart.

Now, seeing Delphine, of whom she had been

particularly fond and had missed terribly in the years since her departure, the girl smiled, a vivacious and dimpled smile that gladdened Delphine's heart. Even though she was wearing a shapeless and threadbare woollen dress, it was clear Maisie was growing up to be a beauty. There was a radiance about her that would attract men like bees to nectar—the worst kind of men. Little wonder Will Kelly had his sights on her.

Delphine gave her a motherly hug. 'How are you, my dear girl? I've been thinking about you.'

'I'm all right, miss.'

'And just look at you. How you've grown. Why, you'll soon be as tall as me.'

'I'm twelve now, and can write more than my own name,' she said proudly.

Delphine smiled at her. 'I know you can. You're a clever girl, Maisie. I've been talking to my aunt about you and wondered how you would feel about coming to work for me.'

Her eyes widened. 'In your house?'

'Yes—in Cornwall. It's a lovely house, Maisie—by the sea. What do you say? Would you like that?'

Maisie's eyes stretched wide with awe. 'Oh, yes, miss. I would.'

'Then go and get your things together. You can come with me now. We won't be going back to Cornwall for a little while, but I'm sure we can find something for you to do until then.'

'Are you quite sure about this?' Celia asked as they watched an excited Maisie scamper away.

'Absolutely. The last time I saw Meg I promised her that if anything happened to her I would take care of Maisie. I feel responsible for her.'

'And your husband? What do you think he will have to say about your taking a young girl out of the orphanage and finding her employment in his house?'

Delphine knew exactly how Stephen would react, but she would not be deterred from doing what was right. 'No doubt he will have a seizure. He has no objections to my charity work—in fact he has always admired what I do—but taking unwanted children into the house is another matter.'

When Delphine and her new ward arrived back at the house, Delphine enlisted one of the maids to have a room made ready and to see that Maisie was bathed and dressed in clean clothes. In a house as fully staffed as this one with countless female servants, there must, Delphine guessed, be plenty of cast-off clothes.

It was by this time early afternoon, and Delphine awaited Stephen's return in a state of nervous apprehension. The minutes ticked by and, try as she might to push her worries aside, it seemed an eternity had passed when she heard his footsteps on the landing outside her room as he passed to his own room next door. Taking a deep breath, she went and tapped softly on his door.

Entering on his command, hesitantly she closed the door and stood with her back pressed against the hard wood, uncertain of his mood. He looked up and an inexplicable, lazy smile swept over his face as he surveyed her from head to foot.

During the daytimes at Tamara, when he was at the mines or occupied with estate matters, he was able to think about something other than his sexual frustration for his wife. But when he was with her, he would take one look at her and desire invariably led to frustration.

So fragile was his remaining hold on his self-control that instead of joining her for the evening meal, he went to a local hostelry or dined with friends. Here in London he could escape to his club. He cursed himself for the agreement he had made with Delphine. He should never have let her talk him into this ridiculous notion of celibacy. It was pointless and juvenile and he was determined to put an end to it. Actions, not words, would be the only way to make her lower her guard and surrender herself to him.

'This is an unexpected surprise,' he said, removing his coat. 'My wife in my room. Now, why is that, I ask myself? I shall not flatter myself with the notion that you have come to see me.'

'It's about my visit to the orphanage,' Delphine admitted, unable to meet his gaze.

'I thought it might be,' he said, picking up a pile of unopened letters that had been delivered to the house earlier and studying each one in turn. 'Tell me—and then I think a change of clothes is in order, if you would still like to go to Hampstead.'

'Yes—yes, I would. But—I wanted to tell you that…I have brought one of the girls from the orphanage back with me. I thought we could take her to Tamara with us—to employ her in some capacity in the house.'

'Girl?' He moved to the window, his attention caught by one of the unopened envelopes. 'Mmm,' he murmured. 'Spain.' He opened it, momentarily distracted from what Delphine was saying. 'How old is she?'

'Just twelve—very young, I know, but she is in trouble.' She watched him uncertainly.

He stopped and slowly turned to face her. His face was totally without expression and Delphine, who had followed him and was right behind him, almost bumped into him. Her spirits sank, for though she knew he was a fair man, he was her husband and master of his house, and she realised she should have asked him before installing a strange girl in it. If he said no to her request, how could she help poor Maisie, whose lovely face had attracted the attention of the despicable Will Kelly?

Stephen stared at her blankly. 'And who is she?'

'It is Maisie; a girl, you might remember, who I was particularly attached to when I used to visit the orphanage. It wasn't safe for her to remain there, so I—so I've brought her here.'

Stephen drew himself up to his full height. Putting down his letter, he folded his arms over his chest and looked at her with an unfathomable expression. 'A girl from the orphanage? I do remember you telling me about her. It was because of her that you were at the brothel on the night we met. I also recall you telling me that her mother was a whore.'

Delphine almost wailed in despair. 'You cannot condemn Maisie because of her mother.'

'I have not condemned her.'

'Please let her stay, Stephen. Would you have her live on the streets?'

His face remained impassive. 'Of course not, but I'm sure a suitable position could be found for her. She could be a maidservant. Maidservants can always find employment.'

'At twelve years old, and without any training? Girls are being abducted every day in London, snatched from the streets and dragged to houses where they are used for men's gratification. Maisie's mother is dead. She has no one. We can offer her a position here, with us. Stephen, I promised Meg—her mother—that if anything should happen to her, I would take care of Maisie. I must honour that promise.'

'I agree, you are duty bound to do so, but how long will it be before you take pity on another girl at the orphanage and bring her here to work?

Before I know it, you'll have every waif and stray in London living with us.'

'Maisie is my main concern; I have made no promises to other girls. If I don't take her away, Will Kelly will surely get his hands on her. I told you about him, but it's so long ago now I doubt you will remember.'

'As a matter of fact, I do. Your concern for this girl is commendable.'

Lounging against the window frame with his hands thrust deep into the pockets of his trousers, his eyes watchful, Stephen was far more interested in his wife than what she was saying. His mind hardened with resolve. He had mentally ticked off the days since his return from Spain—the days Delphine had withheld herself from him. He had noticed the change in her that motherhood had brought about—she was not the charming innocent he had left behind. The transformation both unnerved and enthralled him. The breathtaking woman who stood before him dressed so finely, her eyes alight with passion for her cause, was a lady fit to take her place in the most glittering houses in the land. Stephen had the odd sensation that Delphine had become someone else, but there was no mistaking those brilliant eyes or that entrancing face. She moved a little closer, the scent of her gentle perfume wafting over him, and his decision to have her no matter how much trouble she put him to now became an unshakeable resolution.

Her time was up!

A slow smile drifted across his face. 'What a changeable young woman you are, Delphine.'

Her eyes widened with indignation. 'Changeable?'

Stephen bit back a laugh, trying to keep his eyes off the alluring display of smooth flesh exposed by the neckline of her gown. 'I meant,' he said levelly, 'that you are a gentle, caring mother one minute, and a firebrand fighting for her cause the next.'

Thrown off balance, Delphine was not unaware of the odd, possessive gleam in his eyes as they roved over her, but she was momentarily distracted by the disquieting discovery of how handsome and elegant he looked in his dark trousers and the white shirt that emphasised the muscular width of his shoulders.

'If I am, it's because I am passionate about what I do. Maisie will not be a problem, I assure you. But if we turn her out… She will be in very grave danger. She's a marvel with the little ones at the orphanage, extremely capable, and Aunt Celia has taught her the basics of reading and writing.'

'Then I'm amazed Aunt Celia can bear to part with her. Will a charity school not take her?'

'Will Kelly would soon find her. Oh, please, Stephen,' she begged, 'let me take her to Tamara. She'll earn her keep, I promise you that. Whatever her mother was, Maisie is a good girl. I care about her so much—as I did her mother. I would no more think of abandoning her child than I would my own. Please don't ask me to send her away. I feel it is my duty to take care of her. I swear she won't make any trouble.'

'And what if this—this Will Kelly comes looking for her? What then? Have you not thought of that?'

'Yes, I have,' she replied passionately, her lion's heart pumping hot blood through her body as she leaned forwards, her lovely breasts almost escaping the flimsy lace at the bodice of her gown. For a moment Stephen was totally bewitched and his breeches became uncomfortably tight at the crotch. 'We must stand up to him,' she went on, completely unaware of his suffering. 'You know why he wants Maisie. There are hundreds of disgusting and depraved men who will pay him a fortune for her. Stephen, she is still a child. Please give her a chance. Oh—I truly hope you won't ask me to take her back to the orphanage because—because it would break my heart.'

Stephen hesitated, uncertain how to reply as Delphine waited expectantly, a small bud of hope blossoming in her heart. He longed to go to her, take her in his arms, tell her of his deep, yearning desire for her, tell her that she was his world and if she would only come to him and tell him she wanted him as much as he wanted her, then she could bring every child in the orphanage to live with them.

'No doubt you have fed her and bathed her and clothed her and got rid of the lice and whatever infestations she might have?'

Delphine stared at him. 'Yes, she has been bathed, but she doesn't have lice or any other infestation. Stephen, you must let her stay. I cannot bear to think of that child being exposed to the likes of Will Kelly.'

'Dear life, Delphine,' Stephen said, moved by the intensity of her plea, 'have I said I would do that?'

'Then help me. Will Kelly is the most ruthless and dangerous man one could meet. He must have access to almost any woman he wants in his world, for he is handsome enough in a coarse, vulgar kind of way—and there are whores, pretty ones who would be pleased to accommodate his perversions—but he wants Maisie.'

'Maybe she reminds him of her mother.' As soon as the words had left his mouth Stephen could have bitten off his tongue for uttering such an unfeeling, insensitive remark. He took a step towards her, holding out his hand. 'Forgive me. That remark was unfeeling.'

She glared at him, her face rosy, her startling dark eyes brilliant with outrage. 'I will not let Maisie become a *whore*.'

Stephen winced. The word she uttered seemed to besmirch her, to sully her own purity. She was no virgin, he acknowledged, remembering the times she had spent in his bed before his return to Spain, but her body had been given to no one but him. She stood still, frozen like a statue, such a look of contempt on her face he wanted to throw himself at her feet in abject apology.

'I am surprised at you, Stephen. You should be

ashamed of yourself for your callous, unchristian attitude. I had no idea you could be so brutal.'

He paled visibly beneath her onslaught. Her words were arrows that pierced his heart. 'You are at liberty to think so. That is your prerogative, but—'

'Yes, it is,' she cut in, carried away by her anger, mistaking his attitude and thinking he wanted to send Maisie away when he had no intention of doing so. 'I am appalled by your attitude. Appalled and deeply shocked, for I mistakenly thought you were different. For the time being I will have the housekeeper put Maisie to work in the kitchen and there she will stay under Cook's supervision until we leave for Tamara. When she is old enough to make up her own mind about her future, she can do whatever she chooses to do, but until that time she is as much my responsibility as Lowenna.'

She was ablaze with fury and Stephen felt an even greater passion arise within him. He wanted to go to her, tear the clothes off her, throw her on to the bed and subjugate her to his will. *His will.* Dear Lord, she was glorious in her fury, her magnificent deep-red hair flowing about her shoulders and down the curve of her spine like a vibrant, living mass. But the army had instilled him with a discipline and self-control that he could not fight.

'You are mistaken, Delphine. Lowenna is *our* responsibility.'

'And Maisie is mine.'

She did not allow him the opportunity to respond; without another word she whirled around and hurried from the room.

Stephen listened to her footsteps dying away until there was silence. Shaking his head, his eyes lit on the letter he had received from Spain—a letter that was no longer of any interest to him.

Deciding to give her a moment to cool down before confronting her again, he wandered to the window. The remark he had made about Maisie's resemblance to her mother had been insensitive and he wondered how he could have said anything so crass. But it was too late. He had said it, though it was not in his nature to be callous. Pushing his hand through his hair, he stared sightlessly down into the quiet street. Did she really think he would turn the child away?

His mind was focused on the problem when a movement beneath a towering beech tree across the street caught his attention. Curious, he continued to watch the spot. After a few moments the figure of a man emerged. His movements were furtive, the garish, shabby clothes he was wearing out of place in the heart of Mayfair and he seemed to be watching the house.

Stephen realised with a shock that this man's appearance was no coincidence and that in all probability it was Will Kelly. So he had followed Delphine from the orphanage. Delphine had been right—he was handsome enough in a coarse way, thickset and with a thatch of untidy fair hair beneath an ill-fitting hat.

Suddenly Maisie's problem had indeed become his own. But what could he do about it? Delphine was right: the girl had to be protected. Stephen waited until the man disappeared round a corner before turning away himself.

At the moment he had another more serious matter to deal with—how to placate his irate wife. He had some grovelling to do if he was to make amends. Better to reconcile her by honest persuasion than to force her hand by the weight of his displeasure. It would certainly be a more pleasant course.

* * *

Half an hour later, Delphine was still smarting over her clash with Stephen, but more than that, the probable contents of his letter from Spain had struck at her heart. Was it unreasonable of her to be suspicious—jealous, even—of another woman?

She was sitting at her vanity, securing her up-swept hair with pins when she heard the light knock on the door. Sensing it was her husband, she called for him to enter; when he did, she lifted her head, straightened her back and raised that stubborn chin of hers, which he was getting to know so well. One of the maids was present; Stephen didn't even look at her. His gaze was locked on his wife.

He quirked a speculative brow at her. 'Has your disposition improved?'

His infuriating, unshakeable calm, combined with his arrogance, nearly choked her. After a moment during which she fought to dislodge the word from her throat, she said, 'Yes.'

Satisfied, Stephen moved further into the room. As he came closer, Delphine quivered—half with apprehension about his reason for seeking her out and half with relief that he cared enough to do so. As he approached, she was filled with a disturbing surge of desire for him, despite her anger and hurt.

'What is it you wish to say to me?' she asked coldly.

His gaze flicked to the maid. 'Please leave us.'

The maid gave a respectful bob and then scuttled out of the room.

'What do you want, Stephen?' Delphine asked. 'Can I expect an apology—or do you still condemn me for bringing Maisie here? If you do, please spare me the reproof and go away.'

'I do not condemn you—far from it, as I would have explained, had you given me half a chance. I think we should discuss this.'

She gave him a dubious look. 'Discuss it?'

'Before you make any more rash assumptions.'

Her eyes narrowed and she rose from the vanity table. 'Rash? Everything I have done where Maisie is concerned has been well thought out. It may surprise you to learn that I had made up my mind to rescue her from that brothel-monger Will Kelly before I left Cornwall. Long before. So do not dare accuse me of doing anything rash.'

'I apologise.'

His apology took her off guard. She raised an eyebrow. 'Indeed? Wholeheartedly?'

'Absolutely and completely.'

She eyed him warily. 'Why should I believe you?' she countered, remaining on her guard, resisting her weakness for him. 'How do I know this isn't simply a strategy to placate me?'

'It's the truth. You were right to take the girl and it was wrong and insensitive of me to say what I did. I would not wish such a fate on any young girl. I am sorry, Delphine. I'm a callous brute. Maisie can stay, if that is what you want. Of course she can, and you may fill the house to the rafters with such strays if it makes you happy.'

Delphine's heart swelled to almost bursting with gratitude. 'Oh, thank you, Stephen. I couldn't bear to leave Maisie behind.'

'But what I will not allow is your total preoccupation with the girl,' he said reasonably. 'You have a good heart, Delphine, and a generous nature that will not allow you to turn away from whoever needs you. For that I admire you. So— just what do *I* need to do to get your attention? Present myself at the orphanage on Water Lane and declare myself an orphan?'

Delphine found it difficult to suppress a smile. 'You're far too big for that. They'd never let you through the door—unless, of course,' she murmured, giving him a sly look, 'you were to present them with a rather generous donation.'

'I would do more than that. I would even buy the charity that is so dear to your heart some new premises, if you will forgive me for upsetting you—although as I said, I was not about to turn Maisie out on to the streets.'

She stared at him, seeing the softening in his deep-blue eyes, wondering if she had heard correctly. 'Are you serious—about buying some new premises, I mean? You would do that—for me?'

'Indeed I would.'

'But—why?'

'Because I can afford it and I know it would make you happy.'

'I don't want you to do it for that reason. I want you to do it for the children—but it will make Aunt Celia happy. The orphanage on Water Lane is full to capacity and she has been trying to raise funds for larger premises for a long time.'

'I am aware of the situation.'

She stared at him, her eyes wide with surprise. 'How…can that be?'

Moving to stand directly in front of her, he gave her a smug, smiling look. 'Because, my dear wife, I have made my own enquiries into the state of the orphanage in Water Lane. So you see I am not the uncharitable, unchristian brute you accused me of being earlier. If I provide the money, you must promise me that this is the last time you play Lady Bountiful. No more orphans. Is that understood?'

'Yes, Stephen. Thank you.'

'There are plenty of waifs and strays in Cornwall to be taken care of. I'm sure they will be as appreciative of your time as the ones in London.'

Suddenly Delphine's throat was tight with tears. She wanted so much to go to him and throw her arms about his neck to show her gratitude, but something made her hold back. Afterwards—a long time afterwards, when she looked back— she would realise that that was the moment when she began to love him.

She raised a smile to him, realising she was feeling far better than she had felt in a long time. Indeed, after seeing evidence of his generosity toward complete strangers, her spirits had been buoyed by a rekindling of hope. The day now seemed much brighter.

'Maisie can come with us when we go back to Cornwall,' Stephen said. 'Until then she must remain indoors. You were right about Will Kelly. Someone was watching the house earlier—a disreputable-looking character with untidy fair hair. Does he fit your description?'

Delphine started with alarm, her blood running cold. 'That does sound like him. Is he still outside the house?'

'No. He left. But I expect he'll be back. Men like him are persistent. Don't worry. I've had a word with the staff to keep a lookout for him. Maisie is quite safe.'

'Then I'll just go and make sure—'

He caught her arm as she made a move to go to the door, holding her back. 'No, Delphine. Maisie is being well taken care of. Oakley has charge of her and I assure you he is taking his responsibility very seriously.'

Tears clouded her eyes. 'Then I know she'll be all right. Thank you for your consideration towards her,' she said with heartfelt gratitude. 'She hasn't had much of a life since her mother brought her to London—and Meg's death and the manner of it, however it came about, affected her terribly—but she'll have a much better one in the future.'

Stephen's eyes softened as he looked down into her eyes. 'After seeing your gentle nurturing of our daughter, it comes as no surprise to find you calming the fears of a homeless waif in need of loving care. You are goodness personified, my love.'

The endearment tore at Delphine's heart. How she wished that were true. The corner of her mouth turned upwards tantalisingly. It was absurd for her to be so warmed by his remark. She was annoyed at herself for wanting these crumbs of approval from him, but she did.

'I shall remind you of your words if you ever have reason to be cross with Lowenna.'

A slow grin curved his handsome lips as his eyes glowed into hers. 'I may not have your admirable qualities, but I shall remember—about you.' Briefly his gaze descended to caress her breasts. 'I shall not by any degree forget those rewarding moments when we first met.' Seeing the heat of a blush flooding her cheeks, he smiled. 'So now, for the first time since we arrived in London, can we forget about Maisie and the orphanage? It's important to me that it pleases you, but it's time we spent some time together. We arranged to take a picnic to Hampstead Heath, remember? The food is prepared and the carriage is waiting.'

Delphine hesitated, her eyes drawn to his. Yes, perhaps something would come of spending some time together as a family. There would be plenty of time for lazy conversation. Her lips curved in a smile. 'Then all that's missing is Lowenna. I'll go and get her.'

The afternoon was glorious, the trees showing the full glory of their late copper-and-gold autumn colours. Even as they climbed into the light two-wheeled cabriolet drawn by a single white gelding, Delphine felt something unwind inside her. With the sun directly overhead, Stephen raised the leather hood to provide them with shade. An excited Lowenna in a white gossamer dress with a bright-red ribbon sash, a frilled bonnet covering her black curls and her face alight with excitement, was sandwiched between them, the carefully prepared picnic basket secured to the back.

With Stephen driving the cabriolet—which

was so well sprung it seemed to float along the road—they left the environs of the city behind at a sedate pace.

Delphine was alluringly attired for their outing in a delicate ivory-muslin dress. The V-neck and the edge of the three-quarter-length sleeves were edged with lace. A matching hat festooned with frothy white feathers was perched atop her head at a jaunty angle.

Had they been alone, Stephen would have been tempted to throw caution to the wind and drive the horse faster, to hear her shriek with terrified delight and to see her lovely eyes opened wide and sparkling with excitement, but for safety's sake he restrained the urge.

On reaching Hampstead Heath, which was a popular place for people to picnic and take the air, sufficiently far away from the fumes of London, they decided to have their picnic beside a pond, shaded by a huge oak tree. Stephen carried the large picnic basket and Delphine supervised an excited Lowenna. After spreading a large blanket on the grass, Delphine sat back on her heels and looked around as Lowenna toddled off to pick some daisies that sprinkled the grass.

With fine views all around them, they were completely alone.

'What a lovely place this is,' Delphine remarked, twisting her body and sitting with her legs stretched out in front of her. Discarding her hat, she turned her face up to the sun and closed her eyes.

Stephen joined her. 'It certainly is,' he agreed. 'I did consider taking you to the gardens at Vauxhall across the river, but I thought Lowenna would appreciate something of a more rustic nature to ramble about in.'

'This is much nicer than Vauxhall,' Delphine said, breathing deeply of the clean fresh air. 'There aren't so many people about and you are right, the Heath is more—rustic.'

He grinned at her and a devilish light gleamed in his eyes. 'Careful, Delphine. If we are too secluded, my imagination is in danger of turning to rustic pleasures.'

Delphine smiled somewhat coyly. 'What on earth can you mean? I have never indulged in any rustic pleasures, so how on earth can I possibly know what you are talking about?'

'Don't pretend to play the innocent,' he said softly, pulling off his jacket and tossing it aside, stretching out his long booted legs. 'Prepare yourself for country pleasures.'

'The prospect is rather open, Stephen,' she said, laughing lightly. 'I do not think this is the place to indulge in such things—and Lowenna would never stand for it. Perhaps we should have gone to Vauxhall after all.'

He smiled at her. 'Do you imagine that I have dark motives in mind, bringing you here?'

'I'd be surprised if you hadn't. Be assured that I think nothing but the worst of you.'

Loosening his cravat, he leaned his weight back on his arms, noticing her light shoes sticking out from beneath her skirts and her stocking-clad ankles. He stared at them, thinking of her legs. With the thought came an ache in his loins; sitting up, he fixed his gaze on the waters of the pond stretched out before them. 'Whatever motives I had in mind, my love, it's certainly a nice way to spend the day.'

Delphine had to agree with him. And it was not a lack of room that caused Stephen to sit so close to her on the blanket. Her pulse stirred as the faint scent of his spicy cologne touched her nostrils and she hastily turned her head to see what Lowenna was doing.

Stephen looked at her. 'What have you planned for tomorrow?'

'We are to visit my parents in the afternoon so I am free in the morning.'

'Good. It will be a good opportunity for us to visit the shops.'

She stared at him. 'Us?'

He grinned roguishly. 'You don't think I'm going to let you go by yourself, do you? While we are in London I want you to have a complete new wardrobe. We've been invited to two balls next week, for which you will need a couple of new gowns. I shall accompany you to steer you away from ordering anything in brown and grey.'

Delphine threw him a look of mock offence. 'Not all my gowns are dull. I do have one in rose pink,' she confessed. A dreamy look entered her eyes when she thought of the pretty gown she had been unable to resist when she had seen it on display in a shop window in Plymouth. In a moment of mad self-indulgence, she had bought it, intending to wear it when Stephen came home. 'I could not resist purchasing it when Mrs Crouch and I visited Plymouth.'

Stephen did not understand how something as trivial as a mere gown could engender such an expression of pure bliss in Delphine, but he did appreciate the effect. He saw a pink blush creep into her cheeks as she tucked a loose tendril of hair behind her ear in a self-conscious gesture. A woman could be as beautiful as she felt herself to be, and it seemed as though his efficient and sensible young wife was not immune after all to the magic of a lovely dress to help that feeling along. But then, the woman who sat beside him was not the same Delphine he had known before he went away.

'I am glad to hear it. You have brought it with you?'

She shook her head. 'It still hangs in my wardrobe at Tamara.'

He grinned. 'Your impulsive action tells me one thing at least, my dear wife.'

'And that is?'

'That you are not averse to a little fashionable frivolity, which will make our expedition to the shops a pleasure.'

Their conversation was interrupted by Lowenna. Holding a few straggly daisies in her little hand, she presented the bouquet to a delighted Delphine before scampering off to find some more.

Delphine felt a momentary glow of pleasure at her daughter's gift. Pressing them to her nose, she inhaled their sweet smell. 'They say flowers have a language all of their own,' she murmured softly. 'Do you believe that?'

'Why not? Some people believe it to be true and have even written books about it—not that I've read them myself. It's quite the fashion to convey one's sentiments with the giving of flowers.'

'What a lovely way to express one's feelings.' She looked at him, a smile curving her lips. 'This small bouquet of flowers is the first I've ever been presented with.'

'Lowenna is as thoughtful and sentimental a soul as her mother. You like flowers, then?'

'Very much—especially sweet-scented ones. I wonder what message a daisy conveys—what is its meaning.'

'I don't know the true meaning of the flower, but I suppose it could mean anything the giver wishes it to mean.' Reaching out, Stephen plucked a daisy from the bunch and Delphine caught her breath as he raised it and tucked the tiny flower into her hair. 'There. Now you truly are the lady of the daisies,' he teased. 'I think

I shall take a cue from our daughter and begin presenting you with flowers of different kinds on a daily basis. Perhaps it is the answer to my problem of how to win you over.'

She glanced at him obliquely. 'Do you wish to win me over?'

'Most certainly. I think I shall begin by giving you roses to soften your heart, then lilies to intoxicate you with their scent, followed by passion flowers to convey my complete devotion. They are quite exquisite, you know—like passion itself.'

A rush of warmth swept over her and she turned her face away before he could see that she was blushing. 'I've never seen passion flowers, so I would not recognise them if they were given to me.'

'You would, for I would tell you—and if you were to eat the fruit of the passion flower—well,' he murmured, his voice low and soft with seduction, 'there's no telling what might happen. There is a danger of you losing your inhibitions altogether and becoming a different person entirely—one you would not recognise.'

The effect of his words and the underlying seduction was devastating. Delphine felt blood rushing to her cheeks and a weak trembling feeling from the pit of her stomach to her knees, as she was suddenly assaulted by memories of his heated kisses and caresses. 'Goodness,' she said, a little breathless, 'these are serious symptoms indeed.' With the treacherous warmth seeping through every pore of her body, she felt quite overcome with embarrassment as she gazed into his mesmerising eyes and tried to cover it by teasing. 'What are you trying to do to me, Stephen, lead me astray by offering me exotic bribes?'

'If it's the only way I have of tempting you into my bed, my love, I shall ensure you eat passion fruit every day of your life. You and I are engaged in a power struggle, Delphine. When I came home from Spain and you made it perfectly clear that you didn't want me anywhere near you, I was prepared to honour your wish and keep away from your bed, allowing you to torment me for ever with the unspoken promise that eventually you would allow me access. Too clearly I remember the fire and the passion of our union before I left; I know that same fire still burns deep inside you. Do you not see how much power you have over me?'

Slanting a speculative look at him, Delphine wondered if that was really true, or if he was being deliberately provoking. She licked her lips, feeling so out of her depth with him. 'I do not feel that I have any power over you. Quite the reverse, in fact.'

His fingers gently brushed a tendril of hair back from her cheek. 'What do you think I am? Have you no idea how I am tormented, being close to you day after day and forbidden to touch you? You have been like a shadow beside me for weeks. I am a man with a man's needs, and I cannot stop wanting you. Do you think I am made of stone?'

Feeling herself weakening in the face of his confession, she averted her eyes. 'Are you saying I was unfair and unreasonable in my request?'

'Yes. Look at me, Delphine.' His fingers turned her face to his. 'If I hurt you, I am sorry—but you hurt me, too, and we both felt the pain of it. We can either continue to strike out at each other in our pain or we can stop now and learn to heal each other. Which course do you wish to take?'

Gazing into his intent eyes, Delphine realised that he meant what he said. She stared, her face vulnerable and uncertain, her eyes dark with confusion. Finally she swallowed and said, 'I have never wished to fight you, Stephen.'

He looked at her a moment longer, then, taking her hand, he pressed the back of it to his lips. 'Good. That settles it.'

'Yes,' she murmured, 'it's settled.'

That was the moment when Lowenna pushed herself between them, giggling, for she thought it very funny that mummy was wearing a daisy in her hair. Delphine proceeded to make a daisy chain and placed it like a crown on her daughter's head. Lowenna was so delighted that she hardly dared moved her head lest it fall off. But when her eyes lighted on the small boat they had brought with them, to her parents' amusement she picked it up and forgot all about the daisies.

'Papa, come and sail the ship with me,' she demanded, tugging hard on his hand.

'You go.' Delphine laughed. 'Keep her happy while I unpack the basket.'

Stephen got to his feet, but did not leave her side immediately. Bending low, he placed his mouth against her ear. 'While I amuse our daughter, my love, perhaps you could give some thought to what we discussed.'

Mesmerised, Delphine stared into his fathomless blue eyes while his fingertip traced the curve of her flushed cheek and his deep voice caressed her, pulling her under his spell as he continued, 'And although no aspect of our marriage has been ordinary, think how happy our daughter would be—we would all be—if we were to give her a brother or sister.'

As if entranced, Delphine watched him take Lowenna towards the pond. She'd already thought long and hard about taking Stephen into her bed. Could they forget their differences and behave like a normal wedded couple? She was thoroughly tired of fighting him all the time, but could she put aside her vow not to succumb to his passion while another woman occupied the place in his heart where she so desperately wanted to be? And yet, by becoming his wife in the true sense, was it possible for her to banish the Spanish woman from his heart altogether? Perhaps it was time for her to abandon her fears and confront him with the truth.

Chapter Nine

After spreading out the delicious food the cook had packed into the basket, Delphine spent the better part of the next half-hour sitting on the blanket. Sun bathed her face as she watched Stephen and Lowenna kneeling beside the pond on which they sailed the small two-masted boat painted blue and white. It was attached to a line that Stephen was careful to keep hold of lest it got away from them. Lowenna watched as it bobbed and dipped in the swirling, shallow water. Delphine was utterly captivated by the scene. Their heads were so close together that it was impossible to distinguish where Lowenna's gleaming black curls stopped and Stephen's began. Something Stephen said caused the child to release a peal of happy laughter and Delphine's eyes crinkled with a smile at the joyous sound.

When Lowenna became tired of playing with the boat, she sat close to her father watching two swans pass majestically by. Delphine's heart warmed as she listened to Stephen inventing stories about pirate ships and buried treasure. Wide-eyed, Lowenna listened, enraptured, clutching the little boat between her tiny hands.

After eating the delicious food, they flew the multicoloured kite with streamers attached to its tail. Lowenna clapped her hands and danced about excitedly as it became caught on the wind.

'Higher, Papa,' she kept begging. 'Make it go higher—right up in the sky.'

Stephen reeled the kite out further. Delphine shielded her eyes to watch it soar into the blue sky as it tugged against its tether to be free. When the wind suddenly dropped, it plummeted to the ground, landing with a thud.

Lowenna picked it up and threw it back into the sky, but it was not quite windy enough to get it properly airborne again. Laughing loudly at his daughter's chagrin, in a sure attempt to quell her disappointment, Stephen scooped her up and lifted her on to his shoulders, telling her that if she was a good girl they would stop at Gunter's tea shop for an ice cream on the way home. Gunter's in Berkley Square was a popular rendezvous for the *beau monde*, who flocked there to eat ices and sorbets. The promise of ice cream won Lowenna over and she was in the cabriolet without further complaint.

The following morning found Delphine being whisked off to the shops by her attentive husband. The carriage rattled over the cobbles in the direction of Bond Street. When the carriage pulled up, Stephen told the driver to wait for them at the end of the road before jumping down and assisting Delphine to the pavement. After she took his arm, they joined other elegant shoppers strolling along the street. She couldn't help casting a glance at Stephen. Tall and worldly, suave and elegant, she knew she would be the envy of every woman who passed.

Bond Street was lined with fashionable shops: milliners, haberdashers, shoemakers and expensive jewellers, with their expanses of plate-glass windows and awnings. Taking note of the numerous signs of modistes and wondering which one Stephen would eventually choose, she raised a brow when he stopped outside one of them.

'Why do you choose this one?' she asked, side-stepping two dandies as they minced along the pavement, garbed in wasp-waisted coats and chin-high shirt points dripping with fobs.

'I have heard that Madame Lasalles's is the best. She's been here for many years and is noted for superior style and true elegance.'

Delphine fixed an openly enquiring gaze upon his, her expression a combination of amazement and more than a touch of amusement, for she had not for one minute thought her husband's interest stretched to ladies' fashions. 'And may I ask how you came about this information, Stephen?'

He grinned down at her. 'Suffice to say my mother always favoured Madame Lasalles's expertise—that's how I know.'

Delphine had never shown any interest in shopping—although she had often accompanied her mama and older sisters on their expeditions—but with her husband, so full of surprises, shepherding her into Madame Lasalles's establishment, she felt a strange thrill of excitement.

Liking the look of the elegantly dressed and handsome gentleman who entered her shop, with a charming smile Madame Lasalles welcomed him and his lovely wife into her expensive and fashionable establishment. When introductions had been made and she had astonished him by remembering his mother—who'd had an exquisite eye for style and colour—she got down to business.

'My wife must be outfitted with a complete wardrobe. I'm sure a modiste of your experience knows all that will entail,' he said, making himself comfortable in a large winged chair, prepared to let Madame Lasalles take complete charge of the proceedings.

'*Oui*, of course, monsieur,' she said, smiling with pleasure as her eyes slid over his wife, who was still in the youthful bloom of womanhood. There was something naïve in her manner, almost innocent, refreshingly unique, and yet she was a temptress. The gowns she was already planning would fit those slender yet voluptuous curves perfectly. She watched the young redhead stroll gracefully down the long room to take a closer look at the bolts of materials stacked on shelves, casting a glance at the sketch of a dress on an easel, seeming blissfully unaware of the covert glances she drew from other patrons—although when Madame glanced at the young lady's handsome husband, his long-booted legs crossed and his arm draped over the back of the chair, sublimely at ease with himself and the world, it was difficult to know which of them drew the most admiring glances.

'Your wife is very beautiful, Lord Fitzwaring.'

Stephen's eyes lifted slowly to his wife's back. 'I must agree with you, *madame*. She is the most beautiful woman I have ever known—but then,' he said with a playful wink of his eye, 'I am her husband and completely biased.'

The couturiere went to Delphine. 'Please— step this way, Lady Fitzwaring,' she said briskly. 'We will go into the fitting room where we will begin by taking some measurements before deciding on the style and a selection of materials for gowns and chemises of your choice—and your husband's, of course.'

'I am in your hands entirely, Madame Lasalles— whatever you think is best.'

'I think you should come with us, Lord Fitzwaring. I have some lovely sketches of the latest styles.'

Unable to utter any objections to having Stephen present, Delphine followed Madame Lasalles through some curtains and into a small room at the back of the shop cluttered with fabrics and sketches, motioning Stephen to a chair.

She turned to Delphine. 'When we have removed your gown I will take your measurements.'

Delphine turned her back so the couturiere could unfasten her dress. The room was so small there was hardly room for the three of them. When she stood in her shift, as Madame took her exact measurements, turning her this way and that, lifting her arms and making her breathe in and out, every time she turned she couldn't avoid touching Stephen.

She felt stifled by him, his thigh a hard rock against her leg, his eyes holding her captive. She felt like a fly in a web, yet to all outward appearances she looked unconcerned—until she caught sight of herself in the mirror. In mute horror, she gaped down at her display, for her bosom was only thinly concealed beneath the delicate batiste of her chemise. Her round breasts pressed wantonly against the filmy fabric, their soft, pink crests seeming eager to burst through.

She was so embarrassed she hardly dared to look at Stephen; when she caught and held his unrelenting gaze in the mirror, she could not look away from his face. Aware of his slow, unhurried regard, her skin burned from its intensity. Gritting her teeth, she glared at him before looking away.

Sitting back on her heels where she was kneeling in front of Delphine, Madame Lasalles looked up and smiled. 'You are perfect, Lady Fitzwaring. It does my heart good to make a wardrobe for someone with as fine a figure as yours. Your body is beautiful—full breasts, yet a waist slender enough to fit a man's hands—and your legs—your hips—*mon dieu*!' She turned to Stephen. 'Do you not agree, Lord Fitzwaring?'

Stephen's eyes were devouring as they moved over his wife slowly, glowing with a strange light. The soft light gleaming on her satin skin was a rousing sight for him; his mouth was suddenly dry and his breath a hard knot in his throat. Like a starving man, he stared at the full, ripe delicacies before him, and it nearly sapped his strength to keep his hands off her.

'Most assuredly, *madame*,' he agreed softly.

While Delphine closed her eyes, embarrassed beyond bearing as the couturiere spoke so freely of her body, Madame Lasalles lowered her head and smiled to herself. His lordship had a look on his face she had seen many times in her fitting room. Already he was impatient to leave, to get his young wife back to their bed, where he would use her well, she was sure.

'You flatter me too much, *madame*. I have always thought myself nothing out of the ordinary,' Delphine managed to say, thankful that her voice sounded normal and did not shake. 'I have four older sisters who are infinitely more elegant.'

'Then you must send them to me so that I can dress them all.' Madame Lasalles laughed, getting to her feet and draping her tape measure round her neck. 'I will go and fetch some sketches of different styles for you to look at. You can put on your gown.' Her gaze swept to Lord Fitzwaring, her eyes twinkling gently. 'I am sure your husband can manage perfectly well to fasten you up.'

She left the room and Delphine was more than willing to don her gown, though when Stephen got slowly to his feet and proceeded to fasten the tiny buttons up the back she felt most distracted. His long fingers seemed like firebrands on her bare flesh. She cursed herself silently for allowing his appraisal to make her nervous. When he stepped back she breathed a sigh of relief. But her comfort came to an abrupt end when he stood behind her and dropped a gentle, burning kiss on her neck below her ear.

'That was a rewarding experience, my love,' he murmured easily, terribly confident of himself. 'I admit I have never felt quite so moved upon witnessing a lady disrobe.'

For a moment their eyes met in the mirror, his warm and devouring, hers nervous and uncertain. But under his openly admiring regard, her heart pounding fiercely with emotion, she flushed crimson and lowered her head to adjust her skirts.

Her nervousness did not escape Stephen's observant eye and he laughed softly as she bent low. He watched her breasts swell over the low neckline of her gown and tremble slightly as she shook out her skirts.

'Why so nervous, Delphine?' He grinned. 'All I did was fasten your gown.'

Her reaction was to stand up straight and pull her bodice up a little higher, which proved to be a futile effort.

'Worry not, my love. You are quite decent—besides, there are no eyes here but mine.'

'Please be quiet, Stephen. Madame Lasalles will hear.'

As if on cue, the couturiere swept in with her sketches. Delphine bent her head over the drawings. They were excellent and, for the most part, definitely to her taste. Stephen offered his opinion, rejecting some and selecting those that appealed to both Madame Lasalles and Delphine, even going so far as to suggest the fabrics and the shades that would suit the design. Delphine was quite astounded by her husband's talent. When they had finished, small squares of material were attached to each design—silks, satins, rich velvets and soft wool. One creation in particular he chose for her to wear to their first ball: a deep-red gown the same colour as her hair, a gown that was the epitome of stylish elegance, combining simplicity with the richness of expensive fabric.

Their business concluded, Delphine was aghast by the colossal cost of this new wardrobe.

Sensitive to her thoughts and aware of her dilemma, Stephen leaned in. 'I told you before that no expense is to be spared, Delphine. Do not be hesitant about spending my money. The sketches you have chosen are excellent and I agree with them all. Madame Lasalles approves and I admire your taste, so if you are satisfied we shall see what the rest of Bond Street has to offer.'

He turned to the proprietress. 'I would like two of the gowns to be ready in the next two days, Madame Lasalles—since we are to be in London for such a short time. And make the first of the gowns out of the red.'

Madame's mouth dropped open in surprise. 'But, Lord Fitzwaring—two days for two completed gowns is impossible! A week, at least.'

'I am sorry, *madame*, but we are to attend the Chevingtons' ball three days hence and my wife has not brought any gowns suitable for such a grand event.'

'But it will take my experienced seamstresses a minimum of two weeks.'

'Then hire more.' He took the sting out of his words by flashing her a rakish smile and writing a bank draft for an amount that made her eyes widen.

'That is indeed generous,' she said in a dazed voice.

'It should cover the costs,' he said, knowing it would pay for the entire wardrobe and half as much again. 'If there are any more bills, forward them to me. Naturally there will be extra profit for you if they are ready and well sewn. Can you do this?'

Madame Lasalles thought for a moment. Lord Fitzwaring's mother had been one of her best and wealthiest clients and she couldn't let such an order go. The Chevingtons' ball was to be a truly grand event, and the opportunity to show off one of her creations worn by the beautiful Lady Fitzwaring was not to be missed—even if her seamstresses had to sew round the clock to complete the order. Not only was Lord Fitzwaring appreciative of style and exquisite cloth, he also struck a hard bargain, yet it was clear he was used to giving orders and having them obeyed. He was to be admired, for he would accept nothing but the finest work.

'*Oui, monsieur.* I will do my very best.'

'Thank you, Madame Lasalles.'

When they at last reached the carriage waiting patiently at the end of the street, having forayed up and down the thoroughfare, halting now and then to purchase a miscellany of smaller items— some to be delivered and others Delphine insisted on taking with her—they headed for home.

After a light luncheon, they set off to call on Delphine's parents. Lowenna was full of excitement at the prospect of seeing Aunt Rose's baby, her cousin Thomas, and playing with the toys in her mama's old nursery. The same could not be said of her papa, as he irritably contemplated the impending confrontation with Delphine's father, but it had to be faced, there was no help for it.

Sensitive to how he was feeling, Delphine tried to lighten the occasion. 'Try not to worry, Stephen. I'm sure everything will be all right.'

Despite his cold detachment, Stephen felt an odd sensation of gratitude to his young wife. 'Thank you, Delphine, but I do not expect to be treated as a long-awaited and much-loved member of the family. I intend to get this ordeal over with as quickly as possible. I have no doubt your father had plenty to say about me when you called on him with Lowenna.'

'Nothing in particular, although both he and Mama did voice their concern.'

'What about?'

'Me. They—want to be assured that I am being well looked after.'

'And what did you say?'

'That it is difficult for a man to look after his wife when he is in another country.'

'I see. Then I shall have to convince them otherwise.'

When Lowenna had been whisked off to the nursery by one of the servants, Stephen and Delphine were shown into the drawing room where the family was about to have tea. The group who awaited them reacted with diverse emotions. Lady Cameron, Delphine's mother, looked relieved that her daughter's husband had deigned to favour them with a visit, the twins—identical in looks but one in pink and the other in blue, seated together on a striped green-and-yellow silk sofa—looked fascinated, openly admiring their breathtakingly handsome brother-in-law with small, self-conscious smiles, while her father looked apprehensive as he considered Stephen's superior frame.

Delphine was delighted to find that Aunt Celia was paying a rare visit to see her niece and to become reacquainted with her handsome husband.

'Lord Cameron,' Stephen greeted in deep, melodious tones, offering a smile to each in turn. 'Lady Cameron.' He inclined his head to Celia before turning on that devilish Fitzwaring charm to the twins and kissing each of their hands.

'We are pleased to meet you again, Lord

Fitzwaring,' Lady Cameron said as she looked at her son-in-law, with his lean, noble features and tall, broad-shouldered frame, wondering how in the world she could possibly have forgotten how handsome this dynamic and forceful man was. 'Much has changed since last we met—and we are so happy to have the chance of meeting our lovely granddaughter at last.'

'Lowenna is certainly that, Lady Cameron. She has everyone in her thrall—including her besotted father.'

Smiling with relief that Lord Fitzwaring did not appear to hold a grudge for the way he had been forced into marriage with Delphine, Lady Cameron swept a hand towards the sofa, where Delphine was already ensconced. 'Please do sit down and tell us about Spain and the places you've visited since last we saw you.'

'Mama,' Delphine was quick to say as Stephen sat beside her, very close so that they sat snugly together—no doubt putting on a show of togetherness for the benefit of her parents, she thought. 'You make it sound as though Stephen was taking the Grand Tour, not fighting a war. He was much too busy to look at the scenery.'

Stephen smiled at his mother-in-law. 'Nevertheless, Spain is a very beautiful country—although the summer heat can be extremely wearing. It is certainly not what we're used to in England.'

While her mother busied herself with pouring tea and asking the twins to hand it out, Delphine eyed her husband obliquely, speaking quietly. 'I can move over if you need more room, Stephen.'

Her gentle barb was not lost on Stephen. The roguish grin he gave her as he took her hand in his made her heart somersault with incredulous joy. 'There is no need for such measures, I assure you. I am quite comfortable, my love,' he murmured, leaning close to breathe in the scent of her hair and lowering his head further still until his warm breath brushed her cheek. Delphine nearly closed her eyes at the unexpected pleasure his nearness elicited. Indeed, it seemed as if her efforts to remain detached from her husband were being seriously undermined by the yearning she felt within the depths of her body—a yearning that grew stronger by the day. Looking up, she found her father watching them keenly.

'Sir, the last time we met was at your wedding to my daughter. I trust she is being well looked after. I am sure you will understand our concern about her living so far away while you were fighting with your regiment in Spain. It was unfortunate, that—' he cleared his throat '—that business—not the kind of behaviour I can excuse or condone. My wife and I always gave our daughters the best advice. Obviously Delphine never took it in. Still, she was old enough to know better.'

'She probably never realised she had a father who cared enough to protect her,' Stephen remarked. Recalling the dressing down he'd received from Lord Cameron two years ago, in retrospect he had to admit that the dressing down had been well deserved, even though he would not have admitted it at the time. It was madness, but at that moment he felt a stirring of admiration for his father-in-law—a deeply concerned parent, the sort of father his own had been, that he himself wished to be, with strong principles about what was acceptable and what was not, a man who expected the same behaviour from those around him—yet Stephen wished the gentleman had shown Delphine the love and consideration she had lacked growing up.

'Allow me to put your mind at rest, Lord Cameron,' he went on, 'and to assure you that as

my wife Delphine is protected and cherished—
is that not so, my darling?' He kissed her hand
and smiled again at his father-in-law. 'Delphine
wants for nothing. Now I am home I shall make
sure of her happiness. I will always keep her
safe.'

'No one can promise that,' Delphine said.

'I am quite determined,' he said quietly with
a tender smile.

'I am sure Delphine is relieved to have you
back home, Lord Fitzwaring,' Lady Cameron remarked. 'It is plain to me that she holds you in
high regard. Are you enjoying London?'

Stephen smiled graciously. 'We recently endured a most exhausting shopping expedition,
from which I am unlikely to recover without in-
tensive convalescence.'

'You've been shopping?' Fern trilled, sitting on
the edge of her seat, suddenly interested, since
the beginning and end of her world revolved
around every fashionable street in London where
she could shop to her heart's content.

'A whole new wardrobe—would you believe
it?' Stephen smiled.

'You were the one who said I needed it,'
Delphine declared with mock indignation. 'I

was quite content with the clothes already in my possession. Why, anyone listening to you would think you the victim of an attack!'

Stephen's gaze narrowed on her smiling lips, then he leaned back his head and laughed a rich throaty sound that warmed Delphine's heart. 'And I would tell them that when a man acquires a treasure, he does not argue over a few pounds.'

Her eyes shone with humour. 'You really are wicked, you know.'

'But not beyond redemption, my love,' he murmured with a definite gleam in his eye.

As she met his gaze, Delphine's lips curved in a smile. 'I never said it was a failing.'

'Well, Delphine,' her mother said, more than a little surprised by this open display of affection. After two years of worrying about her wayward daughter, she was delighted to see how well matched they were—and so obviously in love. 'I am pleased your husband managed to get you to the shops. It is more than I could achieve. And I hear you are to attend Lord and Lady Chevington's ball—which is another achievement.' She smiled at Stephen. 'Delphine never enjoyed socialising.' She glanced back at her daughter. 'I'm happy to see you making an effort at last. You must make a pretence of enjoying yourself, even if you are not.'

'Aye, Delphine could never see further than that blessed orphanage,' her father grumbled. 'Night and day, that was all she could talk about. Everything she had of value she would pawn for the orphanage. She was stubborn as a child, so she will not change now, try as you may.'

'I would not wish to change her,' Stephen said softly. 'She is an angel; so I have always considered her and I love her just the way she is. I am happy to have married a woman who thinks not just of herself, but would give all she has to those less fortunate. Her bravery and compassion compels my admiration and respect.'

Delphine stared at him and thrilled to that small endearment—that he loved her. Then she looked down at her lap with furrowed brow. He had said she was an angel. Angel? The word set her mind racing. *Angelet*: the comparison was close—too close for her comfort. She struggled to remember the exact wording of the utterance, so many weeks ago, that had first driven them apart following his return from Spain.

'Something vexes you, my dear?' A soft, gentle voice roused her from her thoughts.

She recollected herself and glanced fondly at her Aunt Celia. 'I'm glad you are here today, Aunt Celia. We have something to tell you that will relieve you of some of your worries.'

The older woman smiled. 'That would indeed be welcome, but first tell me how Maisie is settling in. The other children miss her, but, considering the circumstances, it was for the best that she left.'

'It was, and she is doing well. Her happiness was a delight to see when she first put on her new clothes. She is so very good with Lowenna that I'm considering having her work in the nursery. But what we want to tell you is that Stephen has offered to donate the money you need to buy the new orphanage. You told me you have seen the ideal place in Islington—is it still on the market, do you suppose?'

Celia's eyes widened in amazement. 'But— Lord Fitzwaring—that's extremely generous of you. Oh—really,' she said, so overwhelmed her pale complexion turned a delicate shade of pink, 'I don't know what to say.'

'You are not required to say anything,' Stephen countered. 'Delphine has told me how hard you work seeking contributions for your charity and how desperately the children, whose welfare is most dear to your heart, need a more suitable location. I shall be happy to invest in such a noble cause. I shall also approach some of my friends to contribute.'

Celia stared at him in stunned disbelief. 'That—that would be wonderful.'

'Naturally I shall personally inspect the property you have chosen to make sure it is structurally sound before you move your orphanage. We can undertake the trip together and you can tell me what you will need to make it habitable. I shall make an appointment to see the property agent directly and let you know when we can inspect it.'

Overcome with emotion, Celia dabbed at her eyes. 'Thank you so much. This means a great deal to me—and I know it will mean a good deal more to the children.'

'Think nothing of it. I am glad to do it.'

After that, conversation was easy and relaxed; by the time Stephen had smiled and charmed his way through the next hour, when it was time for them to leave, both Lord and Lady Cameron were of the opinion that despite the sordid circumstances that had brought Delphine and this man together, as things had turned out, perhaps it wasn't such a bad match after all. Considering Lord Fitzwaring's large estate in Cornwall and his vast wealth, she really had done rather well for herself.

On the night of the Chevingtons' ball, trying to calm her fears, Delphine pulled the deep-red gown up over her shoulders. Without her maid she was unable to do up the fastenings at the back.

Stephen entered, immediately standing stock still. A strange expression crossed his face. The Delphine he saw walking towards him in her lovely high-waisted gown was not the charming young woman he'd become accustomed to seeing. In a transformation that both unnerved and enthralled him, the breathtaking young woman was a princess fit to take her place in the most glittering courts in the world. Her hair fell like a shimmering deep-red waterfall, waving over her shoulders and halfway down her spine, where it ended in thick curls. The scooped neck of her gown accented the fullness of her breasts, falling gently over graceful hips to her slippered feet. The deep rich colour of the gown had darkened her brown eyes until they appeared almost black; her flawless skin shone startlingly white against the deep red.

Stephen again experienced the odd sensation that his wife had become someone else, but when she drew near, there was no mistaking that entrancing face. She stopped in front of him, and his decision to have her, no matter how she might argue, now became an unshakeable resolution. A slow, admiring smile drifted across his face.

'Do you like the gown?' he asked, unable to keep his eyes off the alluring display of smooth flesh exposed by the neckline.

'I confess that it is not a shade I would have chosen for myself—and not with the décolletage so low, but I like it well enough.'

'Good—although I'm beginning to regret choosing this particular gown for you to wear for the ball.'

'Indeed? Was that not its intended purpose from the start?'

'I'm beginning to wish I'd bought it solely for my own private admiration,' he said softly, 'not for the pleasure it will give other men when they look at you. You will cause quite a stir.'

Delphine's cheeks flamed. 'Oh—I—I truly hope not.'

'Perhaps you should wear the other gown Madame Lasalles made for you—which, as I recall, is a little less revealing.'

'No—I think I shall wear this one,' she said with a mischievous laugh, 'for no other purpose than to keep your attention on me and not to wander to anyone else.'

'My attention will remain on you, no matter what you wear. You may keep it on—but make sure you wear a cloak when we go out.'

'I always do. Please would you fasten me up?' she asked softly, her stomach fluttering wildly in anticipation of his touch. 'My maid must be busy elsewhere.'

Unsure how he would react to doing this small task for her, she turned her back to him. He obeyed and she felt his fingers on the back of the gown, on her bare flesh, his breath on the back of her neck sending fire down her spine. When the last button was secure she turned back to him, flushed with relief.

'Well—will I do?'

Stephen tilted his head to one side, studying her with narrowed eyes. 'Perfect,' he said, 'almost. There's something missing.' He studied her for a moment longer, the frown still creasing his brow, and then, light dawning, he darted from the room. He returned a few moments later, a merry grin on his lips and a long black leather box in his hand, which he opened to reveal a lustrous pearl necklace and matching earrings.

'Oh,' she gasped. 'I fear I shall cry.'

'You don't like them?'

'They're beautiful—but I do not deserve them.'

Stephen smiled, pleased with her reaction. 'I shall be the judge of that.'

Taking the pearls from the box, gently drawing her hair to one side, he fastened the necklace around her throat, leaving her to secure the earrings. Delphine was not unaware of the possessive gleam in his dark-blue gaze as it appraised her, but she was momentarily distracted by how elegant *he* looked.

It finally dawned on her that he was looking at her hair and Delphine belatedly realised that her maid had yet to attend to it.

'My maid should be here any moment to arrange my hair in a more formal style,' she explained quickly.

'Leave it. It's lovely as it is,' Stephen said, watching her. 'I prefer to see your hair unbound.'

She half-smiled at him, admiring the way his expensively tailored dark-black jacket clung to his splendid shoulders. His face was so tanned, his hair so dark—apart from the flecks of silver at his temples, which gave him a more distinguished look—and his white shirt and neckcloth stood out in dazzling contrast. 'You are bent on charming me this evening, Stephen. I'm beginning to think there must be something behind it.'

'Should a man be rebuked for complimenting his wife?'

'No, but you must be aware that it is not usual for married ladies to attend balls with their hair hanging halfway down their backs.'

The grin he gave her was positively wicked as his appreciative gaze slid over her hair and breasts. 'Then maybe you should set a precedent and display your charms.'

She looked at him askance. 'What? All of them?' She laughed lightly, her small teeth gleaming white between her parted lips. 'Do you forget that it was Eve who tempted Adam by displaying her charms, Stephen?'

'It always seemed to me, my love,' he murmured huskily, bending his head and placing a light kiss in the curve of her neck where a pulse was beating erratically, 'that it was the apple that tempted Adam, and therefore his downfall was not brought about by his lust for Eve, but gluttony.'

She looked at him with mock reproach. 'I might have known you would twist it to your own way of thinking.'

'So is it decided? Will you shock society and leave your hair free of adornment? I want you to enjoy yourself tonight, Delphine. I intend for us to come to London often in the future and it is important that we socialise. Are you nervous about the ball?'

'No, not nervous,' she said, pulling on long gloves that reached well above the elbows. 'As you know, I have never been partial to the kind of events that always excited my sisters and two years in Cornwall have done nothing to change that. Still, as the wife of such a high-profile figure, I realise I must conform. I am not complaining. I have yielded to the temptation to allow myself to enjoy the evening, which already holds the promise of enchantment.'

Stephen arched his dark brows and eyed her

with dry amusement. 'I like your use of the word conform, my love. Dare I hope you will be willing to conform in other areas of our marriage before the night is over?'

Laughing lightly, she picked up her cloak and handed it to him to drape around her naked shoulders. 'As to that, Stephen, you will have to wait and see.'

As he escorted her down to the waiting coach, Stephen's mind was already drifting ahead, to the moment when that glorious mantle of deep-red hair would be spilling over the pillows of his bed and his bare chest, and her supple, silken body would be writhing in sweet ecstasy beneath him.

As they left the house, a figure came creeping along the far side of the street, silent as a shadow, and disappeared down the basement steps.

The long black coach sped through the streets, the four black horses tossing their heads in the pouring rain. Glowing shards of light from the lamp posts flickered over the gilt trim of the coach as it splashed onwards. Inside the equipage, rain drummed on the roof. In a strange mood, but by no means dispirited by the rain, Stephen looked across at his wife.

Euphoric anticipation seemed to increase inside him the closer they got to their destination. He was exhilarated at the prospect of appearing at the ball with Delphine by his side. Ever since he'd returned from Spain he'd been dreaming of the time when he could show her off—what better place to fulfil that dream and present her to London society as his wife than at the home of the Earl and Countess of Darrington? The ball, which was being held at Chevington House, their magnificent mansion in Piccadilly, was seen as the most important event of the year.

The reason for his desire to be seen in society with Delphine eluded him. He told himself that after two years of marriage it was high time they were seen together as man and wife, but it was more than that. Delphine was in his blood, in his heart, and her smile and most innocent touch almost sent his desire spiralling out of control. There was a provocative sensuality about her, a natural sophistication, a sparkle and vivacity of spirit that drew people to her, and he wanted everyone to know, tonight, that she belonged to him.

He brushed off any dark musings he might have had as the carriage slowed, reaching its destination. A footman hurried forwards to open the door, holding an umbrella high to shield them, running to keep up with them as he escorted them under the portico. They entered the mansion's interior, almost blinded by countless chandeliers and candles in crystal sconces.

When the formal announcement of their arrival had been made, they sauntered casually through the crowded hall. Several people glanced curiously their way before realising who they were. They knew Delphine because of her connections, but the devastatingly handsome Lord Fitzwaring had not been seen in society for a long time. As whispers began to spread, completely impervious to the stir they were creating, Stephen tucked his wife's hand possessively in the crook of his arm, pleased that she'd done as he asked and left her hair loose, drawing it back in a ribbon to match her gown. Elegantly they ascended the elaborately curved staircase to the ballroom, the music growing steadily louder.

Reaching a long landing, they passed several reception rooms where tables had been set up for the customary light supper served at midnight. Stephen lifted two glasses of red wine from the tray of a liveried footman, passing one to Delphine.

'For courage.' He grinned. 'You might need it.'

Entering the ballroom, they stood against one of several columns to sip their wine and watch the dip and sway of the dancers, not unaware of the hundreds of heads that swivelled to ogle them. Almost immediately people converged on them in an endless stream, good-naturedly welcoming Stephen back to London and utterly charmed when he proudly introduced Delphine to them, pressing invitations on them before moving on.

'I do wish everyone wouldn't stare at us so,' Delphine whispered apprehensively when, miraculously, they found themselves alone. Yet there were moments when she sensed a jealous malevolence in the attitudes of some of the ladies, whose eyes openly admired Stephen from behind a fluttering of fans, drawn by the aura of restrained power and masculine vitality that emanated from him.

Stephen flicked a glance at those around them, then looked down at Delphine's lovely upturned face. 'I can see that,' he agreed drily. 'Does it bother you?'

'No, but I have an aversion to being the object of everyone's curiosity.'

'Then let us dance before we are inundated once more.'

Disposing of their glasses, he held out his hand to her and Delphine automatically placed her hand in his. She could not remember the last time she'd danced, but she managed to follow Stephen as he began to guide her through the first steps of the waltz. His arm was tight about her waist, forcing her into nerve-racking proximity with his powerful body. He danced, she thought, with the same relaxed elegance with which he wore his superbly tailored black evening clothes.

Two hours later, having danced every waltz with her husband and drunk more champagne than she had ever consumed, she was feeling delightfully gay and light-headed—so much so that she was bolder than she had ever been when Stephen held her in his arms. On meeting his gaze, she was mesmerised by the tenderness she saw in his eyes.

Holding her close, Stephen allowed himself to indulge in savouring her supple grace in the movements of the waltz, undressing her with his eyes. His pulse drummed in his ears. He wanted so much to touch the line of her neck, the curve of her cheek, to feel her silken skin beneath his fingertips, to explore the lush ripeness of her body with his hands and his lips. No man could look at her without feeling the stirring of desire. But there was something more in his hunger— a deeper need.

'I enjoyed our picnic,' he said. 'What are your plans for tomorrow?'

'I haven't had time to think. Suggest something—something we can do together. Something we'd both like to do.'

Stephen's heart slammed into his ribs. He stared down at her, tracing with his gaze the classically beautiful lines of her face, the brush of lustrous ebony eyelashes, and saw the invitation in her imploring dark eyes. Hope and disbelief collided in his chest. His arm tightened about her waist and he bent his head to hers. 'Would you like me to suggest something we can do together before that? Something we will both find—pleasurable?'

Delphine trembled with happiness as she felt his warm breath caress her cheek. She knew what he wanted. Her body recognised it instantly, making her flush and shake as she always did when he touched her. She slanted him a look from beneath her long sooty lashes, a mischievous gleam entering her eyes, knowing perfectly well what it was he wanted, but deciding to play the innocent.

'Well—we could play cards—or chess.' She smiled up at him playfully. 'I'm very good at that.'

His lips curled in a half-smile. 'Minx—I'm sure you are, but if my memory serves me correctly, you are also very good at something else.'

'Why, what can you mean?' she gasped, pretending innocence.

'You know perfectly well.'

His voice was rich and hypnotically deep. He did not release her. His hand encircling her waist tightened, and his long body pressed itself closer to hers. She remembered how it had been between them in the beginning, the muscular hardness of him and the icy, needle-sharp chills that were her own response to his touch. The smile slowly faded from his lips and those compelling, incredible dark-blue eyes stared down into hers. His powerful, animal-like masculinity was an assault on her senses. She was unable to resist him. With a melting deep inside her she felt her body offer itself to this man and in that instant they both acknowledged the flame that ignited between them. Right there in the middle of a ballroom in full view of London's elite, they exchanged a silent carnal promise as binding as any spoken vow.

'I want you,' he breathed, his eyes locked on hers with a smouldering intensity. 'Come with me.'

In those three quiet words, three simple words, somehow there was a promise of an entire life to be lived if only she could take the chance. A sense of possibility came over her then—a kind of lightness. She took a deep breath and stopped dancing.

'What are we waiting for?'

As if moved by forces beyond his control, Stephen inclined his dark head in recognition of the contract conjured between them. He escorted her from the dance floor; within minutes they were in the coach.

Sitting next to Delphine, Stephen took her hand. 'Is this more to your liking?'

His voice was seductive, persuasive; in the moonlight shining through the window, his eyes gleamed darkly. She could smell his skin, his hair, and she could feel his presence. Like a magnet, it was drawing her to him; she no longer had the will to resist, nor did she want to. A smile played on his lips. Looking at him, she was filled with a delicious sense of expectancy. He moved nearer and touched her hair.

'At last I have you where I have always wanted you, my love.'

'And you're a rogue, sir, do you know that?'

'I don't deny it.'

'I'd be an utter fool to let you take advantage of me.'

'Be a fool,' he begged, lowering his head, his lips nuzzling the warm, pulsating hollow of her neck. 'We shall have some more champagne when we reach the house, to celebrate your folly.'

'I suppose you think it will be easier if you get me drunk.'

'You have me all wrong,' he protested. His devilish grin was irresistible, especially to his young wife, already well on her way to being totally captivated. 'I want to keep you well refreshed so that you stay awake. We have a long night ahead.'

'You have been very patient with me, my lord.'

'I'm glad it has not escaped your notice. I did not wish to rush you. I wanted you to be sure.'

'I am sure, Stephen. Very sure.'

And so she was until they entered the house. Mr Oakley was waiting for them, beset with anxiety. The news he had to impart was dire, for Maisie was not in the house. She had been abducted. That was the only explanation there could be for her disappearance.

Chapter Ten

Delphine was plunged into a nightmare. Her expression was one of deep shock, of the agony one feels when someone dear has been hurt. She closed her eyes, trying to shut the ugliness out of her mind.

'Oh, God, no. It's Will Kelly. He's got her, I know it.' She stood for a moment, doing her best to calm herself, for the thought of innocent little Maisie in the hands of that evil man was almost more than she could bear. She wanted to get to Mrs Cox's bordello as soon as possible, for it was where the trail started. Pulling herself together, she rushed towards the door.

'Where are you going?'

She turned and looked at Stephen. 'To find her. Oh, Lord, Stephen, we have to find her. How did he get into the house? Why did no one see him? We must find out where he's taken her.'

There was a stiffening in the lines of his face, a gleam of anger in his eyes. 'Mrs Cox's?'

'That would be too simple. He'd know it would be the first place we would look—but it's the only place we can go. We shall need help if we are to find Maisie. Will Kelly will have her well hidden, you can count on that. We need a first-class housebreaker, someone who can enter a building in moments without making a sound—someone who knows Will Kelly's habits—the places he haunts—someone who is willing and able to help us. I know just the man, a man whose loyalty I can ensure—although you might find it shocking that I should. His name is Fergus Daley and he works on the door at Mrs Cox's.'

'You're right,' Stephen affirmed coldly. 'I am shocked—shocked to think my wife counts criminals among her acquaintances.'

'Fergus was always kind to me when I went looking for Maisie at the brothel. He's gathered a harvest of hatred over the years for Will Kelly. He has always looked out for Maisie and will not take kindly to Will Kelly taking her into his clutches at last. Fergus may be able throw some light on their whereabouts.' She strode towards the door. 'We must go to Mrs Cox's at once.'

'No, Delphine. You must stay here—'

She whirled round. 'Do not tell me what to do, Stephen Fitzwaring. Maisie is *my* charge—in *my* care. We go together.'

'No, Delphine. I absolutely forbid it,' he began, his voice harsh, but she merely shook her head.

'How are you to prevent it, Stephen? You surely know by now that I shall do as I please.'

He cursed and passed a hand over his forehead, knowing it was useless arguing with her. Besides, she had more idea where to find the girl than he had.

'As you wish. It will be all right.' Resting his hands on her shoulders, he gently massaged her flesh, then turned her around and pulled her into his arms. She longed to let him console her, longed to melt against him and cling to his strength, but she was afraid they were losing time and pulled away.

'I have to find her, Stephen. That poor child. I can't let him…'

'Stop it, Delphine. Do not allow yourself to think the worst. Look at you—you are trembling.

I'll order the carriage and in the meantime we must change these clothes, which would attract unnecessary attention.'

They had dressed in their darkest, plainest clothes in order to pass unnoticed among the labyrinths they might have to follow in their search for Maisie. The hour was after midnight when they reached Water Lane. Even at this hour it was a hive of bustling activity, with men and women propped drunk in doorways or carousing as they wended their way home. Stephen knocked on the door of Mrs Cox's bordello. After several moments a bolt slammed back and the door opened.

Fergus stood there. On seeing Stephen, believing him to be a client, his expression relaxed, but when he saw Delphine it sharpened with curiosity and then his lips broke into a grin.

'Miss Delphine? Well, I never. What brings you here at this hour?' Then he frowned. 'It can't be good.'

'It isn't, Fergus. We desperately need your help. A few days ago I took young Maisie away from the orphanage and I'm afraid Will Kelly found his way into the house and took her. We have to find her, but we don't know where to begin looking. Have you any idea where he might have taken her?'

Fergus caught on straight away. His face took on a hard, murderous look and his huge hands clenched into fists. 'He's got young Maisie, you say? God help him when I get my hands on him. He had a falling out with Mrs Cox and he's not been here for months. He's got a place of his own off Fleet Street towards the river.'

'Do you know where it is? Do you think he might have taken her there?'

'Aye, more than likely.'

'Will you take us?'

He nodded, looking at the carriage. 'We can only go so far in your carriage. After that the streets are too narrow. We'll have to go on foot.'

Delphine felt her spirits begin to lift as they left the brothel. Now at least they had a specific trail to follow, but the look on Fergus's face boded ill for Will Kelly.

They left the carriage on Fleet Street and headed in the direction of the river. It was an area notorious as a hiding place for criminals and brothels, which indicated the depths to which Will Kelly had sunk. The place they were looking for was called Maiden Yard, indicating the character of the place. A strong smell of chimney smoke was in the air and a low mist had descended, shrouding everything in a shifting, diaphanous whiteness. The buildings closed in on them, almost blocking out any remaining light. Delphine kept close to Stephen. They went through a labyrinth of winding, cobbled alleyways, each identical and none giving any indication of where they might lead, but they hurried after Fergus, intent on finding Maisie.

At last they arrived at Maiden Yard, a foul, reeking place. In the centre was a gutter in which all kinds of unspeakable matter flowed. There were decrepit buildings on all sides, sultry lights showing from several windows. Fergus pointed out the brothel tucked away in a corner, but it seemed startlingly clean in comparison.

Fergus's face was gleaming with anticipation. Then it darkened, caution reasserting itself. 'If Kelly's here, he'll be caught red-handed.'

Standing close to Stephen, Delphine felt her body shake as if her heartbeat were violent enough to choke her. Had Will Kelly seen them from a window? Was he even now trying to escape with Maisie out of the back of the house?

'We cannot wait,' Fergus murmured. 'We must go in at once.' With Stephen and Delphine close on his heels, he set off across the yard, moving light and easily despite his size, his huge feet making no sound on the stones.

They found Will Kelly alone in a gaudily furnished room stinking of cheap perfume and liquor. He sat at a table pouring gin from a bottle and gulping it down. He looked up when they burst it, staggering to his feet. 'What the hell…?'

Bent on avenging young Maisie, Fergus lost no time in grasping him by the throat. Caught off guard, Will bore no resemblance to the swaggering, roving-eyed Will Kelly of old. He was a big, well-built man, but Fergus had the advantage.

Will stared into the maddened face of his attacker. 'Damn you, Fergus. I might have known you'd know where to find me!'

Fergus would have hit him, but Stephen stepped between them, thrusting Fergus back. Fergus protested, but on seeing the glint of a pistol in Stephen's hand levelled at Will Kelly, he moved back.

'Where's the girl, damn you?' Stephen demanded. 'By God, if you've hurt her in any way, I'll make you rue the day you were born.'

'She's where you'll never find her,' Will hissed with a show of defiance, but when he felt the cold steel of the barrel press against his chest, fear overrode his brief show of bravery. 'All right,' he growled. 'She's here—upstairs.'

Without relinquishing his position, Stephen ordered Fergus to fetch the constables and to tell them that Lord Fitzwaring required their urgent assistance in Maiden Yard.

It was with reluctance that Fergus left to do his bidding, for he would dearly have liked to stay and dole out his own kind of punishment on Will Kelly.

Unable to wait another second, Delphine immediately began to climb the narrow flight of stairs, lit by the occasional candle in sconces on the crumbling walls, pausing at the top to look around. Meticulously she went from room to room, each occupied by an unsavoury assortment of scantily clad women who made Will

Kelly his fortune. Just when she was beginning to despair of finding Maisie, she spied her in the last cold and filthy room. The girl lay on a bed, her face to the wall. Her body was hunched, her knees drawn up to her chin. She looked so small and vulnerable.

'Maisie?'

The child turned her head, distraught and terrified. On seeing Delphine she uttered a cry and scrambled off the bed, flying into her arms and clinging desperately to her.

'You found me,' she wept, as Delphine held her trembling young body close. 'Please don't let him get me.'

'He won't—I promise.' Holding Maisie at arm's length, Delphine bent and looked close into her eyes. 'Maisie, tell me—did he—hurt you?'

She shook her head. 'No, but I was frightened.'

Delphine gathered her close, a sense of relief overwhelming her. 'Oh, bless you. Thank goodness we found you. Now come along—I shall take you home.'

Together they descended the stairs. Stephen still had Will Kelly pinned to the wall, frightened to move, for he knew from the look in

Fitzwaring's eyes that he wouldn't hesitate to shoot him if he tried to make a run for it.

'How is Maisie? Did he hurt her?' Stephen asked quickly, his face darkening. 'Because if he did...'

'No, she is merely shaken,' Delphine replied, standing aside when Fergus entered the house accompanied by two constables.

With relief Stephen handed over his prisoner, explaining as they fastened the manacles to his wrists that his crime was the kidnapping of a juvenile and the possible murder of her mother.

When the constables had led Will Kelly away, Stephen took Delphine's hand and kissed it, then bent forwards and kissed her cheek. 'I am very proud of you, Delphine. Most women would have had hysterics at the thought of entering a district such as this.'

'That wouldn't have done any of us any good. I was just so afraid Will Kelly might have harmed her.' Delphine looked at Fergus. 'Thank you, Fergus. Thank goodness the constables weren't long in coming.'

'I didn't have to look very far. With any luck they'll lock him up for a long time. He'll not be troubling Maisie again. Will Kelly will harm no more young girls.' He looked at Maisie huddled against Delphine. 'Young Maisie?' he asked anxiously.

'Apart from being terrified out of her wits, she's unharmed. Thank God we found her in time.'

'That's all right, then,' he said gruffly, more relieved than he was letting on. 'I'd best be getting back to Mrs Cox's. There'll be the devil to pay when she finds I've deserted my post.'

'I'm sure when you explain where you've been she'll go easy on you, Fergus. Mrs Cox always had a soft spot for Meg. She wouldn't wish harm on her daughter any more than you would.'

After thanking Fergus and pressing some money into his palm, Stephen led Delphine and Maisie back to the waiting carriage. Delphine sat quietly in the corner on their return journey to Mayfair. Holding Maisie in her arms, she stared out of the window, her gaze unfocused. Stephen could see she was tired. There were shadows beneath her eyes and her exquisite face was pale. After attending the Chevington ball and anticipating a wonderful night of lovemaking ahead of them, they had been thrown into a nightmare.

They had spoken of nothing but Maisie and rescuing her from Will Kelly's evil clutches, but Delphine seemed to have become softer in her distress for the young girl. He admired her compassion—how she was willing to put her own feelings aside and stand loyally and protectively next to those who needed her. He also admired her independence of spirit and intelligence, and he adored the vulnerability and softness within her. She was the embodiment of everything he liked in a woman—she was feminine without being vapid or helpless, proud without being haughty, assertive without being aggressive—and he had fallen hopelessly in love with her.

Not a trace of light penetrated the heavy velvet curtains in the master bedroom as the two people within removed each other's clothes. Slowly, expertly, Stephen unfastened Delphine's gown, freeing her arms from the sleeves, and he pulled the bodice slowly down over her hips. She kicked off her shoes before stepping out of it. Removing the rest of their clothes, they became entangled in their haste to get between the snowy-white sheets. Having removed her filmy underclothes, Delphine tumbled on to the bed, gazing up at her husband who stood tall and naked. He slowly perused her curving form, soft skin pale and lustrous in the gentle light.

Bending on one knee upon the edge of the mattress, Stephen leaned across the bed, bracing an arm on either side of her, admiring her attractive features and softly parted lips, but the temptation to do more than look proved stronger than his power to resist.

Gazing up at him, Delphine raised her hand and stroked the black curls from his face. Her eyes were drawn to his mouth. She wanted him so badly. Threading slender fingers through the short, raven strands at his nape, she drew his head down to hers, kissing his mouth softly, before moving on to caress his cheeks, her lips as light as a butterfly's wings, before returning to his mouth.

Following her lead, Stephen's mouth responded by kissing her back, moving on down her creamy throat; soon he was savouring the sweetness of a delicately hued breast. Moaning softly, Delphine arched her back to receive the best of his attention. He gave it eagerly, his fingers continuing their fervent dedication until she was all but writhing beneath his tender assault.

'Please, Stephen,' she begged with an agonised groan, running her hands down his muscled back as warmth glowed and spread through her body. 'I don't think I can stand much more. I think I'm going to faint.'

Pressing her down flat upon the bed, he leaned above her and looked down into eyes that had grown luminous with desire. 'Would you really have me stop now?' he murmured, stroking from her breast to her belly, moving down between her legs.

'Don't you dare,' she whispered, the scent of his cologne drifting through her senses. She gazed at him with something like awe, and she knew that she loved him, knew that she had dreamed of this moment and couldn't believe it was finally here after two long years.

She lay quivering beneath his touch until she could stand it no longer and pulled his face down to hers to kiss him again, their mouths and tongues joining in an avaricious search. It was as if her body had been made for this, had been shaped and created specifically for the giving and receiving of this pleasure.

With their arms entwined, they rolled to one side, their bodies bathed in a dim, red-gold glow. Delphine's hair spilled all over him like a waterfall. She ran her fingers over the taut muscles of his belly, making him moan low in the back of his throat. He reached out with both hands to stroke her hips, her back. Sliding out of his grasp, she bent to scatter hungry kisses across his chest, biting, licking, brushing her lips against the soft hairs that formed a denser line leading down from his navel to his groin. With a soft groan, he took her head and pulled her closer. She could feel his heart beating fast against hers, then he rolled her over like a pebble on the shore, so that he was above her once more, lying between her legs, but holding back so she almost cried out for him to enter her as his maleness awakened that part of her that was most sensitive to stimulation.

Chuckling softly at her mounting impatience, Stephen yielded to her urgings and pressed fully home, causing her breath to catch in the onrushing waves of pleasure that almost swamped her.

It was sweet, sweet torment, delirium and bliss, a torture that must end in sanity or shatter. She held him to her, flesh filling flesh, his strong and firm, hers soft as velvet, she clutching, clinging, her body arching to meet him, to bring him closer still until the oblivion of ecstasy claimed them both. Their skin was warm, moist with perspiration, hair damp, breathing deep, then they slept.

In the night there was more loving, not as frenzied, but lethargic, leisurely. Arms and legs entwined, they slept again.

In the morning when a thin pale light filtered into the room, they smiled at each other. Delphine felt him grow hard and she shifted beneath him; then there was more splendid love, joyous, beautiful love.

Later, steam clouding the bathing chamber, where a long copper bathtub dominated the room and was spacious enough to comfortably accommodate them both, Delphine lounged back contentedly against her husband's chest as he lathered the tempting terrain of her body with scented soap, marvelling at how pale and lustrous her skin looked in comparison to his.

'You seem distracted, my love,' he said, bending his head to nibble the fleshy lobe of her ear, thinking her a fetching sight with her hair piled on her head, a few loose curls dropping coyly to her shoulders, her body sleek and glistening with droplets of scented water.

Delphine's eyes were cast down to his assets, those same assets with which he had afforded her so much pleasure throughout the night. 'I fear you are right, Stephen,' she replied, laughing lightly, turning her head and pecking his grinning lips. 'I fear I shall suffer from such a distraction whenever you are near. I sincerely hope you don't expose yourself before other women as casually as you do with me.'

'What you see is yours alone,' he assured her, carefully avoiding any mention of past involvements. 'I always assumed a certain degree of experience was needed for lovemaking to be at its best—now I find in that I was wrong. I have never tasted joy so sweet as that which you have given me.'

'You are not alone.' She smiled, turning her head and gazing at him with love. 'I regret having wasted so much time.'

'You beseeched me not to touch you, remember? Because of the circumstances that forced you into marriage, you played the avenging angel and I had to abide by your wishes and stand by helplessly whilst you feasted on my heart. You swung your hips and smiled and tossed your head to tease my eyes from their sockets and were so damned tempting I nearly took you by force a thousand times.'

She laid her cheek against his shoulder and ran her fingers idly through the damp hair on his chest. 'It had nothing to do with what happened in London, Stephen. I laid that to rest when you were in Spain.'

He looked puzzled. 'Then perhaps you'd care to enlighten me, for your insistence upon celibacy escapes me at present.'

'The night we were together in the Blue Boar aroused feelings in me that I didn't know how to deal with.'

'What kind of feelings?'

'Wanton feelings. I found them shocking. After that I could not trust myself around you and that desire, rather than anger, was at the root of my resistance. And—I thought you were in love with another woman—a woman you were close to in Spain. You told me you despised the ideals romantics call love. I felt that not only must I love, but I must be loved equally in return.' She sighed. 'I became trapped by my own nature. You see, I could not bear to lose you.'

The smile faded from Stephen's face and Delphine felt his body tense against hers. Each word she had spoken was like a knife thrust into his heart. With her eyes cast down, she looked dejected, like a child. When he spoke his voice was gentle.

'You do me a grave injustice, Delphine, to imply that I would love another woman when you are my wife. There is no other woman—but when I first went to Spain I did possess those ideals you spoke of. I met a girl—a Spanish girl called Maria. I knew her father and visited their house. He was not a well man; he worried for his daughter's future, and thrust us together. She was beautiful and appeared shy and innocent. I thought I loved her. I proposed to her. Respecting her innocence, I never laid a hand on her, but on the eve of our wedding I discovered she was pregnant with another man's child—a man who was married to another, a man she told me she would continue to take to her bed after we were married. I left her then, but later I was set upon by a group of thugs and beaten senseless. I can still hear Maria laughing as they left me for dead. Some of my friends found me and I recovered. Perhaps now you know why I lost faith in that which you call love.'

All the colour had left Delphine's face. When she spoke, her voice was heavy with sadness. 'Stephen, why did you not tell me this at the beginning? I understand your cynicism, but it has nothing to do with us.'

'I realise that now. At the time I was shocked to realise how close I had come to losing control and I vowed that my emotions would never again be engaged by a woman. I wanted none of their treachery and deceit.'

'But I am not Maria.'

'No, indeed, and I thank God for it. You are nothing like her. I love you to distraction, Delphine. Your belief in my duplicity, however, explains a great deal—for one thing, your behaviour at the Saracen's Head that day.' He spoke quietly. 'I think it mattered very much to you.'

She raised her head and turned slightly to meet his gaze, her breasts glistening with droplets of water. 'It did. How I wish now that I had not let my pride keep you away.'

He lifted a brow. 'What made you suspect there was someone else?'

'From something Mr Oakley told me when first we met, I knew you had a woman in Spain— that she was there to tend you when you were wounded in Salamanca. And then when you came back and all the correspondence from Spain kept coming, you were often distracted and preoccupied—and when you were ill—when you were delirious—you talked of your love for a woman—a woman called Angelet. It was plain she meant a great deal to you—that you loved her.'

He frowned thoughtfully. 'Angelet? I know no woman by that name. If I was as delirious as you say and I spoke of loving a woman, then that woman was you, Delphine. Angelet is the Cornish name for angel. I always referred to you as my angel. I am astonished that you could so easily believe in me loving another, although it does explain why you once accused me of being a hypocrite, when I said that, had I not come back from Spain, you would have moved on and married someone else.'

'I would never have done that.'

'Maybe not, but there would have been no reason for you to remain at Tamara had I been killed in action. The letters that keep coming are about military matters—I may be discharged, but there are still issues to be dealt with, hence my visit to Woolwich when we arrived in London. And the woman who assisted Oakley in tending me in Salamanca was a good woman, but she was fat, homely and a grandmother of ten.'

Delphine's heart began to beat with such joy it quite alarmed her. He had said that there was no one else, that she was the woman he loved. It was just too incredible for words.

'How foolish I have been. I see that now. It was because I loved you so much—there were times when I couldn't bear it.'

'I'm sorry, my darling. If I appeared distracted it was because of what I had seen.'

'Tell me,' she urged gently. 'Tell me what it was that made you want to leave the army.'

'In truth, my love, I don't know when that bleak

realisation came over me, but when I left you and returned to my regiment, things were never the same. I missed you and I resented the army for keeping me from you. It was at Badajoz when my disillusionment reached its zenith. We lost a thousand men in January at Ciudad Rodrigo, and after that we marched on Badajoz. We lost over five thousand men. That was when everything became too real, when I was brought into personal contact with some of the simple facts of life, of how brave and gallant men can become infected with madness and behave with sickening savagery.

'The French troops were treated honourably as prisoners, but where the local population was concerned, the very same people we had come to liberate were beaten, raped, killed and robbed. After that I knew it was over for me. It was only later, when you wrote and told me of the birth of Lowenna, that I noted she was born on the very day of that battle.'

Tears misted Delphine's eyes. Listening to him speaking quietly of his torment, she had felt his pain. There was little she could say to comfort him. The memories he carried were heavy for him to bear, but she hoped that with the passing of time they would fade.

'I did not wish to press you to tell me about Spain. I did not want to disturb the delicate balance between us—that seemed more important than any questions I might want answered. But I wanted to know. Why did you not tell me when I asked you about it that day we rode to the Saracen's Head?'

'I drew back from such confidences. I wished neither to burden you nor to reveal myself as a man suddenly disappointed in his chosen career.'

'I am sorry. Knowing how important the army has always been to you, I realise how hard that must have been. It would seem we have both been foolish.'

Placing a finger beneath her chin, he turned her head to face him, his dark-blue eyes aglow. 'Indeed we have. I see our marriage was full of misunderstandings,' he murmured. 'You had the mistaken idea that there was another woman in my life and my desire for you had lessened—and I was sure you couldn't bear my touch, that you'd fight me if I tried to have you. It's strange how our minds have played against us. We should have followed our instincts.' He bent his head and kissed her shoulder. 'But it is over and time for a new beginning. Are you happy, my love?'

'Very,' she said.

'Your cheeks are pink. Your eyes are gleaming. You look radiant.'

'I attribute it all to you.'

He lifted a brow. 'Why to me?'

'Because you are a wonderful man.'

'A lucky man,' he amended, a half-smile curling his lips.

She dipped her eyes to a certain growing part of his anatomy. 'And immodest,' she remarked with a little giggle, 'albeit most endearingly.'

Seeing where her eyes were directed, laughing softly he dropped the bar of soap. It hit the water in front of her face and the splash left her spluttering and gasping for breath. She opened her eyes and, with a gasp of indignation over his outrageous audacity, playfully batted the water into his face, drawing a protesting shout from him, whereby he returned the favour, which soon evolved into a childish contest of playful splashing.

The game ended when they heard someone

knocking on the chamber door. Hungry now, their minds turned to food. They extracted themselves from the tub to eat their breakfast in more civilised circumstances.

The orphanage project was well underway. Delphine threw herself into making lists of what would be needed. Bedding was essential and the children would have to be clothed and fed and caretakers found to care for them. Aunt Celia also intended to open a school—the premises were large enough and, thanks to the enormous sums of money generously donated by some of Stephen's friends, they were able to purchase books and slates and chalks and anything else to do with educating the children. Medicines and herbal remedies were also bought in, since children were always going down with fevers and sniffles.

On the day of the opening everything had been in order and everyone involved with the old orphanage had rallied round to help with the move. The children—some of them never having ventured beyond the grim alleyways of St Giles—

revelled in their new home and the surrounding countryside. In no time at all they were chasing one another around the walled garden.

By the end of the day, everything to do with Water Lane had been left behind. After hugging a tearful and enormously grateful Aunt Celia, Delphine, Stephen and young Maisie had left for their rented London home.

In bed that night, an exhausted Delphine nestled in her husband's arms. 'Thank you,' she whispered. 'Without you none of this would have happened. The children would still be in Water Lane.'

'I was glad to do it. You make me see something that all my life I have been aware of, but never really stopped to consider—that there are others out there not only without food and clothes and somewhere to lay their head, but worst of all without hope. You are a beautiful woman, Delphine. You are sincere and dedicated and passionate in what you do. You are also kind, caring and loving and strong.' He placed a tender kiss on the top of her head. 'Is there any wonder I fell in love with you?'

Deeply touched by his words, she nestled closer

into his arms. 'I'm so glad you did, because loving you as I do, I couldn't bear it if you didn't love me.'

'I do, desperately, and I will support you and cherish you all the days of my life. I have been fortunate—I didn't realise how fortunate until I saw the orphanage in Water Lane for myself. I never wanted for anything when I was a child and was guilty of taking what I did have for granted. I think the children will be happy in their new home; when the older ones move on to begin apprenticeships, there will be room for more children who find themselves destitute through no fault of their own.'

'Sadly there will always be destitute children. I wish it were possible to provide homes for them all.'

'You can't take care of all of them, my love. When I took you to Tamara, I remember you telling me that you'd always found something missing in your life, while having a sense of knowing there was so much out there you could not see. You said if you could find it, it would make the whole world shine.'

Tilting her head, she stared at him in disbelief. 'I'm amazed you should remember that.'

'I often thought about you and the things you said when I was in Spain. It made life more bearable. So, Delphine, have you found what you were looking for? Does the world now shine for you?'

She looked at him lovingly. 'I found it the moment you came back from Spain. It shines more than I could ever have imagined. May we go home now—back to Tamara?'

Stephen smiled, pulling her further down the bed. 'Anything you wish, my love.'

Epilogue

They had been at Tamara for six months. The day was wonderfully warm, the first suitable day of the season when at long last Delphine found the opportunity to drag her husband down to the beach. She waded into the surf, feeling the caress of icy water on her legs. Facing the gentle breeze blowing off the water, with her hair free of pins she felt it ripple against her back and laughed with the thrill of it.

Turning to her husband, she held out her hand. 'You promised to teach me to swim, remember?'

'How could I forget? Ever since we returned from London you've nagged me about it on a daily basis.'

She threw him a look of mock offence. 'I never nag.'

Tearing his gaze from his lovely young wife,

Stephen made a slow scan of the calm sea, considering how best to teach her. The waves lapped and sucked at their bare feet. 'You do realise how cold it is?'

'I'll survive.' She cocked him an impudent smile. 'Perhaps it is you who fears the cold. Is that it, Stephen?' Unable to resist teasing this handsome husband of hers, Delphine waded out until she was knee deep in sea water and, bending over, scooped up a handful and doused him.

It was all the encouragement he needed. With a shout of laughter, in an instant he was wading into the water after her as she ran headlong into the waves, wearing nothing more than her chemise. The shock of the water hit her when it reached her thighs. It snatched her breath away. Her body went rigid and she sucked in her belly, bracing herself as the waves lapped higher.

Stephen was naked to the waist, clad only in black trousers that fitted him like a second skin rolled up to his knees. The long white scar on his chest provided a brutal reminder of the time he had been wounded at Salamanca, but these were happier days indeed.

Stephen caught her and pulled her to him until only their heads showed above the water. She held on to his shoulders as her senses reeled. She could not believe that the strong arms holding her to him, the lips tenderly, urgently devouring her own, the warmth, the smell, the lean, sinewy body were all real, were all hers for the taking. Pinned against his broad chest, she tasted salt water on his lips. His hands stroked soothingly up and down her spine beneath the waves.

The unexpectedness of his action triggered an instant reaction in Delphine. It flashed like a powerful current, charging the air between them. Dizzily she slid her hands up his chest, trying to cling for support to the very object that was destroying her balance. Despite the coldness of the water, her blood ran warm with pleasure. When he eventually tore his lips from hers, he grinned down at her.

'Has that warmed you up, my sweet?'

She laughed at him. 'It certainly doesn't feel as cold as before.'

'Right, my lady,' Stephen said. 'If you want me to teach you to swim, prepare yourself for your first lesson.'

'What do I do first?'

'Watch me.' He demonstrated by striking out with long, expert strokes, showing her how to push out with her arms in an arc and work her legs at the same time.

Captivated, Delphine watched as her husband propelled himself with steady strokes, his body a dark, sleek mass skimming the surface of the sun-kissed water, unable to tear her eyes away. As always when she observed his vigorous maleness, her response was immediate. She felt a shifting, an upheaval deep inside her. From the very beginning, it was as if the essence of herself, the very rhythm of her being, had been altered to beat time with this man's heart. Suddenly his body rose in an arc before he disappeared from sight. She held her breath until the moment he broke through the surface, planting his feet on the sea bed and shaking his dripping black hair like a dog.

'Did you observe my movements?' he asked, walking back to her.

She laughed hysterically. 'You looked like a frog!'

'Exactly.'

'It isn't very dignified.'

'Nobody said it was. Now you do it. I shall support you with my arms.'

'Don't you dare let me drown.'

'I won't.'

Delphine bobbed down beneath the waves and looked ahead of her before stretching out her arms. Feeling Stephen's arms beneath her chest and her belly, she lifted up her feet. He held her while she floated and then she tried to work her arms.

'Open your legs wider,' he instructed.

She spluttered and laughed out loud. 'For you, my lord, any time you desire it.'

'Minx,' he chided, chuckling low. 'Keep your mind on trying to swim. Keep your body horizontal and bring your arms round. That's right.' With his arms beneath her, she managed a few strokes, her hair floating behind her on the surface of the sea. 'You look like a beautiful red-haired mermaid,' he remarked, his eyes dropping to the delectable shape beneath the surface.

'Hopefully I shall be able to swim like one before long.'

'You're quite determined, are you not?'

'Absolutely.' No sooner had she uttered the word than he relaxed his arm supporting her chest and she sank like a stone. Striking out with her hands, she opened her mouth, gulping in a mouthful of sea water before she came spluttering back to the surface, choking and gasping for breath.

'You let me go,' she cried, wiping away the streaming hair covering her eyes.

He laughed loud, his eyes glittering. 'You'll take a lot more dunkings before you learn to master it. It takes practice—a lot of practice— and we have all summer to do that. Come, let us rest a while.'

Despite the cold water and her sodden chemise, trying to swim was invigorating and she revelled in the freedom of it. 'No, I am not giving up until I get the hang of it. Let's try again—and don't you dare let me go until I tell you.'

'I am at your disposal.'

They tried again and again until Delphine at last struck out with her arms and lifted her feet from the sea bed, not realising until she had succeeded in accomplishing two strokes by herself that Stephen wasn't holding her. When the realisation hit her, she put down her feet and shrieked with delight.

'I did it—and I didn't sink! Did you see?'

'I did. I commend you, Delphine. Now there will be no stopping you—but you are not to try it alone—not until you are a strong swimmer.'

Scooping his jubilant, dripping wife up into his arms, he began to wade back to shore. Not until then did they realise they had an audience of three. Maisie and young Davy, who had been the girl's devoted slave from the moment she had appeared at Tamara, sat side by side on a boulder, their faces alight with laughter, while Lowenna, who had been playing in the sand, scrambled to her feet on seeing her mama and papa coming out of the sea. She ran toward them with her arms held high, her little face shining with glee, her cap of black curls bouncing delightfully.

'Papa, teach me to swim like Mama,' she squealed. 'I want to be a mermaid, too.'

Placing Delphine on her feet, Stephen swung his daughter up into the air. 'And so you shall be, my darling girl—and then Papa will have two beautiful mermaids.' Sitting her on his hip with one arm around her, he placed the other round his wife's shoulders and, drawing her close, placed a loving kiss on the top of her wet head. 'As long as you don't join forces and swim off into the deep blue yonder.'

Delphine tipped her head back and gazed at him, loving him so ardently she could scarce believe it. 'Never—not unless you turn yourself into a merman and come with us.'

He grinned. 'What a wonderful idea.'

* * * * *